AWARDS & PRAISES FOR K.L. BRADY

Winner — Next Generation Indie Book Award for Multicultural Fiction (2010)
Winner — Next Generation Indie Book Award for Multicultural Fiction (2013)
Winner — Next Generation Indie Book Award for Multicultural Fiction (2014)
Finalist – Next Generation Indie Book Award for Multicultural Fiction (2015)

Publisher's Weekly calls K.L. Brady's work "comic and charming..."

RT Book Reviews calls Brady's work "Hilarious!"...and says she "draws readers in immediately...and propels them straight through the drama, humor and the various twists and turns that will leave you exhausted but satisfied."

"K.L. Brady delivered again with Her Perfect Catch. This is a quick but fulfilling romance novel and combines two of my favorite things, football, and love."   – Goodreads Reviewer

"Her perfect catch is the perfect read for the romantic at heart. Add sports and you have a recipe for the perfect love story." – Goodreads reviewer

"As always, K.L. Brady does not disappoint with her hilarity, her sensual moments, and tension. Her Perfect Catch is a perfect read." Amazon Reviewer

The 12 Daves of Christmas

A Novel

K.L. Brady

LadyLit Press
Cheltenham, Maryland

The 12 Daves of Christmas
A Novel

LadyLit Press
P.O. Box 461
Cheltenham, MD 20623

Copyright © 2016 by K.L. Brady

Without limiting the rights under copyright reserved above, no part of this publication may be reproduced, stored in or introduced into a retrieval system, or transmitted, in any form, or by any means (electronic, mechanical, photocopying, recording, or otherwise) without the prior written permission of both the copyright owner and the publisher of this book.

Publisher's Note:

This is a work of fiction. Names, characters, places, and incidents either are the product of the author's imagination or are used fictitiously, and any resemblance to actual persons, living or dead, business establishments, events, or locales is entirely coincidental.

December 2017

First Edition

Rest in Heaven, Sweet Buddy

Chapter 1

December 23rd – Two Years Ago

Gabrielle Garrett's relationships had never unfolded as beautifully in reality as she visualized them in her mind. Her life, her memories, all served as the evidence of this truth, starting with Spunky Corsetti, her ping-pong champion high school beau who ditched her at senior prom for Marlene (a bimbo…and her cousin), and ending with Derek Matheson, who took a restroom break during a romantic pre-engagement dinner; he disappeared forever…and left her with a hundred-dollar check.

Her marriage to Leo Drake would be different. He was a sure thing, a safe bet. The beautiful government economist suspected the "guarantee" played a part in the reason she'd consented to marry him…in addition to what felt like love, or something like it.

Attention had been paid to every detail of Gabrielle's Christmastime wedding. Leo had practically arranged and planned everything himself. He'd selected the venue, the music, even her dress—his mother's. She handled the décor as everyone expected, but as he dictated.

Red and white poinsettias and candles lined the altar. Gold ribbon intertwined with pine garland and cones had been strung down the length of the pews, each capped with a bouquet of white roses. The air smelled of rose, spice, and jasmine, and the schedule had been timed to Swiss perfection. An arch of twine and white lights would greet them before they took the final steps and said their "I dos."

This was it. After all these years, at the age of twenty-eight, five years later than the age at which her older sister had married, she'd finally take the plunge. Today promised to be the *wedding* of her family's dreams, and the *marriage* of hers…sort of.

During moments of boredom, she attempted calculate, as a percentage, their marriage's potential to succeed; under the most optimal conditions, the answers peaked at eighty-two percent, a couple of times eight-three, give or take a plus or minus five margin of error. Not bad. Certainly, the highest of any of the men she'd dated in the past.

Her nagging doubts around their compatibility represented the most critical risk and had piqued around their sixth date. When she asked him his thoughts on the Federal Reserve raising interest rates, a move that could impact his real estate business, she never expected him to declare, "I don't think there should be any charge to visit wildlife parks." Her every instinct told her to sprint out of there like Usain Bolt, but she gave him the benefit of the doubt, stuck it out, took a chance on him, and it all worked out exactly as it should, exactly as her family had wanted.

After all, he was a beautiful god of a mortal. Physically he exceeded every standard she'd ever set. His six foot two frame towered a full five inches above her own. He thrived as a top seller at one of the county's biggest brokerages. So, what if he thought America's central bank was an animal sanctuary? Wouldn't be the stupidest thing she'd heard a human say, although perhaps in the top twenty…ten.

Too late for second thoughts now. The ceremony was set to begin. She fought back the pangs of inner doubt as the hunger rumbling in her gut now distracted her. There'd be no tummy pouch from an ill-timed snack to ruin the clean lines of the column skirt on her mother-in-law's ode to frumpy wedding gown. Only one tiny detail remained unaddressed, and she rifled through every bag she'd brought with her to find it.

"Oh, no! Where is it?" she muttered, her eyes scanning the room in panicked flashes.

Her "something borrowed," her mother's pearl necklace, had gone missing, exacerbating her consternation. Her angst was driven by an irrational, superstitious nature, quite peculiar in one who worked as an economist analyzing facts and figures all day, every day. But the necklace had been handed down through two generations of Worthington matriarchs and all lived happily ever after. She'd emptied the room to finish dressing and take a moment's pause to process the enormous commitment she was about to make, suppress the ebb and flow of apprehension, try to enjoy her last few minutes as a single woman, a free woman, but her missing heirloom and a stuck zipper yanked her out of her calming thoughts.

She cracked open the door and called for assistance from her mother or sister. "Mom? Vic? Somebody please bring the pearls and zip me up."

No sooner than the word "up" passed her lips, a jittery Leo, her groom, walked into the vestibule. She saw him and then he saw her see him.

Bad juju.

Wedding. Doomed.

She slammed the door shut and clenched her eyes tight.

"Oh, no, no, no, no! This can't be happening."

Seconds later, Vic burst into the room, the missing necklace dangling from the tips of her fingers, only to be greeted by Gabby's flustered expression. Vic gripped her by the shoulders. "Calm down. I've got the pearls, and I'll take care of the zipper. What else is wrong?"

"I saw Leo. Don't you know it's bad luck to see the groom? It's a sign."

Vic rolled her eyes and ignored Gabby while tending to her dress and clasping the string of pearls around her neck. "Please, not with the signs again. Everything's fine. You always panic, but don't. Marriage is wonderful. It's absolute bliss. Reggie is my soulmate…and Leo is yours. You'll see. You two complete one another."

Gabby narrowed her eyes. "Please don't Jerry Maguire me…and who are you? Did you see Leo's expression?

His was not the face of a soulmate. More like the face of an escaped convict."

"He's panicked, but not because anything's wrong. He's running a little late. That's all. He hates being behind schedule. You said it yourself."

"I'm telling you, Vic, disaster lurks. I can sense it."

Her mother whipped open the door and practically floated in wearing a stunning gold, floor-length gown. She glowed as usual; the rich hue contrasted perfectly against her chestnut colored skin. She and Vic, who could pass for sisters, radiated loveliness in whatever they wore, whether formal gowns or jeans and T-shirts. It was Gabby who took after their dad, handsome in his own right but geeky and a touch awkward; he had wild curly hair and a dearth of social sophistication. The likeness between Vic and her mother is what she simultaneously loved and envied about them. "Oh, honey. My sweet baby," her mom said tearfully. "You look stunning. You're perfect. You're a vision. You're—" She stepped back and gave her a once-over. "A wreck. What in Satan's pajamas is going on here?"

"I saw him."

"It's Armageddon. She caught the briefest, tiniest of glimpses of her groom ... a millisecond at best," Vic added with a heavy side of snide.

Her mother's expression pinched. She folded her arms across her chest, tapped her foot, and glared the sanity back into Gabby. Her daughter snapped her back straight and focused her eyes forward as if a general had barked an order and she'd complied.

The pianist began to stroke his fingers across the keys, filling the air with the sound of Stevie Wonder's "Ribbon in the Sky." Also, Leo's selection. She preferred classical but she compromised...or gave in, really. The coordinator, Gloria, poked her head into the door. "That's our cue. It's time. Let's line up!"

In that instant, the wedding's pace quickened to the point at which Gabby's brain could barely catch up.

"You see? Everything's fine. Gloria wouldn't start the ceremony without the groom." Vic forced the corners of her lips upward and appeared more constipated than happy. "All that drama for nothing."

Vic finalized the positioning of Gabby's veil then gave her a warm embrace and a careful kiss. "You ready, Gabby? You've got this."

Gabrielle didn't feel like she "got" anything. On the contrary, she'd sensed an unraveling, but she'd been wrong before. Maybe she'd gotten her signals mixed. Perhaps this time, for once in her life, everything would proceed as she envisioned instead of appearing as the picture of perfection in her imagination and then falling apart in spectacular fashion in reality.

With that glimmer of hope, her nervousness dissipated, and she revealed a sliver of a smile. That's when her phone sounded. The "Wedding March" ringtone played. In her engagement euphoria, she downloaded and assigned the song to Leo shortly after he proposed.

"Leave it," Vic said, flapping her hand toward Gabby, gesturing for her to lose the phone. "It's time to go," she urged with a determined tone in her voice. But Gabby knew this call was the one she needed to take above all others.

"It's Leo's ring," she said. "It may be important."

All eyes locked on her as she dug into her purse and stared at the screen.

The words paralyzed her.

All sound evaporated except her heartbeat's slamming into her chest. She couldn't say how long she'd been standing there before her mother's voice pierced through the fog. She read his text aloud, or so she thought.

> We're not right for each other.
> I'm calling it off.

The screaming in her head did not breach her lips. Her breath caught in her throat, and the room started to spin.

"Gabrielle Renee Garrett! Listen to me. What does it say?"

She held up a finger and banged out a reply in angry taps.

> Are you kidding me?
> You're twenty feet away.
> You couldn't tell me face to face?

He replied.

> I left. It's easier this way.

Her jittery fingers typed.

> Easier?
> ~~For who~~
> ~~For whom~~
> For who?

He replied.

> For me. :(

Gabby's hand dropped to her side, and her phone to the floor. She peered up with tear-filled eyes.

"It's over." The deep throaty rumble of a muscle car engine started and seconds later screeched off in the distance; Leo drove a Mustang GT.

"What's over?" Vic asked.

"Our marriage. Our relationship. Everything. The wedding's off."

The devastating blow sucked the air out of the room. Everyone deflated. Her mother and Vic rushed to Gabby's side and enveloped her in a group hug.

"I know you're not okay," Vic said. "But I promise you will be."

"The spineless son of a—" Her mother grabbed the phone while Vic placed a consoling hand on Gabby's shoulder. "I'll make the announcement."

Pain flooded her cheeks. She'd drained her strength fighting to stem the flow, all for naught. "Given my record, raise your hand if you didn't see that one coming?"

She lifted her hand and sobbed.

Chapter 2

Two Years Later

Black Friday held a whole new meaning for Gabby after Leo deserted her, bolting from their cancelled Christmas, his wheels screeching and smoking. The day after overdosing on dry turkey and expressions of sympathy during her parents' Thanksgiving dinner, she peered out from her fourth-floor row house window, and her eyes followed the snow drifting over the Capitol dome. She dreaded the start of her now least favorite season. Each flake, new and different, would leave a thin blanket of white to delight children across the area, frustrate morning commuters, and remind her of the brutal heartache, gifted by a man who refused to stop calling despite her persistent cold-shoulder. She glanced at the empty corner where she used to set up the Christmas tree, couldn't bear to fill the void. Perhaps a metaphor for her romantic life.

Two years. Still too soon.

She needed new memories to supplant the old, but every time she wandered downstairs to the storage unit to retrieve the boxes, she pictured the aisle she didn't walk down, and the gown never seen beyond the bounds of the dressing room, and the seventy-five people she faced alone as she suffered the ultimate humiliation due to her spineless coward of a fiancé who fled the scene of the crime like Dale Earnhardt, Jr. on the Indy 500 track.

Her Christmas had been stolen from her, except her villain wasn't a Grinch, rather he was the man who'd consented to love and protect her for the rest of her life.

As she pondered how she'd use the vacation days she'd taken to hide and hibernate until January second, the doorknob jiggled. For a moment, she thought Leo may be trying to use a key that no longer worked, but she'd long ago changed the locks. The noise stopped, and she feared she might be losing her mind when the door flung open.

"Gabby! Hey, Baby Sis! The decorating committee has arrived. I've come bearing ornament kits, holiday Shrinky Dinks, and the joy of Christmas," Victoria bellowed. She scanned the area conducting a motherly visual inspection. "Gosh, I hate your house. It's always perfect, like a Crate and Barrel ad. The beigey yellow paint looks perfect against the espresso-colored furniture. You've done quite well."

"Thank you." Gabby clutched her chest and breathed heavily. "But you can take back the stuff you brought to wherever you got it. We don't do joy here."

Vic burst in looking as if she'd gone to the Christmas Store for seasonal garb, asked for one of everything—then wore them all at once. From the Santa Snoopy jacket to the ugly sweater underneath, to the Rudolph headband with antlers and blinking nose, Gabby didn't know what to focus on first. She resisted her sister's show of affection, keeping her arms at her side and frowning as Vic wrapped her up in a tight embrace.

"Sorry for the fright. Didn't mean to scare you. Why didn't you answer your phone? I've only been calling you for an hour. Not trying to avoid me, were you?"

"Crud! My cell's going wonky, again. Sometimes it rings, other times not so much. Half the time I can't maintain enough bars to call two houses down the block, but I can send a text message to Zimbabwe without missing a letter. What's that about? I think I need a new service."

"And a new attitude. I'm here to deliver. I will not allow another holiday to pass with you sitting here like dreary death on a stick, moping around and depressed in funky pajamas."

Usually, her mother sent in Vic to spy, ensure the memories of the almost-wedding hadn't caused Gabby to blow out the pilot light in the oven, so to speak. She'd arrived in snoop-and-lecture mode, her perpetual state ever since the dreaded day…but that didn't explain the suitcases, which drew a curious glance from Gabby. She sniffed her armpit. "I've got one more day in these pajamas before I reach funky town city limits. What's with the baggage?"

"I'm staying with you for a few days…or a week…or longer. That's not gonna be a problem, is it?"

Gabby's posture collapsed, and her head tilted to the side as she pursed her lips.

Before she could fix her mouth to form her next question, Vic said, "Marriage sucks. It's a total and complete sham. If Reggie's my soulmate, I'm Oprah Winfrey. But I'm not about to allow that man to steal my joy. So, please don't ask for any more details, at least not until I've poured us a tall glass of holiday cheer."

Gabby answered with silence, offering only a nod as she watched her sister settle in. Vic was clearly not ready to do a deep-dive into her emotions.

"Good. Put on your shoes. Let's grab the decorations out of the storage unit."

"Viiiiiic," Gabby whined. "I don't wanna."

"You move your butt right now, or I'll call Mom."

Gabby shrugged.

"And tell her you begged to be set up on a blind date with that Freddy character. You know the one who still lives in his mom's basement?"

"I'm up. I'm up. You fight dirty."

Vic laughed evil villain style, dropped a load of bags on the dining room table, and they headed downstairs. Within fifteen minutes they'd dragged the containers upstairs from the storage space. Piles of dusty plastic crates loaded with Christmas decoration were strewn about the room waiting to find their places in Chez Gabby, including one containing their dad's old Santa suit. He wore it each year while they opened gifts until his heart attack. It'd been two years since they'd seen the light of day. She and Vic glanced around the living room to survey and assess the decorating damage they were about to impart on her row house.

"Before we get this party started. We are in serious need of cocktails." Vic strolled into the kitchen, and

Gabby heard cabinet doors slam, glasses clang, water run, and ice cubes clink.

"I've decided I'm getting you a new phone for Christmas."

"Don't bother. After I switch services, it'll be fine."

"You don't need a new service, you need a new phone...and a new life. You've had that thing since your sophomore year excursion to New York, how many years ago? Ten?"

The memory of that perfect summer brought an instant smile to her face, even though her dream seemed farther away today than ever. One glance around her swanky, expensive home nestled in the heart of the Hill told her everything she needed to know about the chances, the slim chances, that she'd ever return to being that daring girl, so adventurous, so full of hope, so broke and unencumbered by mortgages as she'd been way back then.

"It's ancient, big enough to kill an elephant. Time to upgrade, Gabby. You'd be amazed at how far technology has come since the nineties. There's this new-fangled invention. It's called an iPhone."

"First of all, my Nokia isn't ancient, it's classic, an antique if you will. And it's my 212 phone, a classic area code, from my second pancake summer. So, I'm keeping it. As for the rest of my life, well, I'm definitely considering some changes—including resurrecting Gabby's Designs."

"Second pancake summer. Really?" Vic muttered. "Nobody wanted you to settle. Nobody wanted to kill your dream of owning your own interior decorating business. We just didn't want you to set your sights so high that you couldn't get what you wanted."

"But if I base my wants on possibility rather than my heart's desire, doesn't that limit my dreams? Isn't faith extending your hopes beyond what you think is attainable?"

"Perhaps for normal people, but you're always in your head imagining a life that hasn't come to fruition. Maybe being a little more realistic with that list of yours means you won't live a daily existence filled with disappointment," she said.

"So lower my expectations. Is it so much to wish to make a living with my art, with my passion? Make a connection with a man that begins up here?"—she pointed at her temple—"and not here." She circled her hands around her boobs.

Gabby had longed to meet someone who challenged her intellectually, who understood her, who accepted her quirks, her desire to be together and alone at the same time. But hopes for "something more" had landed her single and unmarried. She began to fear Vic may be right, and yet...

"Disappointment seems to be inevitable, a part of living. You married the man of your dreams, yet you're here with your suitcases keeping your lips locked about what's going on with you and Reggie."

"Ouch." Vic shifted her gaze in the opposite direction. Gabby could tell the words stung even though she hadn't intended them to. "Fine, whatever, keep the phone. You just better hope you don't have an emergency that requires you to call for help. The police in Zimbabwe don't service this area. Now to start the party!"

"Yes, indeed."

Frankly, Gabby didn't want to be reminded of what could've been. She spurned the thought of her first pancake life—a term she coined to describe not only her second-class family breakfasts but also perceived slights from her most beloved.

While she was growing up, Gabby's parents always served pancakes for Sunday breakfasts—the Garrett family tradition. The maple-soaked treats remained one of her favorite meals to this day, but she'd hated, with an admittedly irrational passion, the first pancake. Not just for its appearance but for what it stood. From a nutritional perspective, there was no difference between the first pancake and the fifth.

Tasted the same as all the others.

But it didn't look like them.

The coloring was always just a little off, never browned evenly. She much preferred the golden-brown ones with the wide nooks and crannies thirsting of her father's famous maple butter. Everyone understood it.

Yet, Dad had never been served the first one, neither had her mother nor Vic.

Only Gabby.

They'd conspired to force the first one upon her.

She, perhaps wrongly, translated the action as an intentional subliminal message, an order to settle for whatever she'd been served, choke down the half-brown carb cake and be happy it wasn't cornflakes, even if everyone knew she'd wanted something different.

She deserved something more.

Vic dug around into her bags and pulled out the ornament kits, laid them out on the kitchen table, and separated the packages of beads. She and Gabby had made tree ornaments every year since they were small girls. The activity, mandated by their mother, proved very effective in keeping them busy during holiday vacations.

"Before we begin, how strong do you want your drink? Merry or merrier."

"The merriest. I'll take a large glass of spiked eggnog...minus the egg and the nog."

"Merriest coming right up," Vic said as plastic bags rustled in the background. She returned a few moments later and handed Gabby a red party cup with something tempting on the rocks. "A tall glass of spiked eggnog without the egg or the nog. Drink."

Gabby snatched the drink from her hands and drew in a long sip, allowing the elixir to heat her throat and warmed some part of her body that might be characterized as a cockle, if she knew what they were. "You're always late but right on time! Just what I needed."

"Rough day?"

"Not so much rough as utterly depressing."

"Po-tay-to, Po-tah-to."

"I've been trying to pull myself together all day. Maybe I'll find my Christmas spirit in one of those boxes," she said, looking at the decorations littering the floor.

The 12 Daves of Christmas

As Vic returned to the kitchen to fix her own cocktail, she called out over her shoulder, "It's been two years since you last enjoyed the holidays. What you need is a sweet date with a hot guy."

"Hot guy? Been there, done that, remember? My problem isn't finding a date, it's finding 'the one.'"

Vic poked her head out of the kitchen. "You're going through life, looking for this perfect ideal. Newsflash, this gift of the gods doesn't exist among us mortals and never will....and, yes, you are still mortal."

"Don't remind me. And for the record, I've given up my quest for the 'gift guy.' None of mine are of the gods. No, they seem to come from Walmart...the bottom of the discount rack."

"You just need to loosen up. You won't spend the rest of your life alone. As a matter of fact, if you want to know how to find the perfect guy, I've got the secret."

Then Vic fell silent as if she weren't required to follow up that statement with full and complete details.

"Well, don't just stand there. Share!"

"This is what you do. Take out a sheet of paper and draw up two lists. On the first list, write down every single quality *your heart* tells you that you need to be truly happy, the ones that are the stuff of your every dream and wish. Next, list of all the qualities that *your mind* says need in a partner to have a healthy, normal relationship."

At that point, she stopped as if the conversation had ended. Gabby waited practically on the edge of her seat for the rest of the answer. Finally, after what felt like forever, Vic finally looked up. "What?"

"What do you do next?"

"Oh, I should think the answer is obvious," she said, quickly phasing back into assembling her craft project.

"Really, Vic? I'm practically frothing at the mouth waiting for your response. You can't drop this bomb and fail to detonate. What? What do you do?"

"Duh! You tear up the heart list. Rip that baby to shreds and burn it if you need to. It's filled to the brim with unrealistic expectations. After that list has been destroyed, make yourself 'at one' with the mind list. And then quit giving me that look."

"I know not of what you speak."

"Oh, you know the one I'm talking about. That *you burned down my treasured Barbie Dream House* look."

"But you did."

"Accident! What part of accident do you not understand? How many times do I have to apologize? I was a kid, for goodness sakes. I didn't know the embers would jump out of the fireplace and melt it into a puddle of goo. Mattel forgot the smoke detectors. Is it my fault Barbie and Ken weren't insured? I offered them a full policy when they signed the closing papers."

Even at the age of eleven, Vic loved real estate and catering to high-end clients. She bought and sold numerous houses to Barbie and Ken over the course of their entire childhood. Lincoln log cabins, Lego skyscrapers. Even helped Gabby build a cardboard addition to her most treasured Barbie McMansion (until the unfortunate incident). Also, to this day, she remained the family Monopoly champion, fifteen years running. Gabby so admired her—she'd followed her calling from the start. Then again, she'd always lived her second-pancake life.

The 12 Daves of Christmas

Only Gabby had succumbed to family pressure to seek the right job, the security of a good government job. Gabby's "thing" had always been decorating. She loved color, making things orderly and beautiful.

"Anyway, the point is, stop imposing unrealistic expectations on real people. Nobody's perfect. In your quest for perfection, you're going to eliminate some really good guys who could make you happy. After all, I mean, you're beautiful, smart, and wonderful but no picnic to deal with all the time."

Gabby collapsed in the chair and pouted. "Why do I feel like I can never have the life I imagine?" She watched Vic set the beads in her ornament and anticipated opening her own kit, before saying, "I'll be right back."

Taking advantage of a lull in the conversation, Gabby stole away a moment in her bedroom. She pulled her journal from the nightstand and flipped it to the center page. That's where she kept it. Her list. Years ago, she'd enumerated the qualities representing her ideal. An update was in order, the addition of some realism. After all, she'd known little of the world when she drafted 1.0. Too naïve, too stupid to understand what she'd asked for. Now, she'd revise as Vic suggested. Maybe if she pinpointed those characteristics most important to her happiness, she'd seek relationships with men who possessed them. By the time she finished, her list had changed—drastically.

1. ~~Gorgeous~~ Not repulsive with a thick head of hair

2. ~~Exciting job, 6-figure salary~~ Employed, no newspaper delivery boys (too young), no roadkill scoopers

3. ~~Owns a mansion~~ Not living in his car

4. ~~College degree, master of anything~~ Some college
5. No vegetarians! Must be a carnivore ✓
6. ~~Acceptable Cars - Mercedes, Lexus, Porsche, Range Rover, BMW~~ Engine turns over by the third try
7. A kind heart, caring, sensitive ✓
8. ~~Aquarius, Sagittarius, or Aries~~ Earthling
9. ~~Genius~~ Sane (two or fewer medications)
10. ~~At least 6'2"~~ Can see over the steering wheel
11. No kids ✓
14. No pets ✓
15. Regularly reads books without pictures in them; has read Shakespeare. Major bonus—can quote a play or Sonnet. ✓✓

There. It was done…and filled to the brim with acceptable, attainable standards. Now her original dream man in the list was almost imperceptible, exactly as Vic and the rest of her family would have it. She scanned the draft once more, this time to conduct a quick assessment. At a basic level, only number seven mattered. She didn't have anything against kids and pets, per se, as long as they belonged to other people. Not that she didn't want them someday, she just didn't believe she could ever establish her own business and work for herself with the little rug rats in the picture. She barely could keep goldfish alive.

On second thought, numbers seven, one…and two—they should be the focus of her efforts. Fourteen was probably way too much to ask and should remain last. If she found a man with the revised qualities, perhaps he wouldn't meet every requirement, but maybe he'd meet enough.

The 12 Daves of Christmas

She expelled a deep breath signaling she'd conceded her dreams for realism. She peered out the window and noticed a bright beam of light blaze across the sky. In the D.C. area, that usually meant a plane was flying in a holding pattern before landing. On the off chance the streak belonged to a Christmas star, she made a wish to the universe that she'd meet a nice guy and wouldn't have to spend the holiday alone. Maybe he'd be the one.

Hardly a minute passed before her cell phone sounded. A text message banner filled the screen. She hoped Leo hadn't sent it. He seemed to sense when she'd begun to move on emotionally. She huffed and clenched her eyes shut, then glanced over and read the message.

> Come, come, you wasp. I'faith you are too angry.- Petruchio

Shakespeare? She chuckled, looking up at the heavens with her brow crinkled. Then she stared in disbelief. *Really? That was fast.*

She studied the number. A 212-area code. She didn't recognize it.

Color me intrigued, she thought.

Someone had texted the wrong person, but the contents begged a response—from her. What harm could one reply do?

Chapter 3

A knot formed in Dave Williams' stomach as he eyed the tabletop Christmas tree his assistant, Lexi, had forced onto his drafting table.

Not that he didn't love the holidays, he did.

Or at least he used to.

Recalling those of days gone by brought back difficult memories, reminded him of the looming pressures he faced today.

His new year would bring with it a new city and job, and, somehow, he must prepare a home and holiday for the family who'd meet him there.

Now that it was too late to turn back, he questioned the wisdom of employing his life-reboot strategy at such a hectic time, with so many emotional and logistical hurdles to overcome. But the truth was he couldn't endure another Christmas in Manhattan.

He glanced out of his Fifth Avenue window and reminisced about holidays past. He and Tina met at Columbia University and fell in love during their first study group meeting. They'd been inseparable from that day forward, until breast cancer ruthlessly stripped his life of the only woman who'd ever given it any meaning. They'd built their lives in the City of Dreams. Every street corner from Harlem to the Village held priceless memories that were too painful to remember and impossible to forget.

Ice skating in Central Park during staycations at The Plaza. Elevator rides to the top of the Empire State Building with her face buried in his shoulder because she feared heights but was determined to be with him. Trips to the tree lot to buy biggest Douglas Fir and lug it home ten blocks and up seven flights of stairs because they were too broke to afford a car, and the building's elevator stayed broken. Midnights on the roof terrace drinking hot cocoa and talking about everything and nothing.

Three years had passed since she transitioned, and he could no longer endure the constant reminders of her absence.

The time had come to rebuild, start anew.

On her final day, Tina had made Dave promise not to linger in his grief, threatening on multiple occasions to return from the heavens to haunt him if he didn't get on with life (after a suitable period, of course). After all, his responsibilities required his presence of mind and heart. He couldn't afford to check out, not with so much riding on his stability, his ability to put the past behind him and move forward into whatever the future had to offer. But what length of time constituted "too long?"

Until this year, recalling their short but thrilling life together had sustained him, woke him up each morning, propped him up as he pretended to live. But he'd finally reached the point at which his longing for some semblance of happiness (or something closely resembling his memory of it) surpassed his present sorrow.

He wanted more, needed more.

And not from the high-maintenance cougar-client Diane vonWolfraddt, who'd hunted him as if he were jungle prey.

No, he desired someone a bit more easy-going, someone who'd rather spend an evening at home decorating a tree and drinking spiked eggnog than going out to some ultra-formal party rubbing elbows with the wealthy and feckless. Someone who'd rather dress in an ugly Christmas sweater in front of a handful of people than a Christian Siriano gown in front of hundreds. Someone who'd prefer to quote a Shakespearean Sonnet over a Vogue article citing ten ways to love your loofah. Someone who liked to laugh and joke. Someone who'd rather be with him, beside him, than any place else in the world.

As he gazed up at the twinkling in the night, Dave whispered toward the sky, made a wish of sorts, that he'd meet someone special. This time perhaps someone of his own age with whom he could spend the holidays . . . and maybe always.

The jingling sound in his reception area shook him out of his thoughts. Seconds later, Lexi entered bearing a gift box wrapped in Santa paper and a big red bow replete with bells.

"Ho ho ho!" she said. "I'm on two missions, and this is the first." She handed over the present.

Dave shook his head and smiled. "You shouldn't have." He reluctantly grabbed her offering. "I haven't had time to do any shopping yet. But I promise you will receive something before Christmas day."

"Are you kidding me? You've already given me more than I could ask for—the best boss ever. And that bonus wasn't too shabby, either. Besides, I had to give you something before the big move, although I still can't believe you're deserting me."

"I wish I could take you with me. I'll never find another assistant who knows me so well and will so graciously suffer my quirks. Honestly, I wouldn't be able to make this move to D.C., to one of the most prestigious architectural firms in the city, if it you didn't make me look so competent."

"Trust me, I'll never have it this good with the next person who fills your shoes. I'd go with you if it weren't for that pesky husband of mine who makes three times my salary on Wall Street. But…can I say something? I hope you won't be offended."

"Please! It's me."

"Well, ever since you announced your move to Washington, I don't know…I've seen this new energy surrounding you. A new *joie de vivre*, if I may say. You seem, happier, livelier, more hopeful. I see that spark of life in your eyes again…the one before, you know."

"I'm not back, not quite yet."

"Of course not."

"But I'm ready to take the journey."

"It's going to take time, but…baby steps," she added. "Obviously, I hate to see you leave, but if this is the change you need to get back to your old self, then it's a change well worth making. And while we're on the subject of changes, go ahead and open your gift."

He unpeeled the paper carefully and then more quickly when Lexi spun her hands in circles, gesturing for him to pick up the pace.

"Two tickets." He read them. "A Candlelight Christmas at the Kennedy Center."

She shrugged. "Well, I figured as the new guy in town, you may need a night out...with a date."

He tilted his head to the side and paused.

"Fine, it's a longshot but you never know. And speaking of dates, I've been telling you about my sister for years. She's a little rough around the edges. The pink hair and three nose rings can be a little off-putting, at first, but you don't even notice after a while. She's the sweetest girl."

"Yeah, okay." He pulled a second envelope from the box. "A gift card to Fogo de Chão. Perfect. Nothing says you care like an American Greeting card containing a free meal at the Brazilian meat factory. I'm really going to miss you."

"How will you ever survive?" She snickered and offered a teasing pat on the shoulder.

"Now that we've dispensed with all the pleasantries, you said something about another mission?" he asked.

"Oh, yeah." Her face curled into a frown. "The Baroness VonSnob, Di-annnnne called." Her voice sounded like a constipated British aristocrat. "She's peeved because you haven't replied to *her order*...I mean, *her invitation* to accompany her to the Annual Christmas Tree Ball at the *Gaaaah*-den."

The forty-something socialite widow, one of the firm's biggest clients who unfortunately had marked Dave for marriage, had been the bane of his existence. The Madison Square Garden ball, an annual event for the charitable rich, brought in loads of money for the Boys & Girls Club but suffering her presence for four hours was a bit more than the universe should ask two years in a row.

"I take it you haven't broken the bad news about your relocation yet," she continued.

He tightened his lips and shook his head. "I'd hoped *to escape*...I mean, *leave town*, maybe remarry...retire in Jamaica, first. Guess I can't hide any longer, huh?"

"You're gone in a month. Tell her. Gently, please. We can't afford to lose her millions. She's hired us to renovate two penthouses and build a vacation home all because she likes your...*work*."

Dave chuckled. "Why does drawing blueprints sound so seedy when you say it? Eli has agreed to take over her account and schedule meetings for the new addition to the Hampton home. She doesn't need me, but I suppose a clean getaway was too much to ask. I'll call her...*or something*."

"You can't punt this one. You've got to follow through. Yes, you're leaving and will be three hundred miles away, but the rest of us will be stuck with the fallout if you don't do the right thing."

"Okay, okay. Fine. I'll call...or something. I promise."

"Well, I've got to head home. It's getting late, and somebody's got to order the pizza. Four phones in the house and apparently only mine works."

He chuckled. "All right. See you tomorrow."

After the office door opened and closed, signaling Lexi's exit, he picked up the receiver on his office phone to make the call. His fingers hovered over the buttons far longer than necessary; he just couldn't bring himself to push. He didn't want to talk to her, and neither his fingers nor his common sense would allow him to call. With her constant yammering about walls and skylights, nothing he wanted to hear, she was tough to tolerate, even under the best of circumstances. He feared a week of dodging her calls may have pushed her to the edge, resulting in a lengthy conversation drowning in passive aggression.

So, he chickened out, decided instead to feel her out with a text first. He picked up his business cell, intentionally avoiding the use of his personal one (as he had since he'd known her) and sent her a short message. As long as she didn't reply with fury, he'd give her the phone call for which she'd been waiting. He tapped in what he thought was her number and left a few simple words

```
Come, come you wasp. I'faith, you are too
angry. - Petruchio
```

It'd take her ten minutes to Google what this meant. By that time, maybe he could bear to hear her voice. He rubbed his tired eyes and began packing his briefcase for the trip home. When she didn't respond right away, he grew concerned and checked his screen to ensure the message was sent. That's when he noticed the number. Somehow, he'd sent typed in the wrong one. It wasn't surprising that he hadn't caught the mistake sooner as he usually made Lexi place all calls for him on his desk phone. He'd inverted the digits—2-7 instead of 7-2.

One digit off.

Just as he decided to send a quick apology for the intrusion, his phone buzzed.

> `If I be waspish, best beware of my sting.`
> `- Katherine`

His head jerked back as his lips crawled into a wide smile. The response was far beyond what he expected. He stared in amazement. The receiver could've tapped out a "bug off" or replied with plain old-fashioned silence.

She could be an ax murder or serial killer or even worse, another Diane.

Still, he was intrigued.

He opted not to ignore the message. Some mysterious stranger had replied in the name of Katherine from "Taming of the Shrew." She (he hoped) not only had read Shakespeare, but she also quoted it.

He'd be insane to extend this conversation with another text; she may not offer a second response. But she'd intrigued him enough that he risked it.

Chapter 4

Gabrielle stared at her screen in disbelief. She'd returned a text to a complete stranger and sat on her bed practically holding her breath, waiting for him to respond. Pure insanity, especially as she thought about all the things that could go wrong with this scenario. After all, he could be a pervert or a serial killer or one of those guys who took better care of his car than his mother. Or maybe he lived in his mother's basement. As bad as those scenarios would be, none of them discouraged her from waiting.

"Gabby, what are you doing in there? Did you get lost?"

"I'll be out in a sec!"

Just as she stood up to return to the living room and rejoin her sister, another text buzzed in. *Okay, I'll bite. Favorite sonnet.*

She bounced back on the bed and tapped out a response with her thumbs, now unable to suppress her wide smile. *Easy. 116. Yours?*

This time the reply came more quickly. *Believe it or not—same.*

She chuckled. *You lie. :P*

Within seconds, he replied. *It is the star to every wand'ring bark.*

No way he looked it up, she thought. His response came too quickly. She shook her head and grinned. *Not the usual quote, but you spelled "wand'ring" correctly, so it must be true.*

She wanted more details on him, all of them at once. She refused, however, to ask point-blank for fear he'd suspect she was doing the very thing she was attempting to do — building a profile.

She replied with laughing emoticons and typed: *Quoting Shakespeare on a Tuesday. You must be a hundred years old.*

He answered: *I can pretend to be a hundred if you like older men. :)*

She celebrated for a moment. Hallelujah, a man!

Then after a beat, he continued: *Alas, I'm thirty-two.*

She pumped her fist in the air and shouted "Yes!" in a loud whisper before she caught herself. What the heck was she thinking? Pure madness. But, then again, given her fortuitous wish, she couldn't deny the timing…and she believed in signs.

"Gabby! Come on before you miss out on the brown stuff!"

Part of her wanted to stay and chat, to see where their words and their imaginations might carry them. There was something kind of freeing about connecting with a man based on nothing except his ability to quote Shakespeare.

The irony of the day's events wasn't lost on her, either. Leo cancelled her wedding day with a deliberate text two years before. Now she'd found a person of interest with an accidental one. A peculiar universe, indeed.

Almost as quickly as she allowed her trip down the rabbit hole, she reined in her wild thoughts. In her life, there was no such thing as fortune. Things never worked out in reality as they did in her mind. If she had an ounce of respect for her past mistakes, she'd end the conversation by telling him he'd made one by texting her—have a nice life.

But, in her heart, she believed everything happened for a reason, that every person who entered one's life was sent for a season, no matter how short. That's why she couldn't ignore him, the text, or the timing. That's why she replied with the next message: *Hate to cut this short, but can we continue later? Sister's here. Decorating frenzy to commence.*

Took a long time, but finally, his response appeared. *Of course. Ten, okay?*

Her answer was a no-brainer. *OK :)*

It'd been ages since she looked forward to interacting with a man in this way; she'd given no one a chance since Leo. No suitor had piqued her interest, not in this way. Her reaction to this stranger affirmed for Gabby that her hesitation to date again was never due to persnickety tastes, regardless of what her mother and Vic said. The real issue at the heart of the matter was complicated and yet simple: she didn't want a space-filler, neither on the other side of her kitchen table, nor the other side of her bed.

She wanted a soul filler. She wanted to read a man's thoughts, to know what he was thinking with just a look or a glance. She wanted to laugh with him, to joke together, to communicate though glances and gestures as often as words. She wanted to love eighties music and disco with him, dance around the living room with him until they collapsed, breathless and exhilarated. She wanted to eat cornbread with syrup with him and bake Christmas cookies until the wee hours of the morning. She wanted to spend time with him as a couple while allowing time apart to grow as individuals.

That kind of relationship, that kind of bond, required a connection beyond the physical, founded on friendship and commonality and likeness. The mystery text man may not be the one of her dreams but, at least for now, he represented the possibility.

She pulled herself out of her thoughts and changed into her Garrett family Christmas outfit. She tamped down the butterflies batting around in her belly with the sobering thought that this little spark would fizzle out before it got warm. Even if all else worked out, he lived in New York. She didn't want to do a long-distance thing.

She called out to Vic, "Here I come!" Then she took a deep breath and bounced into the living room where her sister had abandoned the ornament beading to set up the tree. Her arms were wrapped in tangled lights.

"Well somebody's been a busy beaver," Gabby said.

Vic turned toward Gabby, gawked at her outfit, and her mouth fell open. "Now, that's a load of Christmas joy."

Gabby was now the sight to behold, festive on steroids. If the blinking reindeer antlers protruding from her shoulder-length, kinky-curly locks weren't overkilled enough, she capped off her outfit with red stirrup pants speckled with glitter-green polka dots and a sweater that matched Vic's.

"Yeah, look at you! Somebody caught the spirit, and you've been MIA since like yesterday, for goodness sake," she said with a chuckle. She'd been heavy into the eggnog minus the egg and the nog. Her voice had started to sound a little sleepy.

"Well, I'm back in the nick of time it would seem. And I think I'm ready for some actual eggnog in my brown stuff. It's more festive, more Christmassy that way. Since you're the bartender, I'll let you get my drink while I finish detangling and stringing the lights."

"Hold up, wait a minute! You hate stringing the lights." Vic gave her sister the side-eye and then inspected her. "What's with the new attitude? You disappeared into your bedroom as the Scrooge a half hour ago and you've returned as the Happy Elf. You're practically glowing. What gives?" Her gaze scrolled down to Gabrielle's hand which clutched her old Nokia. "Ah, I know what this is about."

Gabrielle shrugged, eyed the phone in her hand, and shrugged. "What?"

Vic pointed an accusatory finger. "You've been sexting. You can't fool me. I saw the way you were clutching that ancient thing on the way out here. Who is he?"

"Nobody," she whined like a toddler, her ears burning with embarrassment. That Vic could even think such a thought left Gabby feeling somewhere between embarrassed and flattered. "You need to lay off the eggnog."

"All right, then. Let me see it."

"You're so high school," she said. "And you can forget it. I'm not handing it over. Not because I have anything *to hide* but because I have nothing *to prove*."

"Uh-huh. You can't fool me. Something happened in that bedroom, and you can't convince me otherwise."

"Listen, there's no intrigue here. I took a minute to pull myself together after a rough day, and now I'm ready for you…and all of this." She gestured her hand in the general direction of the Christmas mess. "So, let's focus *less on* my personal business and *more on* the decorations."

Vic hesitantly allowed that part of the conversation to slide. "Fine, whatever. It'll be nice to breathe a little more life into this space, but it's gorgeous as always. You think you're ready to help me stage a condo? I need to get the place open house-ready in a couple of weeks."

"Of course. Anything for you, Sis."

"I have to tell you, I'm glad to see you phasing out of your depression."

"I wasn't depressed. I was taking a time-out…from life."

"You were taking a depression, and I'm partly at fault. I'm responsible for Leo," she said with a groan. "But you have to admit, he was gorgeous. He's still a top seller at my firm. And he would've made some beautiful babies."

Gabrielle rolled her eyes. "Yes, I'll admit Leo was perfect as a fine piece of eye candy, but you couldn't possibly believe he and I had anything in common. I mean, he wasn't very bright. This is a real estate agent who couldn't spell the word *house* if you spotted him the first three letters."

"Your standards are too high."

"Wanting to marry someone who can hold a civilized conversation for longer than five minutes, someone who can occasionally employ a word with more than two syllables, isn't a high standard; it's a basic human right. You've got that with Reggie, so you couldn't possibly understand. You have everything with him."

"No, not everything." She fiddled restlessly and began chewing on her lip.

Gabby's eyes narrowed with suspicion and curiosity. "What's going on with you two?"

A suffocating silence fell between them, one in which Vic refused to fill with a direct answer.

"Let's wrap this up. I've had a long day, and I'm pretty tired," Vic replied. "Anything we don't finish because we're jabbering, you're on your own."

For the next hour, they listened to Christmas music, Stevie Wonder's "What Christmas Means to Me" on repeat, singing as they sipped on eggnog and finished decorating Gabrielle's place. They infused more holiday spirit in her home in one day than it'd seen in a few years. The decorations lifted her spirits, but it wouldn't take much to do that. She'd almost forgotten about the Christmas disaster of years before. Bigger and better things lie ahead, at least that's what she hoped.

"We're done! Finally! The house is now suitable for guests this year," Vic said. "Now let me hit the powder room and get some rest."

Gabby pecked her cheek. "See you in the morning. First one up makes the coffee."

No sooner than her sister disappeared did Gabby's eyes lock on her watch. It was two minutes before ten, and Vic hadn't yet shut her door. Gabby tapped out a quick message to tell the guy she wouldn't be ready to chat until maybe 10:15, but the minute she picked up the phone, Vic returned to the hall and roamed into to the restroom, eyeing her suspiciously the whole way.

"Ah-ha! Sexting again, aren't you?"

"Go to bed."

When Vic exited minutes later, she muttered something indiscernible as Gabby rushed to her and practically shoved her into the bedroom. "I put a new mattress topper on the bed. You'll sleep like a baby."

"All right. I'm going, I'm going. But when I wake up tomorrow, I'm going to find out why you're sneaking. Don't think I'm going to forget because I'm not."

"Okay, okay," she said. "Now, goodnight...and I love you."

Gabby waited until the door closed and Vic's light shut off before flying back to her phone. She checked for a text message from "him" whoever he was.

She unlocked the screen—nothing.

She glanced at the time. 10:02. Late. Bad sign. She hated lateness. He should've been on time. And if he couldn't be on time, he could've texted early to let her know he'd be late.

Maybe he'd decided not to text at all.

She set the ancient artifact on the nightstand, refusing to be a slave to the screen, staring at it like some desperate spinster.

She decided to forget about him and pretend as if the conversation never happened…until she was struck by a single cogent thought—she'd officially gone insane.

Gabby had never so much as batted an eye at the man. Yet, within a twenty-second time span, she'd jumped on the crazy train and expressed from waiting in anticipation to passing judgment and writing him off as a loss.

She laughed at her nuttiness and decided to use her time more effectively as she headed to the kitchen to wash up the glasses from Vic's mini cocktail party. As she recollected the speed at which her irrationality had devolved, she knocked her head with the heel of her hand and took two steps toward her door when her cell buzzed. It was the standard ring so it could've been the Salvation Army for all she knew; he needed a ringtone. Gabby darted down the hall so fast she created her own breeze. She entered her bedroom and dove across her bed with the form of an Olympic swimmer on a championship lap and grabbed the phone.

Finally!

The tension released from her shoulders as she read his message: *You there? Sorry, I'm late.*

She started typing but stopped herself. She didn't want to seem too eager as if she'd been waiting with bated breath for him to contact her. She played the moment cool, put on her pajamas and brushed her teeth, much faster than usual, but she took time to do it. Then she replied: *Well, well, well. He's back. :)*

His answer was immediate: *To be honest, I've picked up the phone twenty times in the last fifteen minutes wondering whether or not I was responding too quickly, questioning my sanity. Is this weird? Me texting you?*

She rolled over laughing and shook her head. Their likeness was almost frightening. Only she'd never admit the truth to him.

Gabby: *Yes. Totally weird. But it'll be our little secret.*

His reply was simply an emoticon. *:)*

She waited for him to say something more but he took longer than expected, so she jumped in: *I'm Gabrielle, by the way. But we can just stick with Gabby.*

She wanted to make him understand her phone number and first name were all she'd be willing to offer...for now.

He replied a second later: *Nice to meet you. I'm Dave. Just Dave.*

Chapter 5

Dave left his midtown high-rise office and took the number six train to his Harlem brownstone on 141st. All the while, his mind churned over the girl named Gabby, wondering how a mistake that seemed so inconsequential could consume his every thought. After arriving home, he opened the entry door to the foyer, shook off the snow, and hung up his coat on the rack. After kicking off his shoes, he paused to consider his next move.

He opted to ignore the mountains of boxes stacked around the living and dining rooms, deciding instead to collapse into his couch and rest his head against the overstuffed cushions. He loved his sofa. Sinking into it felt like a warm hug after a long, rough day. That's when he heard the thing he had not heard in nearly ten years.

Silence.

He'd enjoy having a quiet house for a change.

Dave thought for a moment about how life could reverse in an instant, from receiving an unexpected diagnosis in one instance to sending a misguided text in the next. When he left work this morning, he'd resigned himself to spend another Christmas by himself. Well not exactly alone, but without a girlfriend or a date. He sought to rectify his status by embarking on this new adventure. The time had come. It was long overdue.

As a widower, the main challenge to beginning his romantic life again remained meeting someone with whom he truly connected, someone who possessed the ideal mix of qualities required for his complicated life. He'd met brash and brilliant upper-class Manhattanites, the nature of his business at his high-powered architectural firm. He'd met fun artsy women who were elusive and flighty, often lacked focus. He'd met laid back women living lives with no structure or order, who often overindulged in pleasure and shirked responsibility. He'd met women stiffened by structure, orderly women living lives that left little room for the unpredictability of his own and zero space for enjoyment.

No single one of these characteristics would suffice; he required fractions of them all. Women who struck the right balance proved elusive. He'd never met a woman willing to accept the complexity, which he'd fully admit was hefty load, more than evidenced by the clutter representing the stages of his family's life.

But with "Katherine," something clicked for reasons he couldn't explain. When she replied to his wayward message, the universe flipped on a switch and a light came on.

A question had been answered.

Yet, he struggled to retain his grip on common sense. An accidental text leading him to anything more than a "pardon me for interrupting" struck him as ridiculous. The possibility lacked all logic. And how creepy must it be for her to have some random guy texting Shakespeare, a line about a shrew no less.

What woman in her right mind would be interested in a guy like that?

He shrugged. Well, Tina for one, he supposed. She'd once been interested, so much so, in fact, that she married him. Could destiny favor him with the same grace twice?

He shook off his thoughts, negative and positive, and checked the time. That's when the phone rang. He glanced at the screen and smiled—his brother, Brian. He answered, and they exchanged their usual greetings as Dave took a seat.

"How are things going?" Dave asked. "I'd planned to check in with you earlier, but I worked late. You've probably got a house full by now, I imagine."

"Yes, two kids, Liz, me, her parents, mom and dad, and Buddy, who seems to be the most well-adjusted of any of us."

"Well, he's an English Mastiff, and he does lick his own balls."

They roiled in laughter.

"I was referring to the fact that he's getting lots of head scratches and attention, but the balls thing might be a contributing factor."

They'd always gotten along, knew nothing of sibling rivalry and had been the best of friends since they could remember. Brian and his closest (non-blood relative) friend, Robbie, were the only reasons Dave had maintained any semblance of sanity after Tina's death.

"I suspect Liz and I will need a mediator or psychiatric assistance by the time the holiday ends. Seven thousand square feet of space, a Granny pod in the backyard, and I still don't think we have enough room."

Dave fell out laughing. "The kids. How are they holding up? Hannah and D.J. driving you nuts?"

"Of course. But that's their job. We spent the day in the mall. They ran around for hours window shopping for themselves and for you and Buddy. Five minutes into the ride home, they were both knocked out. I'd put them on, but they're all counting Z's."

"Sounds like a perfect activity."

"You all packed up?"

"Just about. Two more rooms and we're all set to go. A few short weeks, and I'll be back home in D.C. for good. I appreciate you pinch-hitting for me until then. There's too much chaos here. Better they have time to get acclimated in D.C. than be here trying to maneuver through this maze of mess."

"After all you've done for Liz and me, helping us design and build our house, it's the least I can do. I realize you're making a difficult move, but it's the right thing. You've been stuck for a long time. You checked out on us, all of us, for a while, you know."

"I know."

"I hope this move signals you're ready to check back in. Speaking of which, I told Mindy you'd be here soon, and she's most anxious to see you again."

Dave rolled his eyes and glanced at the time. He had zero desire to see or speak to Liz's sister again; she fell firmly in the flighty artist category. However, he was anxious to chat with his Katherine for a little while and learn more about her. "Listen, I hate to cut this short, but I've uh, I've got plans for the evening, and I need to grab a shower."

"Shut the front door. You?" Brian exclaimed as if Dave had just claimed to invent the car.

"What's with the excess excitement?"

"Are we living on the same planet? You've got a date. This is amazing and long overdue. Who is she? Where'd you meet her? What does she do? Where does she live?"

Dave tried to hold back the laughter but failed. He couldn't answer half of those questions yet. Even if he knew the answers, he wouldn't tell Brian, especially not while he hosted the family. They'd spend the next few weeks planning the wedding for a woman he'd never met.

"I don't have—it's not a date. Not even close."

"A hookup?"

"Dude! No. I think I've evolved beyond meaningless affairs." No answer would appease his brother, especially the truth. "I've gotta go. I'll call you tomorrow."

"Wait, wait, wait."

"What?" Dave responded.

"Is she pretty?"

"Brian!"

"What color are her eyes?"

"Bye, Brian."

"Does she have eyes?"

Dave hung up. The wall clock's big hand rested on the nine. He usually wouldn't cut his brother short, but too much time had gotten away from him already. He ran upstairs to shower and washed off his day. Then he slipped into something more comfortable, the Rudolph the Reindeer pajamas he'd been gifted by the two terrors, and a pair of non-slip socks. He'd miss his hardwood floors, the new place had wall-to-wall carpeting, but he sure wouldn't miss falling on the wood, especially after once spraining his ankle.

A half-hour after exiting the bathroom, the countdown began—that's when the doubts crept in.

Should he text her, or shouldn't he?

On the one hand, he'd agreed to a time, and he intended to stick to it. On the other hand, he feared she'd think he was some desperate creep guy. The truth of the matter is that he was neither a creep nor desperate, and what he searched for was something much more than a hookup, something he could have anytime if that's what he wanted. By most standards—looks, education, job—he was considered a catch, but he didn't want to invest his time and emotions in just any woman. No, what he truly desired was a connection, an authentic, genuine, sincere meeting of the minds, filled with affection and hope. And after marrying and losing his ideal, after knowing the depth of that love and the satisfaction of that perfect combination, he refused to settle for anything less.

That's why the text with the stranger intrigued him so. The speed and rightness of her response ignited the smallest of sparks within him. He wondered if the small flicker might turn into a flame...someday, fire, a raging one. But his doubts lingered. First, based on the phone number, she lived in New York, a place he'd leave in a couple of short weeks, and the long-distance "thing" wasn't an option. It'd be a burden for everyone involved. No, the more he thought about it, the more he thought it best he leave the situation alone and give thanks that it hadn't extended any further than a few messages.

At least, that's what he told himself. The fervent declaration made him question the reason his hand picked up his phone, why he stared at her texts for the next thirty minutes. He leaned into the insanity of it all. One final contact wouldn't hurt. His fingers had typed up the message before his brain caught up. They greeted one another, and he explained his tardiness. Finally, they exchanged names.

Nice to meet you. I'm Dave. Just Dave.

The exchange of names felt as if they'd entered a new realm, the moment signaled they'd consented to take the next step in this short brief journey together, at least for now. To keep the conversation light, he interrupted the pause with his first question: *What are you wearing? :)*

She replied immediately: *Fifty shades of pathetic in a cotton-polyester blend. You?*

He cracked up. Already she'd given him the laugh of the week. Her sense of humor was impressive. He replied. *Same. But with Rudolph. The most wonderful time of the year for you, too, huh?*

Took her a minute to answer. He didn't know if she was distracted or had hesitated. *I plead the fifth.*

She'd hesitated.

Dave: *Pleading is more incriminating than the truth.*

Gabrielle: *Okay. I won't plead. It used to be.*

He questioned whether he should even attempt to go down this road and get personal. On second thought, he decided getting the cards on the table early would be better for all involved.

Dave: *What happened?*

Gabrielle: *Leo happened. Our Christmas wedding didn't. Two years ago.*

Maybe the Fates were being kind since he was leaving the city in a couple of weeks. Her past still pained her, which to him meant she wasn't over Leo.

Dave: *And I thought I had it bad.*

Gabrielle: *Nasty break up?*

She flipped the script with a single question. He definitely wasn't ready to go into details about his past. He hated the expression of sympathy and pity when he revealed his widower status. The looks were the worst.

He no longer wanted to be treated as if he were a broken man. Yes, a piece of him would always ache for his loss, but he remained a living breathing man, of flesh, blood, and soul. He still existed here in this space and time. While it's true that he checked out for a while, he still wanted to live. Part of that meant not burdening her with his pain. Having learned from his past mistakes, he opted to tell the truth...in a different way.

Dave: *No, let's just call it a permanent parting of ways.*

Gabrielle: *Depressed yet? Let's turn the frowns upside down. Favorite Christmas gift. You first.*

Dave: *Age ten. Woke up to the imagined sound of reindeer on roof. Ran to tree. Shiny blue Huffy. Dad assembled. Two weeks later, best broken leg ever. Bike totaled. You?*

Gabrielle. *Today. Weird, dyslexic guy misfires Shakespeare text to the wrong number and forces me to think good thoughts?*

Dave: *Nice try.*

Gabrielle: *Okay. Age nine. A Barbie Dream House. Burned to a crisp by random fireplace spark thanks to meddling big sister. Devastated. May or may not be over it.*

Dave: *A sign you wanted to be a real estate developer when you grew up?*

Gabrielle: *An interior decorator. It's been said I have an eye.*

Dave: *I hope most would say you have two. Kidding. So, interior decorator, huh?*

Gabrielle: *Economist.*

Dave: *My sympathies. Something tells me you'd make a better decorator.*

Gabrielle: *Certainly not living the dream. But things seldom work out the way I picture them. What do you do?*

Dave: *Artist of a different flavor. Architect. Been drawing since I was three.*

Gabrielle: *You like it?*

Dave: *The art of it? LOVE. The business? Not so much. :(*

Gabrielle: *Kinda the point, isn't it? To build for people?*

Dave: *Yeah. That's why I quit the high powered commercial world for a new job. Residential development.*

Gabrielle: *So lucky. You'll create dream homes where people get married, raise families, grow old together.*

Dave: *And you'll create designs that reflect who they are…someday. I know it.*

Gabrielle: *From your mouth to God's ears.*

He questioned whether he should reveal to her what he did for a living. Unfortunately, many women heard the *ka-ching* the moment he told them. But she seemed to be unfazed, further affirming his decision to text her. He found himself wading into dangerous territory. He decided now would be the time to reveal the truth about his relocation. Maybe she'd put this to an end before they could take it any further, before he could like her more.

Dave: *Indeed. That's why I'm actually moving soon. To D.C. for a new job. I'm sitting in a house surrounded by boxes.*

He held his breath, half expecting her to make an excuse about needing to polish her silver or see a man about a horse. Instead...

Gabrielle: *D.C.? Really? Today may be your lucky day.*

He took offense at her apparent elation that he'd be moving away, but pushed his feelings aside, mostly.

Dave: *That's not nice.*
Gabrielle: *Why not? I live there.*
Dave: *Are you kidding me? What's with the 212?*
Gabrielle: *New York City. Best. Summer. Ever.*
Dave: *Care to elaborate?*
Gabrielle: *Yes. But not tonight. Spiked eggnog without the eggnog is kicking in. Need my beauty rest.*
Dave: *Hard to believe.*
Gabrielle: *What? That I drink eggnog?*
Dave: *That you need beauty rest.*

Whether she knew it or not, she was beautiful to him already with her sense of humor, her intelligence. For the first time he'd connected with someone sight unseen.

Gabrielle: *You're a charmer. Good night.*
Dave: *Til it be 'morrow*
Gabrielle: *One last question before you go.*
Dave: *Shoot.*

The 12 Daves of Christmas

Gabrielle: *Federal Reserve — financial institution or wildlife sanctuary?*

Dave: *Trick question?*

Gabrielle: *I wish.*

Dave: *Financial institution. Did I pass?*

Gabrielle: *You had me at financial.*

Dave: *You had me at waspish.*

Chapter 6

Three weeks later...

Gabby raised her window and reached her arm outside to catch snowflakes in her palm. She wore a smile on her face and held Christmas spirit in her heart thanks to Dave. She inhaled a deep breath from the chilled night winds that swirled the frozen powder into loosely formed cones. The air smelled crisp, clear; her favorite day waited around the corner, and her favorite person was one three-hour train trip and nine days away from spending the special holiday with her. She closed the pane and turned to the tree topper to admire its glimmer and the extra twinkle in the star. The dense coating of blinking multicolored bulbs smothering the Balsam fir left her mesmerized, amazed at the abrupt but beautiful turn the holiday had taken.

With one week remaining before Santa's big day, Gabby's spirit had kicked into full gear over the last couple of weeks, and the source of her newfound verve was obvious to her...and Vic, who still hadn't found her way back home to Reggie.

Never mind the fact that Reg had called a zillion times a day, every day since Vic had arrived unannounced, uninvited, but always welcome. She'd struggled to hold her emotions together, but, for Gabby, the situation had been burning on her mind. Vic had so far revealed little. She still did not grasp the "real" reason for the break, which she suspected would differ greatly from the one Vic told her.

Gabby had done all she could do to support her sister at this apparent crossroad, offering her safe haven, a shoulder, a desk and computer to keep her business running. Vic had plenty of space to work through the true source of her confliction, whatever that may be.

After scrambling into her bedroom, Gabby changed out of her jeans and sweatshirt into her coziest pair of footed pajamas. Just before she hit the sofa, she lit the flame in her fireplace. Then she flopped on the couch and stared at the cover of her ancient phone, waiting for her Prince Charming to call.

As she curled her body into the cushions, her cell rang. She and Dave had evolved their communication from texts to voice calls.

"What are you wearing?"

Sweet Dave.

He'd asked her the same question at the beginning of every call. Their hundredth conversation echoed back to the first, making both of them chuckle. They'd become addicted to the sound of each other's voices, to laughing together. She and Dave (still on a first-name-only basis) had hung up barely an hour before, following a three-hour talk. It'd become their after-dinner routine; they also spoke soon after waking up each morning. Now the time had come for pillow talk.

"Hmmm…what am I wearing?" She peered down at what must've been one of a hundred pairs of pajamas in her collection, half of which were Christmas themed. "Jingle bells…and a heart full of cheer," she replied with a snicker. "You?"

"A Yuletide log and a whole lot of joy to the world," he answered. They shared laughs before continuing.

"I call foul. You can't make Christmas songs naughty," Gabby said to Dave.

"Well, you started with your Jingle Bells talk. Man, I really can't wait to see you."

"You made the rules, remember? No photos. No video chats. At least not until you move to D.C. tomorrow, and I upgrade my phone to something manufactured in the last decade."

Her stomach lurched at the sexy gravelly lilt in Dave's voice, one that was especially prevalent when he relaxed or lounged. Except, his voice sounded that way all the time, not just at nighttime. She'd never heard anything like it. The sound made her stomach quiver, her body tingle, especially all points south of her…shoulders. The flurry of excitement and anticipation during their talks kept her stomach rolling and fluttering. She only wished she could put a face to his voice. She still had no idea what he looked like.

"One more day to go. I told you I'd get there before Christmas. Looks like I'm going to make it nine days under the wire," he said. "I can't wait to snuggle up next to you in front of the fireplace. We can even take some selfies so you can post them on your Facebook page. "

"Very important. Because if we snuggled and none of my Facebook friends saw it, did we really snuggle? I personally can't wait to watch Christmas movies…and bake my grandmother's snickerdoodles. They are amazing. Chewy and melt in your mouth."

He sat in silence, didn't respond.

"You do like snickerdoodles, don't you? Because I'll just warn you, for me, cookies are pretty much a deal breaker. Any dislike of snickerdoodles or opposition to braking for animals and we can pretty much just stop now."

He snickered. "It's important to get the critical things out of the way. First of all, I'd love anything you make, including snickerdoodles. I've got a stomach made of steel, so I'm an ideal food tester. And I happen to adore animals. Small ones. Big ones. Really big ones. Doesn't matter."

"Phew! Well, that's a load off."

"By the way, if we hit it off…"

"If?"

"I mean, *when* we're finally together, I will personally buy you a new phone for Christmas. These days, a decent smartphone is not even a splurge, it's a necessity. It's not about FaceTime. They've got features like GPS…locators in case you're abducted by elves and stowed away in a sleigh, and they forcibly take you to the North Pole to work hard labor in Santa's Workshop."

"Believe it or not, I actually think I can reach the North Pole on my network. I just can't text my sister down the hall."

"In the case of your sister, you should probably just holler."

"And I don't really need GPS because I don't drive. Only partly due to the fact that I didn't pass my driver's test."

"Yet another thing we'll rectify. Who doesn't own a car?"

"A lot of people don't own cars in D.C. I've got direct access to every kind of public transportation known to man practically at my front door. Bus, subway, streetcar, bicycles. I could probably find a couple of mules and a Sherpa if we got three inches of snow on the Hill. And, unlike the men, buses really do pass by every ten to fifteen minutes."

"Well, my condo is more upper Northwest. It was apparently the tenth largest building in the city at some point."

"Condo. Wow. As an architect, I'd expect you'd buy a house…or build one."

"I checked out at a few on the market, couldn't find one that felt like…home, so the condo is temporary. It's not perfect, but it's close to my job. Metro stop's about a mile away. The walk might be okay some days in the summer but I'll be driving in the winter. I've never been fond of the cold."

"So, what's the plan for tomorrow, again?"

"I'm on the 2:00 Acela from Penn Station arriving at Union Station at 4:30. I'll meet you in front of the Thunder Grill at 5:00."

"Sounds perfect…except for one thing."

Their first meeting was now only a day away after they'd been talking for nearly a month, and her excitement was now tempered by a string of but critical paralyzing thoughts: What if this man who'd fallen in love with her over the phone met her in real life and hated her? What if he thought she had a beautiful mind but an ugly face? What if every deep conversation, every late-night pillow talk session, every chuckle and laugh, and every flirtation amounted to little more to him than passing the time, and she ended up, once again, spending the holidays alone?

Even worse: What if he fell for her, but she didn't fall for him? What if after a month of falling in love with his mind, he turned out to be the booger man from the Mucinex commercials?

A final troubling thought completed her mental spiral: what if she fell for him and *he* rejected *her*?

She couldn't deal.

The mere possibility triggered her sobbing muscle. Why had she allowed herself to get involved this way? The risk of falling seemed low while he lived in New York, but as time drew closer and his pipe-dream relocation threatened to manifest itself into a reality.

She could handle the fear in two ways: option one—go with the flow, meet him according to destiny's plan and accept the outcome like a grown-up if they didn't meet the other's unreasonable expectations; or option two—spin herself into a frenzy of doubt, sabotage their rendezvous before they ever met, and spend the rest of her life wondering *"What if?"*

Of course, she selected option two. Easier…and less humiliating.

"Listen," she said. "Since the day your stray text turned my life upside down, there's only one moment I've looked forward to more than Christmas, and that is the day you and I will finally meet in person. But I think, just in case something goes awry, we should both get an easy out option."

"Easy out. What do you mean?"

"I just mean establish a contingency plan, of sorts, if either of us should have second thoughts, get frozen feet, or decide maybe this wasn't a good idea. We each should have an option to back out with no pressure."

"I don't need an easy out. There's no place in this world I'd rather be than meeting the woman who has consumed my every thought for the past month."

"You're so sweet."

"I'm not afraid."

"You say that now, and I believe the words are sincere. But if there's one thing I've learned the hard way, things don't always work out in real life as you visualize them in your head. And no one's life is a better example of that than mine."

"Gabby…"

"So, if either of us doesn't show up…how long is the train trip from New York?"

"Two and a half hours on the Acela. Let's call it three hours for safe measure."

"Okay, so the deal is—if the other doesn't show up within three hours of our scheduled meeting, we just accept that the other person bailed and we go on with life. No pressure. No obsessing. No calling the other person to find out what happened or why they didn't show up. No texting to ask questions we really don't want the answers to. And absolutely no social network stalking. We agree to release each other and move on with life."

"I hear you, okay. But what's with the three hours?"

"I figure there's an off chance some great catastrophe happens and you miss the first train…"

"And you won't?"

"No, I live on the Hill. Union Station is a thirty-minute walk. I'd have to make an effort to be an hour late. Three hours late? Virtually impossible, absent a terrorist attack or the Apocalypse."

"I see."

"So, as I was saying, on the off-chance that you missed your scheduled train, you'd have enough time to catch the next one without worrying about missing the window."

"Well, I appreciate the scary level of thought you put into this, but I don't need no stinkin' easy out option."

She chuckled. His joke eased her fears…a smidge. "So, you're not the least bit apprehensive about meeting me?"

"Hmmm…how to put this," he said, taking a brief pause. "Short of dragging yourself into Union Station with a bloody stump and a missing eye, I don't see how you and I can go wrong."

"For me, you're my wish come true. You're the only person I want to kiss under the mistletoe," she said. "I'm just afraid you've oversold me in your mind, built up some fantasy that I couldn't possibly live up to."

"Stop worrying, Gabby. I'll meet you under the mistletoe and I'll make all of your wishes come true, mark my words. My only hope is that I live up to your best thoughts of me."

She couldn't exactly explain her feelings at the moment he spoke those words. They comforted her, wrapped her up like a warm winter quilt, allowed her to believe for a second, just one second, that her fears were unfounded, that their first date would go even better than she imagined. But common sense and past experience told her differently.

"You already live up to my best thoughts of you. Every single day. But, trust me, the way my life is set up…if all my wishes come true in one day, I'll eat the mistletoe."

Chapter 7

After ending his conversation with Gabby, Dave leaned back in his chair. His smile stretched so wide he could feel it in his ears. He'd fallen for an angel. Each late-night phone call drifted into the early morning hours, ending only with their snores. Like teenaged crushes, both refused to hang up first, and he craved the sound of her voice like a drug to his addiction. He couldn't get enough of it, of her. He thought back to the seemingly innocuous moment when he'd peered into the night sky and made a small Christmas wish. Last month's whisper would become tomorrow's reality. They'd finally set the date to meet. He'd admit to himself, if not to her, that he'd questioned his sanity more times than he cared to think about. How could he allow himself to emotionally attach to a woman he'd never seen, especially for three very significant reasons of which she was yet unaware? But Dave's attraction for her crept into his soul and now consumed him. Her appearance concerned him at first but no longer. While he'd initially questioned the wisdom of traveling down this path with no real way ahead in sight, he'd grown more excited than fearful that their future revealed itself only with each step forward, and he settled in for this journey with her.

The ground rules—no picture exchanges or video calls—had been all his "bright" idea; he had no one to blame for that but himself.

The rules allowed him to get to know Gabby without any pressure or false expectations. Talking to her was as easy as breathing. Their conversations drifted on forever; they'd started developing inside jokes, a feat only possible when you're familiar with someone. Even in silences, he often knew what she was thinking; he could predict what she'd say next. It was hard to believe they'd been speaking for only a few weeks. He allowed his growing affection for her to wash over him like a warm rain—but a brusque voice slammed him back into reality.

"Daaaaave," the voice called out from behind him. The ghostly whisper had a Darth Vader-ish tenor. "I am your conscience. You cannot keep concealing the truth from Gabrielle without the situation blowing up in your face."

"Really?" Dave turned to his best friend standing in the kitchen doorway. He'd arrived from D.C. and had been staying in the guest room due to his generous offer to help stack boxes in the dining room so they'd be ready for the moving vans, scheduled to come first thing in the morning. Then he'd drive Dave's car to keep an eye on the van. That would allow Dave to tie up loose ends at home and de-stress during a relaxing train ride to D.C.

"When are you going to fess up?"

"It's not time. Not yet," Dave replied. "She's amazing. One of the most caring, wonderful, sensitive...so funny. If I tell her, I'll lose her. She'll run, and I won't blame her."

"Dude, listen, she may be funny. Hell, she may be the second coming of Whoopie Goldberg, but I can guarantee you that she won't be laughing when the truth comes out. After weeks of so-called getting to know one another, you've conveniently omitted the fact that you're the father of two kids under ten and a dog the size of a mid-sized sedan."

Dave grimaced, swallowed hard, and took nervous paces between his seat and the window. The words sounded harsher coming from Robbie's mouth than they'd played in his head. Perhaps because he'd been lying to himself and the truth hurt. "I know. I know. But you don't understand. If I'd told her about Hannah, D.J., and Buddy, we'd never have an opportunity to meet."

"Well, in all of your discussions, have you even broached the subject of kids and pets? She might be thrilled with a ready-made family. Maybe?" His chipper voice contradicted his skeptical expression.

He groaned. "I've tried several times. She's intimated that while she loves kids, she has goals she wants to achieve before she's tied down. She's afraid the responsibility will prevent her from starting her own business and fulfilling her dreams. I honestly don't believe she'll entertain the thought of raising one child, let alone two…under the age of ten…and a dog."

Robbie shrugged. "So, then what are we talking about here? This is a non-starter."

"Not so fast. There have been other times that Gabby's suggested she's not certain about anything anymore. She's been through a lot. And it's my firm belief that D.J. and Hannah can make anyone fall in love with them. You never know."

"You're setting up yourself for a mighty big disappointment, my friend," Robbie said with a heavy sigh.

"I know…and I didn't mean for this to happen. It's beyond my wildest dreams that a month after sending a text to the wrong woman, I'd feel as if I've known her my entire life."

"She doesn't know you."

"She knows *a version* of me. I needed to let her get to know me—the guy, you know? Yes, I'm a widower, but I'm more. And, yes, I'm a father, but that's not everything there is to know."

Robbie rubbed the back of his neck and avoided eyeing Dave.

"Is it a crime that I don't want to be Sad Dad anymore?" Dave continued. "For the first time in three years, I've shed this cloak of pain and depression. To her, I'm only a guy who's falling for a girl. Most people have no idea about their willingness to tolerate a situation until they face it, and they're forced to make a choice."

"You may be right," Robbie replied with a shrug. "She could meet the two terrors and become instantly enamored. Of course, I'm their godfather and predisposed to love them. Couldn't adore them more if they were my own, but they can be a lot to handle. Motherhood's tough, not the job you want to slip and fall into. It's the one job you've got to really want, especially if the kids aren't your own."

Dave tightened his lips. "She gave me an out."

Robbie's eyebrow curved into a high arch.

"I've gone so far left of where I expected…I dunno. Part of me believes the complications are a sign and I probably should take her up on the deal. I'm beginning wonder if it's even worth trying."

"What's the out?"

"She said that if either one of us decided to back out, we can just bail. Don't show up and it's done. We won't seek each other out, speak, obsess, call, or stalk. No more contact whatsoever. Just accept that, for whatever reason, the other person chose not to pursue the relationship and move on with life."

"Is that even possible? You're not the same man you were weeks ago. I haven't seen you this happy in a long time. It's clear she's had an impact on you."

"More than I imagined. But I'm not fresh out of college, and I'll never again be single without kids. I've got to think about the children."

"You're not going to take her up on it, are you?"

"How can I not consider it? For her sake and mine."

"Listen, not implying in any way that I agree with you deceiving her, especially for this length of time. But, Dude, to back out like a coward without facing up to what you did? You're not that guy. You've got to show up and tell her the truth. Be a grown up; let her choose what she's willing to handle. Otherwise, you'll regret it, and you'll never find peace."

"Really? *You're* telling *me* to be an adult. This from a guy who still builds Lego spaceships and collects *Star Wars* action figures."

"First of all, they're collectibles and a smart investment in my future kids'…futures."

"Not if you take them out of the package and stage lightsaber fights. At that point, they're toys."

"Call them what you want. None of this detracts from the fact that you've got a wet noodle for a spine."

Dave simultaneously wanted to hug Robbie and punch him. The exchange served as a prime example of what he loved and hated about his oldest friend. His legendary brutal honesty had kept Dave on the straight and narrow since college. He wasn't a Boy Scout by any stretch of the imagination, but he always had a knack for cutting through the muck to reach the core of the truth, and he'd spoken nothing but the truth. Dave had made choices, selfish ones, and Gabrielle would suffer most.

He was no better than a fraud pulling a bait and switch. She'd entered into this, whatever they had, with an illusion, a single guy she believed had experienced a routine break up. She had no clue about the widower whose wife died of cancer, who was raising two kids, and caring for a massive hound. He'd kept the most important facets of his life a secret to feel "normal" again, at least for a little while—and he'd done so with absolutely no regard for the fact that he'd have to break the truth to her at some point. His reality very well may turn out to be more than she was willing to handle, no matter how much she liked him, no matter how far she'd fallen.

Regardless, he owed her the consideration of allowing her to choose him—and Hannah and D.J. and Buddy.

"Well?" Robbie asked, filling the lengthy silence.

"Fine, I'll show up, tell her the whole truth, and, as they say, allow the chips to fall where they may."

"Won't be easy, but you're doing the right thing," he said. "Knock back a couple of brews on the train to keep your nerves straight and your spine firm, and you'll get through it."

"You mind taking the kids and Buddy for a night, while she and I work through this? Brian's house is shrinking. He's got like a thousand people over, and he's been keeping the terrors for a month. He's probably ready for some relief."

"You've got it. Rebecca and I need some child labor to help with the outside Christmas decorations, anyway."

Dave shot him an evil eye.

"What? Just lights. The inflatable Santa. Door wrap. I'm determined to win the homeowner's association contest this year," he said. "Since I'm driving your car back with the movers, I'll have Rebecca pick me up from your place after the truck is unloaded then we'll get them from Brian's place. You and Gabby need a chance to talk things out, and something tells me once you confess the truth, you'll work it out."

"I can't thank you enough. I'll think about how to break the news on the train ride." Relieved and grateful, Dave offered his fist and bumped it against Robbie's. "Now let's finish moving these boxes, so I can wake up on time to meet the movers, and drop the key off with the agent. After that, my new life begins."

"Perfect. When you arrive at Union Station, don't try to take the Metro to your new place. Grab an Uber. It'll save you some headaches."

Dave's expression shifted abruptly. He sagged into his chair.

"You look nervous," Robbie said. "You worried?

"Indeed, I am. Tomorrow may mark the beginning of the end, and I miss her already."

Chapter 8

9 Days to Christmas

"Wish me luck!" said Gabrielle, all dolled up and preparing to push her way through the blustery winter winds to meet Dave for the first time. She peered out the window and thanked the heavens for the clear sky. Adding precipitation to the biting cold might've given her an excuse to cancel.

"Who needs luck?" Vic replied, fussing with Gabby's scarf. She'd helped her tie off the pashmina to polish her chic look. Vic had forced her sister to change out of the chunky blue knit sweater, saggy jeans, and rubber ducks on her feet, a combination that drowned her slim figure. She now sported black tights, a knee-length A-line skirt and blouse, Vic's stylish leather coat with faux fur lining, and high calf boots. The scarf and matching slouchy beanie perfectly accented the all-black outfit.

"For what it's worth," Vic began, "I realize I've repeatedly questioned the wisdom of getting emotionally attached to someone you met via a stray text, but I can admit when I'm wrong. From all accounts, he seems like a decent guy. He makes you happier than I've seen since the-one-who-shall-not-be-named. That's all I've ever wanted for you."

"I know, Sis," Gabby said. "I understand that pursuing this man, this relationship, qualifies me as certifiable in most circles, but I've played it safe for my entire life. For once, I'm not obeying the rules or my family's expectations. I'm following my heart, and I'm actually kind of proud of myself for taking a risk."

"This is bigger than a risk. It's more like diving head first into the far end of the deep… blindfolded."

Gabby shrugged. "My every instinct tells me he's 'the one.' He's the Mr. Right who's been waiting for me just beyond my comfort zone. When I finally breach that wall, or in this case, emerge from the subway, he'll be there waiting for me and my life will never be the same."

"Honestly, it's my greatest wish that this, more than any other wish, plays out as wonderfully in reality as I know you've imagined it a thousand times."

"I want the same thing for you. Any progress with the Reggie situation? You two haven't seen one another in a month, and you still haven't told me everything. What's going on with you two?"

"Funny, you should say that. He's been asking for the same thing. He wants to come here and work it out, but, I'm not ready yet. I need to understand what's going on in here"—she pressed her hand to her heart—"before I hash this out with him. The issue goes deeper than what he did and what I saw. Until I figure that out, we can't fix what's broken."

"Reggie's not perfect, but there's no question in my mind that he loves you. I've seen him in action. When I visualize your relationship, I see happily ever after."

"When I visualize my life, I'm married to Will Smith and yachting in Bora Bora. Reggie is proof that life doesn't always work out the way it does in our heads."

Gabby laughed. "Normally, I would agree with you one hundred percent, but today is a new day. The universe keeps sending me signs that everything will work out exactly as I imagine."

"Signs? For instance?" Her expression and voice signaled she didn't really want to hear the answers, nor would she believe them.

"Well, the first sign happened yesterday. I ran into the grocery store to pick up almond milk, you know what kind I like, and it was *in stock*. It's always out."

Vic pressed her lips together, puffed out her cheeks, and stared blankly. She remained unimpressed.

"When I caught the bus, we didn't hit a single red light. Green lights all the way up Pennsylvania Avenue...and no traffic. Now c'mon. You've got to admit that one's pretty impressive."

She released the air from her cheeks.

"Okay, it was after rush hour. But still..."

"What else ya got?"

"My boss called me into the office. I'm receiving a quarterly performance award. I've been there three years—nothing. And then *BAM!* You can't possibly believe that's a coincidence."

"You've been working your butt off for three years without any recognition. Maybe it was just time. You ever consider that?"

"No, no, no. You're missing the point. On their own, they mean nothing, but collectively, with everything happening at once, the universe is signaling that its paving the way for our reunion."

"Union. You haven't met before."

"Whatever, you know what I'm saying." Gabby peered at her watch. "Ooh, look at the time. Gotta to head out and catch the Metro."

"Why are you leaving so early?" It was two hours before they were scheduled to meet.

"Union Station is close, but I have to switch trains twice. And if one is running late or they're single-tracking because of all the construction, I don't want to be late. If I have to break into a sprint at any point you know what'll happen to the nice outfit you've dressed me in; I'll arrive looking as if I went through the spin cycle."

"So, why not Uber? Or, better still, let me drive you."

"Thanks, but no, thanks. I want to take my time, think about what I'm gonna do, say. Try to suppress my inner dweeb."

"Good luck with that."

Gabby sucked her tongue. "Whatever. I'm putting on my girlie act tonight, arriving calm, cool, and collected, and looking hot in this beautiful outfit that my sister picked out for me."

She burst out laughing.

"I fail to see the humor. Picture it—I stroll into the Thunder Grill, all heads turn. I sit down and offer a sexy wink to the bartender, give him a little head nod, and he forsakes all others to serve me. He asks for my order, and I request a Cosmopolitan. Then I take chic-girl sips, without spilling any on myself or dribbling for a change. By the time Dave arrives, I've knocked off the nerves and the rest of the night is butter smooth."

Vic snorted and laughed. "Dare to dream. You sure you don't need me?"

She shook her head. "However, keep your phone handy. If the booger man shows up, then I may text an S.O.S."

Vic laughed. "All right, Gabby. Scram. Call me if you need me for anything. I'll be on the couch bingeing on this *Bridget Jones' Diary* marathon."

Gabby opened the door and cast a glance over her shoulder. "What if he doesn't show?"

"You're kidding me, right? Stop thinking and go! Don't be late."

Gabrielle plugged in her iPod earbuds and trekked to the subway, only three blocks away.

At the Capitol South station, she rode the escalator down one level, and everything went smoothly, just as she pictured. She loaded her SmarTrip card and the machine took her wrinkled dollars as if they were crisp and fresh from the bank. She'd usually spend fifteen minutes jamming money into the blasted hunk of junk as it persistently spat it out.

Today, perfection.

She scanned the reader, entered through the turnstiles, and took a second escalator down to the platform.

Not a minute after her heels clicked against the rust-colored tile on the subway level, her train, the Blue Line going to L'Enfant Plaza, arrived in perfect time. Another sign from the universe affirming what she already knew to be true: today was the day she'd meet her Christmas dream.

Her train ride gave her time to think and also to doubt.

What if she'd been wrong about Dave? What if he turned out to be an ax murder? Or a Jack-the-Ripper incarnate? Or a con man?

What if they didn't meet each other's expectations? What if he wasn't cute...or worse what if he didn't find her so? What if every moment they'd shared was a lie, not because she'd lied to him (she hadn't) but because he'd been untruthful to her? What if he was jobless and homeless? Every negative thought clouded her mind. What if the universe had conspired to set her up, not for the perfect night, rather a big disappointment.

A lump grew in her throat. Her pashmina constricted around her neck; she tugged it loose and inhaled deeply, in through the nose and out through the mouth.

Union Station, her final destination, was only minutes away, but the subway paused and the doors opened at the stop before she reached her transfer station.

Fear seized her common sense and her feet.

She shot out of the car with the speed of a bullet exploding from a Smith and Wesson. The unplanned move baffled her, paralyzed her. Dazed and in disbelief, she watched her train disappear down the tunnel. She'd officially chickened out. Bailed.

The 12 Daves of Christmas

Is this how their relationship would end? With Gabby tucking her tail between her legs and scampering home to hide from her past and her future? Would she allow the Christmas of her dreams, the man of her fantasies to disappear into the day's blustery frost?

Yep. Apparently, so.

She made an about-face and darted toward the escalator as if she could escape herself. She felt as if she wore a scarlet letter "C" and thanked the heavens for the light crowds, fewer witnesses to her cowardly shame. She eyed the exit turnstiles, dragging her feet and second-guessing her decision the entire way.

She glanced at her wrist.

Nearly thirty minutes had passed since she left home.

An hour and a half remained before she was scheduled to meet Dave face to face. But she couldn't muster the courage to take the final leg of her journey.

Before she arrived at the promised land, the Metro exit, the sound of another train approaching rumbled inside the tunnel. She dashed back to the see the direction in which it was headed; it was an Orange Line train going to her scheduled stop. She wavered on the edge of her comfort zone finally accepting that her blessing may lie outside of its boundaries; that it may be waiting only three stops away. An opportunity like this one, to meet a man like him in this way, came only once in a lifetime. The promised land beyond the exit would keep her hostage to her "almosts" and "maybes." She'd had more than her share of those. She wanted to live her life to the fullest, to kiss Dave under the mistletoe, to see her wishes come true.

In an instant, she sucked up sufficient courage to turn and bolt down the jam-packed escalators. The station was suddenly deluged with slothful tourists.

"Excuse me, excuse me, excuse me," she pleaded as she nudged them out of her way. By the time she returned to the platform, the train's doors were only inches from closing. She reached between them, and a considerate bystander helped her pull them open. She jumped inside in time for the doors to slam shut on her purse; she tugged hard until they bounced open. By the time she pulled her bag through, she'd delayed the commute—and nobody in her car was happy about it.

Everyone scowled as she lumbered through the car searching to find a space to sit. With all seats filled, she grabbed a pole and volleyed her glance between the Jack Daniels ad that read "You're going to need something stronger in your stocking" and an adorable baby stuffed in a red snowsuit and Santa hat; her toothless smile phased into a baby fart and a burp which caused formula to spatter on her coat.

At that moment, she sensed a shift. The universe, once paving her way, had taken a turn against her.

The tourist crowds on the escalator. The closing door. The passengers' dirty looks. The puke splatters the baby's mother had rushed to wipe.

She'd begun to meet resistance and obstacles. Her fear had altered her fate, presented a fork in the road that snatched her from Easy Street and dropped her on Predicament Parkway. The only way to escape her comfort zone now would be to press through the challenges and endure until she made it to the other side.

Finally, she reached Metro Center station, her transfer point, two stops from Union Station.

She bolted off the car and trucked up the stairs to catch the Red Line. A quick glance down at her wristwatch revealed she still had an hour, but there'd be no winking, no Cosmo sipping. If she somehow managed to get her hands on the drink she so richly deserved, she'd have to toss that baby back.

Now on the upstairs platform, Gabby had arrived just in time…to watch her train pull off and disappear. She checked the arrival status on the digital sign hanging above her. The next one? Eight minutes away. Eight of the longest minutes of her life, but she quickly shook off the panic, tried to remain positive.

I've got plenty of time.

She turned to face another copy the same Jack Daniel's ad, staring her down, warning her that she may need something stronger than a Cosmo.

Fifteen minutes later and Gabby "enjoyed" her ride to nowhere.

Still no train. She hadn't budged except to pace.

Adrenaline spiked her temperature as she marched back and forth, shifting her position from the concrete walls to the platform's edge to do nothing except stare at the rails, will the train into the tunnel. She yearned to see that glimmer of light signaling hope was on its way.

The universe gave her a big bag of nothing.

Finally, the station manager announced, "The Red Line to Glenmont is experiencing mechanical problems. It will arrive in ten minutes. All subsequent trains will run on a delayed schedule. Thank you for riding Metro."

She rolled her eyes and glanced up at the board. Ten minutes. Eight. Five. Three. Finally, the light. The cars moved in, an extra-long train filled the station from end to end.

The doors opened, and she shoved herself in with the crowds. The car was packed to capacity and beyond. Droves of passengers had arrived from the lower-level and intermingled with those who'd been waiting for nearly a half hour. The station manager announced that a second one followed behind, but she refused to wait. She was now standing on the boundary of her comfort zone; she only needed to persist and press her way through to the other side.

They pulled off smoothly, and she exhaled. Only two stops before Union Station. They zipped in and out of Judiciary Square station with such ease she allowed the corners of her mouth to curve upward, barely discernible but she could feel it.

Home free at last.

A minute into the final tunnel approaching Union Station, and the driver slammed on the brakes, throwing riders into one another, against the walls and the doors. The train screeched and jolted. Passengers rocked back and forth, struggling to stay on their feet; packed into the car like sardines, no one fell. The train crawled along for what felt like a few hundred feet before it came to a complete stop.

Everyone exchanged panicked glances. Voices could be heard saying, "What's going on?" and "I don't know?"

Finally, the operator made his announcement. "We apologize for the inconvenience, but there is a track malfunction before we reach Union Station. We will move out of the tunnel as soon as possible and appreciate your patience. Thank you for riding Metro."

Inconvenience? Patience? Thank you? she thought. He'd spoken the words as if he'd stolen her parking spot or dropped her eggs at the grocery store. No, he'd changed the trajectory of her life, put a big honking sinkhole square in the middle of the road to her destiny.

Gabby channeled her frustration to her eyelids which she clenched shut. In her mind, she yelled, "Nooooo! No, no, no, no, no!"

Then she opened her eyes, and her fellow commuters stood stone quiet; everyone's gazes were locked on her. Apparently, she'd used her outside voice. They thought she'd gone insane, and they probably weren't far from wrong.

"Sorry about that," she said sheepishly. "Late for a blind date with Mr. Right."

From hell, the voice of a crotchety old woman called out, "Fat chance! You'd have better luck asking Santa to send one down your chimney."

Her words may not've been true, but they sure felt like it. Now completely and utterly mortified, Gabby checked the time. Twenty minutes to go. Thank goodness, she'd had the foresight to add a buffer.

Still fearing she'd be late, she pulled out her phone, her ancient Nokia, to text Dave and warn him that she may be running late. "Of course, there's no freaking signal!" she muttered, drawing more curious expressions from onlookers. She glanced up at the confused woman standing beside her. "You wouldn't by any chance have the number for Zimbabwe? I could reach Zimbabwe."

The woman laughed. Gabby wanted to cry.

The universe which previously had rolled out the red carpet was now snatching it from beneath her feet. Why did she allow her doubts to dissuade her? Why did she chicken out? She couldn't help but realize that if she'd stayed on the first train, she'd be at the Thunder Grill now, winking at the bartender and sipping on her Cosmo. Instead, she was sardined between a man in a suit who was a cigar smoker judging from the pungent odor and an older woman who stood only as tall as her boobs.

Three of the longest hours of her life later, the repaired track allowed the train to move through the tunnel. On the bright side, she thanked the heavens for the winter; God help them all had it been summer. She may wreak of cigar smoke, but at least they wouldn't die of heat strokes. She'd missed the first window to meet him, but had enough time, just barely enough, to reach Union Station before the backup hours ran out.

She nervously flexed and curled her fingers and blinked incessantly, wondering if he'd shown up at all. She darted toward the Thunder Grill as close to top speed as possible without falling on her face, first reaching the interior entrance and then remembering they'd planned to rendezvous outside. She maneuvered through the sluggish crowds and toward the door until a blast of cold wind slapped her in the face, battering against her body, and ruthlessly violated her coat and scarf. She checked the time again. Five minutes remained before the deadline, but there was no sign of him.

A steady succession of shivers caused her to tighten her coat and scarf around her neck.

"He should've been here by now," Gabby whispered with her eyes turned up to the night sky.

Determined to stick out the final minutes, she forced a warm smile to every passerby with searching eyes and received a few signs of interest, but none from Dave.

Standing squarely outside of the boundaries of her comfort zone, she allowed the tension to release from her shoulders. She'd hung in there, fought the cold, and waited. She still held out hope despite the absence of signs signaling the contrary. She decided to check on the status of his train, maybe there'd been some catastrophic failure, but first she detoured into the mezzanine level restroom. On her way out, she slammed into a stranger, barely looking up, but begging his apologies before she disappeared. She stared at the status boards—all Acela trains from Penn Station had arrived.

Where is he?

Chapter 9

"This can't be happening to me," Dave groaned, checking his watch for the fiftieth time. His already harried schedule had spun into a nightmare.

Dave had planned every moment of his final day in New York practically to the second. His tasks were simple and straight forward—all he needed to do was execute. He'd scheduled the movers earlier than necessary and allowed four hours to pack the truck. Robbie would follow the moving van in Dave's car and supervise the move-in at the condo. Meanwhile, Dave would wrap up his loose ends: lock up the house and stop by the Realtor's office—she'd manage the maintenance and sale; return his company equipment to Lexi; and then head to Penn station to catch a nice relaxing Acela train to Washington...to Gabby.

The packing and organizing hit nary a speedbump, everything proceeded smoothly, and that's when he got a little cocky. Without realizing it, he'd oversimplified his relocation, inadvertently lying to Robbie, telling him that he had everything under control.

If you want to make the universe laugh, declare your plans to be airtight.

He only had one job—and he'd blown it in grand fashion.

The movers arrived two hours late, using up two-thirds of the hours in Gabby's emergency scenario. The van caught a flat in Jersey. Took them three hours to load the boxes, using up the last hour of his reserve. He not only needed to be on schedule from that point forward, but he'd also need to try to get ahead.

As the truck disappeared and Dave watched as Robbie followed in his car, and then he glanced at the clock. 1pm. He still had to deliver the keys to his realtor and an important blueprint revision, his laptop, and work cell phone to his office before catching a Yellow cab to Penn Station. Unless some miracle helped him sprout wings and fly, he'd miss the 3pm train that would've arrived in Union Station by 6pm as well as the back-up arriving at 7 pm, but he tamped down the panic. In his estimation, he'd still make it in plenty of time to meet Gabby by 8pm. He felt thankful for her foresight. But catching a 5pm train would be tight. He'd need to hurry.

No sooner than he slipped into the backseat of a cab, his phone rang. His brother, Brian.

"You on your way?" he asked.

Dave rolled his eyes as the sounds of Bollywood piped through the car's speakers, and the scent of curry wafted from a Styrofoam take-out container into his nose. "No, I'm heading to midtown. Running late. The movers. Ugh," he grunted. "Everything okay? The kids and Buddy all right?"

"Oh, everything's fine, fine. Unless you count the fact that my house has been hijacked by crazy people. If I ever remotely suggest inviting Mom, Dad, and the in-laws for Christmas at the same time again, bludgeon me in the head with a sharp object. It'll be less painful than this."

"That bad, huh?"

"Geez, Louise. It's like the political Hunger Games in here. Conservative versus Liberal. They argue constantly. I never know who's gonna emerge from the dinner table alive. I've forced a truce for the rest of the holiday. Everyone's agreed to honor it. That should last about twenty minutes."

Dave chuckled. "I don't even want to know how you maneuvered that deal, but I suspect that bottle of Sequoia Grove Cambium you've been hoarding may have played an influential role, along with a couple of those Montecristos the fathers like to smoke."

He laughed. "You guessed it. So now Liz is out the with kids—movie and ice cream. Buddy's napping on his bed next to the fireplace. They're all packed up and ready for Robbie."

"Good, I miss the little buggers. Can't wait to see them."

"Meanwhile, the parents went on a joint outing at Tysons Corner, and I'm watching a Game of Thrones marathon. For the first time in days, the house is quiet," he said. "So, now I'm checking in on you, making sure you're not having second thoughts."

"Little late for those. My furniture's on Interstate 95, headed to D.C., and you've got my kids and dog."

"I'm not talking about moving. You made the right choice in relocating. I'm referring to your date with Gabby."

Dave recalled his brother's warning about the inevitable confession, the truth and the ugly of it. Words had consequences. "No doubts about her, but I've questioned my decision to conceal the full truth every moment since last spoke. If I'd been honest with her from the start, I wouldn't feel so conflicted about meeting her tonight."

"Hate to say I told ya so, but..."

"Something tells me she's not ready to handle…*my life*. I'm afraid today's the beginning of the end. And while I'm not a guy with a lot of pride and ego, I've got just enough to be bruised if she bails on me and decides not to show up at all. I honestly don't want to know."

"Lies have consequences, but nothing bad comes from telling the truth. I mean, it's difficult and facing up to what you've done takes backbone I don't have. You're risking everything. But let's focus on the bright side: if she rejects you, she wasn't the woman for you anyway, right?"

"You're right. I know you're right. Doesn't make it any easier, but"—the taxi cab pulled in front of his building— "Listen, I'm at the office. I'll call you once the verdict is in."

"Break a leg."

"Don't say that. With my luck today, I just might."

Dave checked the time. It ticked close to 4pm. If he didn't catch the five o'clock train, he could hang up meeting Gabby, confessing his sins, and all. He asked the cab driver to wait. His initial plan was to stroll around and say his goodbyes, but the hourglass had nearly emptied of sand. He needed to make this quick.

Jamming his hand in front of the sensors before they shut, he jumped inside the first elevator and caught it, but his briefcase got stuck. He yanked it through and shifted his gaze to avoid the dirty looks from the riders by checking the leather for bruising. When he reached his floor, he darted out and scanned for Lexi, and spotted her at her desk.

Thankfully, he'd caught her. "Hey! I'm running late."

"The expression was a dead giveaway. This everything? Laptop? Phone? Revised blueprints?"

He nodded.

"Great!" She double-timed her steps from behind her desk to walk him to the elevator. "New employee today. I'll wipe your equipment clean and give it to him."

He barely heard her, so busy jamming his finger into the elevator call button as if that'd compel it to arrive any sooner. "Wish I could stay longer but I'm running late, and the cab's waiting. Gonna miss my train."

"Okay," she said after the car arrived. She offered a quick hug and watched him board. "We'll miss you!"

He waved goodbye, and a lump formed in his throat as the doors closed and he descended to the lobby.

Overwhelmed with emotion, Dave grew nostalgic as they drove downtown to Penn Station. He'd miss Christmases in New York, the life he once shared with his wife and children there. The decision to abandon this world he'd built with Tina had been among the hardest of his life, but he finally admitted to himself what he'd refused to tell anyone in his family, or his grief counselor.

When Tina first died, he didn't have the heart to leave the city. Now that he'd begun to heal, he didn't have the heart to stay.

He could no longer summon the strength to drive past the sacred ground where they'd built their memories, to stroll past the constant reminders of before while at the same time focusing on the future. Most of all, he couldn't be the father his children needed living in an eternal state of depression.

So, lost in his thoughts, Dave peered up and found himself facing the picturesque windows framing Madison Square Garden and Penn Station; he exhaled. He'd take the escalators down the platform to leave behind in one station, what he'd willingly embrace when he emerged from the next. The second he took his seat on the train, he'd text Gabby to let her know he'd fallen behind schedule.

Dave clutched his first-class ticket as he boarded the car, thankful for Lexi's insistence that he splurge on a pricier seat. The spacious accommodations would allow him to plug into his MacBook and catch up with his family and friends on social media.

After settling in, he pulled out his personal cell phone to send Gabrielle a text. Perhaps she'd be gracious enough to wait if he warned her that he'd fallen behind schedule.

He swiped his finger across the screen to pull up her phone number. Panic set in when he realized his phone contained no sign of Gabby, her phone number, or a single text message they'd exchanged over the past few weeks.

He shrunk back in this seat, covered his eyes with his free hand, emitted an audible groan when the gravity hit him: he'd been contacting her using the company cell since the first day his text reached the wrong destination.

Bile bubbled in his stomach with the next realization: he'd turned over the phone to Lexi, and she'd probably erased it already—along with the laptop that contained all of his backups (which were months behind). He never kept up with them. Unfortunately, he'd learned the importance too late. His heart pounded in his chest; his head felt light.

What could he do?

Call Lexi.

Even with the slim possibility, he hoped to catch her before she erased them. He dialed her number as fast as his fingers allowed; the phone rang...and rang...and rang before voicemail picked up. He checked the time. She'd left the office for the day.

"Lexi! No," he muttered and then groaned. His head collapsed against the seat, and his eyelids drifted closed. In that second, a buzz alerted him—Lexi.

Hope?

"Lex! Please, tell me you didn't erase my old cell yet."

"O—kay. I mean, I can say those words if you'd like to hear them, but unfortunately, they won't be true."

The deafening silence between them filled with his frustration.

"You okay? Aren't you on the train to D.C. by now?"

"I am, but I forgot to copy some very important contact information to my personal cell."

"You don't remember it?"

"Does anyone remember numbers these days? That's why they call them smartphones. They store stuff so we don't have to clutter our minds with mundane details."

"Your theory's all good until someone hits the reset button. Didn't you back it up?"

"Yes, on my work laptop, which you probably erased right after you finished with the phone."

"No...before. Sorry." Her voice begged his forgiveness. "Wait a minute, Ellen from IT billing handles the accounts. She's on vacation until the New Year, but the second she returns I'll ask her to pull yours. You can get the number from that."

"Thanks, Lex, and good thinking. Unfortunately, January's too late." He let out a frustrated breath. "You're still the best, though."

He hung up the phone, clenched his eyes shut. In his mind, he yelled, "Noooooooooo!"

He opened his eyes to greet curious looks from the elderly couple sitting in front of him, signaling that he'd used his outside voice.

"Sorry about that," he said in a conciliatory tone. "I'm, uh, I'll just be over here napping."

Dave awakened from a power nap as the train pulled into Baltimore station; a streak of drool trailed out of the corner of his mouth. Still groggy, he wiped the spittle with his sleeve and blinked a few times until the couple across from him came into focus. All the late-night packing over the past few weeks had caught up with him. He finally surrendered to the exhaustion. The quick snooze proved to be exactly what he needed.

"Excuse me, but where are we?" he asked a woman who'd buried her face in a copy of Reader's Digest as her husband called hogs.

"Baltimore," she replied.

Relief washed over him. He was only thirty minutes away. He'd arrive on time.

"We've been here for over an hour. There's a fire near one of the tracks. They're inspecting, verifying that it's safe to travel."

He did the math and then bolted upright in his seat and glanced at his wrist. 7:25.

"Oh, no." He banged his head against the seat. "Wait, a fire? It's like zero degrees outside. Who'd set a fire?"

She shrugged. "The conductor's last announcement said we'd be pulling out any time now. That was fifteen minutes ago."

"Ugh," he groaned.

What else possibly could go wrong? He dared not ask. Maybe this was a sign. Maybe the universe was letting him off the hook. His lie would remain concealed and he could avoid facing the truth and Gabby's disappointment, after all.

The second the thought flitted through his mind, the train lurched forward.

Wrong again.

Just before the deadline, they pulled into Union Station. 7:55. Five minutes to spare.

He'd depart the near-empty first-class car with ease and no baggage check worries. Just as he prepared to exit, Dave spotted a frantic mother struggling with three kids, trying to dress them in coats. She was strapping twin toddlers into a stroller and balancing a fussy baby.

Mind your own business, Dave ordered himself. *Walk by. Gabby's waiting.*

But his conscience convinced him to offer a hand. It'd only take a minute, he told himself.

"Can I help? I've got two, seven and nine. I remember these days all too well."

"Oh, my goodness, you're a savior. If you could hold her, just for a second. Then I can finish with these two."

He wrapped the baby in his arms, admiring the sweet cherub face swaddled in pink. "She's adorable."

"Thank you so much. Dad's meeting us, but it's so cold. I'm afraid they'll become biohazards if I don't get them in their coats, the little Germ-inators."

He chuckled and bounced the baby to soothe her fussiness. "No problem."

At once the baby's ruckus came to an abrupt halt. He'd calmed her down. Still had the touch if he did say so himself. Hannah had always been putty in his hands. In the midst of his gloating, it happened.

She exploded all over his shirt. And the sweet baby girl just laughed and smiled.

"Uh, I think we know why she was fussy now."

The mother looked back over her shoulder. "Sweet heavens! I'm so sorry. Let me get you cleaned up."

She apologized profusely, pulling a puke rag from the diaper bag and dabbing his coat. "It's true what they say, huh? No good deed goes unpunished. I truly apologize. Can I pay for your cleaning bill?"

He refused the kind offer as she placed the baby into the carrier. "Please, go. Thank you so much. You've been a lifesaver."

Dave peered down at the remnants of the baby's tossed cookies as he took off running. He debated for a second as he passed a bathroom but didn't want to meet Gabby with the mess on him, making for the most unromantic introduction ever. He ran inside to get wet a paper towel and exited wiping his shirt and coat along the way. Distracted and eyeing his shirt, he bumped into someone, his shoulder almost taking out the poor woman, a beautiful woman whose number he may have asked for once upon time. "I'm sorry. So sorry," she said, moving with barely a pause.

He heard her apologies, but he kept pressing forward.

Full of regret, Dave arrived in front of the Thunder Grill. 8:15. Couples loitered around the entrance waiting to enter, along with a few stray singles. A few people craned their necks looking for rides, but no one's eyes appeared to be searching for him.

After five minutes in the brisk winds, he entered the restaurant hoping to find her sitting at the bar. Everyone present was coupled up, except one leggy woman wearing a little black dress and red scarf. As he approached her, her lips stretched into a broad smile.

This must be her, he thought, and she's a goddess.

Now three steps out of her reach, he opened his mouth to speak, and her date swooped in; their status as a couple was clear from the position of his lips on hers.

Better not be Gabby.

He drifted back outside and scanned the area. She'd skipped out on him or bailed altogether. If she hadn't, she couldn't reach him if she tried. Even worse, she may have assumed he'd abandoned her and disappeared.

A pit formed in his stomach. He'd never wanted so much for a hole to open in the ground beneath him and swallow him up.

How could he ever find her? He didn't know her full name, what she looked like, where she lived. Didn't even have an email address. As he ambled back into the bar, he ordered a beer, and then an Uber. Time to face facts: he'd missed his one and only chance to meet his Christmas dream coming true.

Chapter 10

8 Days to Christmas

Gabby collided against her mattress, drunk with disappointment. Her dear Dave had stood her up, and she awakened hungover with frustration. She'd invested her heart to achieve the most satisfactory of ends —a boyfriend for Christmas—and he chickened out. She'd gambled and lost.

A little over one week before Christmas, and all signs suggested she'd end up alone again, the last thing she'd anticipated. She believed in him. They'd shared something real; they understood one another on a deeper level than some ever realize. They'd taken a risk to avoid muddying the mental clarity and romantic excitement with physical intimacy too soon—all for naught.

Still dressed in her footed Snoopy pajamas, she grabbed her phone from the nightstand and dragged her sulking self from the bedroom and into the kitchen; she needed a hot cup of coffee fresh from the Keurig.

As the scent of hazelnut crème wafted through the air and the sweet elixir dripped into her favorite mug, she tried calling him. Perhaps some unforeseen event had prevented him from showing up as scheduled, as had happened to her. Maybe she should have shut her pie hole before she allowed the easy-out plan to leak from her lips.

She quickly shoved aside those thoughts and allowed her anger to bubble up as she waited for the ring.

He could've called at any point to give her a heads up, to advise her that he'd be late. No, this inconsiderate boob had made no effort to contact her at all. In fact, his phone was now out of service, disconnected. The thought of enduring more humiliation by appearing like some desperate broad hunting down a man who didn't want her was more than she'd been willing to bear. If he could walk away without a word, nothing between them mattered; they had nothing worth holding onto. That was it. There was nothing left to say.

As the last drops of coffee dripped into her cup, she pulled three packets of Truvia from her makeshift coffee bar and ordered herself to let it go. She decided to release all memories of what they shared into the universe and allow them to dissipate into the cold winter winds twisting outside her window.

"How are you hanging in there this morning?" Victoria dragged into the kitchen like the Walking Dead, slippers scraping the floor, wearing pajamas with a decal that read *I Woke Up Like This*. "You look pathetic to the third power."

"Gee, thanks. Self-esteem issues explained."

"I realize you're disappointed. Your evening didn't work out quite the way you envisioned, but let's not sulk all day, huh? It's not the answer to your problems."

"I left all my troubles at Union Station last night and all memories of *him* in the wind where they belong."

"Mmmm hmmm. You say that now, you and I both know you'll obsess if you end your relationship right here. If you want my advice, what you need to do is find him and tell him face-to-face exactly what happened. Leave no ambiguity whatsoever. You'll be forced to live with a lot of stuff in this life, good and bad, and you'll have no choice. You can still choose whether or not regret over Dave is one of them."

She drew in a long sip of coffee and allowed her mind to process what Vic said. "I hear you, I really do, but I'm tired. You have no idea how heartbreaking it is to build these moments in your head, to envision how wonderful things will be, and then consistently watch each dream end in a nightmare."

"I don't, huh? Then what've I been doing here for the last month."

Gabby's eyes filled with tears and her voice trembled. "You've always been stronger than me. I'm not certain whether I have the strength to set up my heart for more disappointment."

"Of course, you do."

Gabrielle's face tightened.

"I didn't mean it like that. All I'm saying is, I've heard you two talk. You use the speakerphone a lot. I haven't seen you this happy and connected with someone since you-know-who. Your whole demeanor has changed. This light glimmers in your eyes, like the ones on the tree."

Gabby looked away shyly.

"I'm serious. The last time I saw you beaming like this was the first of never. He brings out the best in you; he's at the root of this newfound happiness. I should think risking a few minutes of humiliation to find out the truth would be worth every second."

Gabrielle grabbed a cold bagel from the refrigerator and dropped two slices inside the toaster as she considered Vic's advice. She couldn't keep him off her mind, even after she'd ordered herself never to think of him again. She closed her eyes as her toast browned and recalled that sexy lilt in his voice as a whisper in her memory. "You're beautiful for who you are not for what you look like," he said.

What kind of cretin says such a beautiful thing to a woman and then stands her up?

If he were the scum she now believed him to be, she'd never have fallen for him. No, Dave was special, and their relationship had never been a figment of her imagination. Every moment, every word spoken, every butterfly that flitted through her stomach, every smile she revealed when they joked and laughed together was real.

She wasn't crazy and, truth be told, she had arrived late. Maybe he showed up and left think she ditched him.

One thing was for certain: she couldn't abandon him without another word. She believed in him and what he meant to her enough to find out the truth, even if the discovery broke her heart...again.

Better for her to endure a few days or months of hurt than spend the rest of her life wondering if he was "the one."

From that moment forward, her mission was clear.

"Okay, fine. I suppose I'm not completely opposed to finding him, but I have no idea where to begin. We spent a lot of time talking but agreed not to disclose any substantial details."

Vic glared at her with a "really?" expression.

"What? We wanted to build something on a different level."

"You mean to tell me you didn't even find out where the man was moving?" she barked.

"Well, I know he's moving to D.C."

"That narrows it down. I'm a real estate agent not the Great Swami."

"We agreed to exchange details last night…after we met."

Victoria narrowed and rolled her eyes. "How's that plan working for you?"

"Never mind the smart-aleck remarks. Can you help?"

"Okay, let's start with the details he's told you so far, what few there are."

Gabrielle reflected on all of their conversations. Mostly, she remembered the romance, the things he said that made her tingly on the inside. But she recalled one specific detail, a weird factoid, that he'd cited one day. "I'm not sure whether this means anything, but he did tell me that his new condominium is somewhere in upper Northwest. At some point, it was the tenth largest building in D.C."

"Who remembers something like that? Even worse who commits a fact like that to memory."

"He's a little weird that way. But it's cute."

"Not unlike someone else I'm familiar with," Victoria said with a wink. She stood and trekked over to the computer; her fingers tapped the clicky keys at a rapid pace. "Lucky for you I'm a crack researcher, too. We'll start with Google. If I find the building, I can use tax records to find him. Or at least narrow down the list of suspects."

Gabrielle gobbled up her bagel before pulling up a seat next to Victoria so she could supervise.

"Hmmm. When I search the tenth largest, I get Foxhall. Great property, but it's huge. I've sold several condos there."

Gabrielle sensed a new excitement. After leading a complicated life, could finding her David be this easy?

"Let me pull up the tax records. All I need from you is his last name, and we're home free."

Gabrielle tightened her lips and puffed out her cheeks. "Ummm, see what had happened was..."

"What?"

"So, I don't really know his last name per se, but I'm sure he has one, and I'd recognize his voice anywhere."

Victoria let out a frustrated breath. "Really?"

"You just love rubbing it in, don't you? It was part of the agreement. His name is David, and I call him Dave. Maybe there's a listing for David, king of my heart, man of my dreams, I think you're my destiny."

Victoria could only snicker. "Okay. Destiny-Dave."

Gabrielle watched the series of mouse clicks and listened to Vic's fingers tap as she sipped on her coffee. She phased through a range of emotions, from frustration and sadness to anger to hopefulness and now anxiousness.

What if he didn't want to meet her? What if he rejected her after they met?

Part of her wanted to tell Victoria to stop, but she'd already fallen head-first out of her comfort zone. She may as well find him before the delirium subsided.

"Wow, this is a pretty big building. There are nearly three-hundred units."

"Three hundred? Sheesh. I'm not knocking on all those doors."

"I've added another parameter." She tapped her finger and conducted another search. "Hmm. There are twelve Davids. Oh. Crap!"

"What is it?"

"I'm getting an error message. It's not allowing me to see the dates of ownership. Now, I can't tell when the units were purchased, but I do have the addresses for the ones I found."

"You think they'll fix the system today?"

"I'll submit a trouble ticket but probably not. We're looking the holiday in the butt. I'm willing to bet the IT guy is on vacation, like everyone else in my field, except me. The system always breaks down when the IT guys are out."

"Figures."

"Hey, this is our slow season; it's cold out. Buyers don't want to shop in this weather unless they'd be homeless otherwise. But I'll keep checking back. In the meantime..."

"Twelve Daves."

"Yep. And eight days before Christmas. I'll make a list for you. You've got your work cut out for you if you chose to accept this mission."

"Don't forget to check it twice. Get it?" Gabrielle giggled and examined photos of the complex on the computer screen. "Problem! The community's gated...with a doorman."

"No worries. You'll go with me the first day; I can distribute a few fliers, preview some units. But I can't run up there with you every day. I'm trying to enjoy what I can of my holiday and get some much-needed rest and relaxation. So, after the first day, you're on your own...mostly."

Chapter 11

Dave woke up the next morning in his new condo, Unit 430, surrounded by mountains of empty boxes. He felt the onset of a head cold, no surprise after his late night in the frigid air.

He'd planned to spend his evening romancing Gabrielle, convincing her that "they" could work as a couple, despite the fact that he'd conceal the full truth from her. Perhaps even cuddling in the suite he'd reserved at the W Hotel because his condo remained in shambles. Instead, he spent the entire night alone, sulking and angry with himself as he set up the kids' beds, and undertook a search-and-discovery mission to find pots, dishes, and the coffee pot. Most importantly, he pulled out the Christmas decorations.

He had little hope of finding Gabby, so he refocused his attention on returning to his pre-Gabrielle state, obsessing over work, the kids, and the dog.

A glance out the patio door revealed the well-manicured grounds thick with ornamental trees covered in snow. Nothing spoke Washington D.C. to him. He could've been anywhere in the world, well, except for

New York. For the first Christmas in years, he'd experienced a subtle relief—nothing in his view sparked memories of what used to be. In the wink of a moment, he'd considered "accidentally misplacing" the box of ornaments so that they could start anew in every way, but the kids needed to remember more so than he. He'd never abandon all of Tina's traditions, even as he sought ways to move on with his life.

He carefully maneuvered through the stacks of cardboard boxes, trying to reach the coffee pot and make himself a cup of joe when his phone rang. He glanced at the screen and couldn't answer fast enough.

"Morning, Lex," he said. "Lemme guess. You're calling because you found the number."

"Uh, no. I'm sorry. I did check, but our accountant is on vacation until January fourth."

"It's okay. It's not your fault, it's mine. I'm an idiot."

"Actually, as your sister in idiocy, I'm calling to give you a heads up."

"About what?"

"More like whom. Diane."

"Ugh," he groaned. The mere mention of her name made him wish he could lay his hands on a bottle of anything with the word "proof" on the label. The only thing more relieving than escaping his memories was getting away from her. "I brought you all of her files yesterday before I left. What does she want now?"

"She stopped by my desk yesterday, after you left, and claimed she wanted to send a gift to you and the kids. You know, in appreciation for all of your years of hard work. So..."

"Oh, no. You didn't give her my number, did you?"

"Of course not! I would never give away your private cell. You would've been proud. I refused, locked my backbone straight, stood my ground, and told her I wasn't authorized to give out that information."

"Say, what?"

"Yes, I did," she continued. "Then I gave her your home address in Washington."

"No, Lex. You didn't!"

"I did. I suck. My backbone went wet noodle city," she said, her voice filled with regret. "I was stuck between a rock and a hard place, with her being the hard place. What else could I do?"

"Maybe next time try hanging up?"

"She stood at my desk, and you know that look she gives."

"Then you should've run," he said. "But that's fine. A few Christmas gifts can't do any harm…can they? It's okay. No harm, no foul."

"Well, it's not so much the Christmas gifts as it is her presence."

"Yeah, that's what I said. Gifts, presents, to-may-to, to-mah-to."

"No, not presents as in gifts. Presence, as in she's going to be in Washington over the holiday," she said. "I overheard her telling George that she was invited to some charity gala. She paid a pretty penny to receive an invite. Need we ask why?"

Dave grumbled.

"Well the Gala's not for another week, and on the off chance that she does decide to visit, just appease her. Get her in and out for the sake of the firm."

"I no longer work there."

"It's not me asking, it's George," she said.

Whether true or not regarding the request from George, Lexi understood that he'd do anything for his former boss and mentor. George had taken Dave under his wing as a new architect at the firm. He'd taught him everything and eased him into the partnership track. Dave worked all hours, days, nights, weekends, never turned down an assignment. In turn, he was mostly an absentee father who provided well for his family materialistically, but emotionally he'd detached from the home front.

He supposed it was easier.

Dave loved his kids with all of his heart but specialized in managing finicky, ostentatious clients, like Diane, not fatherhood. Neither he nor George had any idea that such a devastating turn of events would upend Dave's life. In an instant, he went from breadwinner to caregiver to widower.

All of his family lived in the D.C. area which proved convenient while protecting the sanctity of his young marriage from his meddling mother, but he needed help with the kids now; he needed his tribe surrounding him.

With George's understanding, Dave resigned without pressure or guilt; George connected him with his new firm which hired him sight unseen and with zero cut in pay. He owed his old boss everything.

"Fine. Fine," he said. "I'll play along. Anything else?"

"Of course!" she said. "How'd your date go?"

"A big flop. I'll call you to commiserate this evening. Right now, I need to go pick up the kids."

An hour later, he stood outside of Robbie's palatial mansion in the D.C. suburbs. He rang the doorbell and heard little feet pattering across the floor before the lock clicked. Robbie opened the door, a wide smile stretched across his tired face. He appeared more relieved than happy to see Dave.

As the kids jumped up and down yelling, "Dad! Dad! Dad!" Robbie slipped in his welcome.

"You made it. Finally! Come in."

Dave scanned his babies from head to toe; he'd missed them so much.

They both appeared taller, but Dr. Hannah, the aspiring surgeon, more so than D.J.; she'd started her growth spurt before he brought them to D.C. The sleeves of her formerly oversized doctor outfits with accompanying stethoscope, now rested high above the wrist. She'd stretched out a half inch if not more. D.J. trotted behind her dressed as her trusty lab assistant; he was constantly annoyed by his big sister while he idolized her. They were thick as thieves. One at a time, each kid leaped into his arms and showered him with hugs and kisses. "Oh, I missed you guys. Where's the patient?"

"In the backyard," Dr. Hannah said. "He's at it with the squirrels again. Almost knocked down Uncle Robbie's fence."

"Yeah," D.J. said. "Don't be shocked when you see him. His paws aren't hurt. We've been practicing our bandaging technique. Come see, Dad."

"Okay, okay," Dave said as D.J. yanked his arm and dragged him toward the patio door. "But put on your big coats first. It's freezing outside."

"Dad, you sound like you're catching a cold. Your voice is froggy. I may need to operate," said Hannah.

"Ummm, why don't we start with taking my temperature when we get home?"

She agreed and disappeared as Dave flashed a sentimental glance at his two munchkins. The past few weeks away had been the longest he'd spent apart from them, even though he'd been the absentee parent in the past. He'd make it up to them during his extra-long Christmas break.

He glanced out of the window at the full-bred English Mastiff with shiny golden fur, the last gift purchased by Tina. He had the body of a small sedan but the mind of a puppy. Dave hadn't been raised with dogs, and neither had she, but he knew those ginormous puppy paws would never belong to a small dog. But who knew that such a sweet little, floppy-eared being would grow into a gargantuan?

"A hundred pounds max," Tina said. "He won't take up much room at all," she said.

A Google search quickly revealed the challenges ahead, but he fell head over heels with the lump of love.

Now all grown up, the ungraceful, 220-pound beauty had no understanding of his weight or its impact. He welcomed his most beloved people by crashing into their bodies. With the exception of a few bumps and bruises from Buddy's exuberance, he'd proved to be the perfect city pet. Dave hoped he'd adjust well to condo life until he found the perfect location for his forever home.

"Where's the Beck-ster?" he said, referring to Robbie's wife, Rebecca.

"Grocery store. Buddy was nearly out of kibbles, and we thought our Christmas labor, I mean the sweet children, would stay for the entire day, especially after your big night."

As Dave began to explain what happened, Dr. Hannah and D.J. dashed back into the family room, grabbed their coats, and headed to the backyard. Still covered with sufficient snow, the yard became the battlegrounds for a snowball fight. Dave and Robbie laughed at Buddy's paws, each wrapped in raggedy bandages, scuffed and dirty from his dashing through the snow. They watched them frolic as Dave lamented over the date that didn't happen.

"Man, Murphy's law worked triple-double overtime," Robbie moaned. "You shouldn't give up on her, though. Somewhere in the world, a very disappointed woman believes you stood her up."

He shook his head. "I'd never in a million years," he said. "I mean, she came up with the easy out. Not me."

"Humph, I dunno," Robbie said with a shrug. "Let me ask you something. When you think back on all the time you invested in getting to know her, does she strike you as someone you can live without?"

"I *could* live without her...but I don't want to. How am I going to find her? Lex reset my cellphone. Her number, text messages, everything, gone. Me and my stupid rules," he said.

"Stupid is much too harsh," he said. "Let's go with absurd."

"My only hope is that the accountant returns and gives me the billing statement. Otherwise, I'm screwed."

Robbie studied his expression. "What's with the face?"

"I'm torn. Maybe I should leave this all to fate."

"Um Hm."

"The kids...and Buddy? We're quite the package. She may not accept us, anyway. And, truthfully speaking, I'd recover from the disappointment if our relationship didn't turn out as hoped, but this one would leave a mark."

He'd at last admitted the truth of it. While he believed himself ready to open his heart and love again, he had not anticipated such immediate regret.

Robbie replied with silence and a nod then patted him on the back; he understood.

"It was nice while it lasted. For a while, I felt like the old me," he said. "All good things aren't meant to last. So, I'll focus on making this a great Christmas for the kids."

Chapter 12

7 Days to Christmas

Gabby questioned her sanity from the moment the winter sun cracked through the broken slat in her blinds. After a bout of indecision, she committed to her quest. She wanted to see, in person, the man who had the *cojones* to stand her up and made the grave mistake of wishing for courage. The universe granted it, thrusting her completely out of her comfort zone, forcing her to find it. Now, Dave's place was located somewhere in the vicinity and the closer they got to his condo, the more she second-guessed her decision.

Her stomach knotted into a tight ball as she and Vic drifted down Massachusetts Avenue, eyeballing addresses. They spotted his on the right, and Vic sharply spun the wheel into the driveway leading to Foxhall, at one time the tenth-largest building in Washington D.C. As Gabby craned her neck and turned her eyes to the sky to take in the high-rise's curved architecture, Victoria wheeled up to the gatehouse. A uniformed guard cloaked in a black London Fog and a dearth of holiday cheer greeted them.

"Can I help you?"

"Yes," Vic handed over her business card.

"Realtor," the guard deadpanned with the roll of her eyes as if they'd inconvenienced her by expecting her to work.

"Yes," Vic said.

Gabby had never seen a smile so fake and so wide on her sister's face.

"We're going to unit 702 to view a property for sale."

"Mmmm hmmm," she said with a grunt. "Use the guest parking ahead, and the concierge will let you inside."

"Thank you," Vic replied. She reached into her purse and pulled out a Starbuck's gift card. Five dollars. "Excuse me, but, here, have a cup of coffee on me. Please."

The guard reached back, grabbed the card, and tipped her hat. Not a word of thanks.

"What's with the generosity?" Gabby said. "I could've gotten more use out of it than her."

"From the look on her face, she needed it far more than you did. And judging from her cheery disposition, I thought you could use some skid greasing for subsequent visits. Can you dig it?"

"Ah, I see. On second thought, thanks."

"You just remember, tomorrow you're on your own. I'll be bingeing on candy canes, *Suits*, and *Scandal*."

"Sounds like the title of a bestseller."

A few minutes later, they headed toward the lobby.

"So, I'll be upstairs on the seventh floor previewing units 702 and 711 for potential buyers. When you're finished, you come get me. Are we clear?" she joked in a patronizing tone, treating Gabby as if she'd sent her on her first big-girl airplane trip. "Now, do you have your list?"

"Really? That's unnecessary. Just pray I find him on the first try. Let's do this!" They took quick steps into the building where the concierge briefly greeted them at the door.

Victoria gave her a high-five, strolled ahead, and disappeared as Gabby walked to catch the elevator. She studied her list to determine which unit she'd visit first, flip-flopping between selection methods — eenie meenie miney moe versus the blind point-your-finger method.

She reached the elevator and proceeded to enter without looking up, and someone rushed out, slammed into her, and almost barreled her over, knocking her off balance. When she peered up, a broad chest blocked her view, and a pair of strong hands gripped her to prevent an inevitable fall.

"Whoa," she said, fixing her mouth to bark at him for not watching where he was going. Two things stopped her: her own guilt and the fact that the beautiful specimen standing before her left her goo-goo eyed and tongue-tied.

"Excuse me," he said before unleashing a barrage of sincere apologies. She glanced at the phone in his hand, likely the source of his distraction. "Are you okay?"

"Oh, I'm fine," she answered while thinking, *and so are you, you hunka hunka burnin' love.* The elevator door she needed to catch to go upstairs closed behind him, but she didn't care.

"Pardon me, I'm going to"—she reached around him and pushed the call button—"There. Another one should be along soon."

They froze in each other's gazes, hers falling first on his eyes and then on points further south. She had no idea whether she'd find Dave or what he'd look like, but almost by instinct, she pushed a small wish into the universe that this Adonis standing before her would by some miracle, any miracle, be the Dave she'd set on a mission to find.

"I, uh, I should be going." He scanned her from head to toe to head again and flashed a smile, the most perfect one she'd ever seen.

The elevator returned. "Yeah, I should, uh…" She gestured toward the open elevator door and stepped past him into the cabin.

"Maybe I'll…see you around?" he asked with a wink.

"I certainly hope so." She smiled and waved as the doors closed, and he disappeared from her sight.

With the adrenaline coursing through her veins following her encounter with Mr. Handsome, Gabby's courage peaked. But with every inch that the cabin crept upward toward her destination, her stomach began to lurch and roll like a boat over troubled water. She took tepid steps down the hall until, finally, she reached the door to the home of her first David.

Now facing Unit 202, she paused in the silence.

Her throat thickened along with her tongue. Her eyes burned with fear. As she prepared her rap her knuckles, she pulled back and turned tail, double-stepping back toward the elevator—she didn't knock on strangers' doors. She didn't search for men she'd never met. Yet, she didn't make it far. Three steps out and she spun in an about-face, returned to the scene of her retreat, and used her left hand to lift the right one and then forced it to knock.

She leaned forward and listened.

Not a sound or a hint of a peep. She repeated the move, this time pressing her ear to the door.

Nothing at first. Then heavy footsteps caused the door to vibrate. When it opened, standing the door way was Richard Simmons—except he was black. She gasped and then attempted to control her urge to laugh.

"Hi, can I help you?" he said, sweat pouring down his face and his hand holding a half-eaten Twinkie in his super Kung Fu grip.

"Uh, hi," she said, staring in disbelief at the man who greeted her. She scanned him, starting with rainbow polka dotted sweatband that cut through his three-inch afro, a blue nylon sleeveless tee-shirt, and a pair of Army-green leggings bearing Richard's likeness and imprinted with the words "Not today, Satan. Not today."

If that were true, he would've picked a different outfit because this one was truly the devil's work.

"Hey there! Sweatin' to the oldies I see," she said with a fake laugh. Must've been a pretty intense workout. Despite his poor choice in snacks, at least he was trying to get more active. She forced a smile and made a hollow wish.

"No, as a matter of act, you caught me right on time. I'm grabbing a snack before I get started. How can I help you?"

"Are you...David?" She might never recover from seeing those leggings stretched to West Cucamonga, clearly meant for a man Richard's new size, which Richard-Dave was not. No, this guy looked as if he'd eaten Richard for dinner and then had another Richard for dessert. Richard Simmons' face was unrecognizable appearing as if he'd inhaled the Whole Foods bakery section. If this was Gabby's Dave, he wouldn't have to worry about rejecting her because she'd silently plotted to kill him for concealing this secret.

"Yes, I am. Would you like to come in? Mother will be back with the groceries soon."

Mother? She tried to process his voice, where she'd heard it before, but he sounded nothing like her Dave. Before he uttered a word, she'd imagined this Richard-Dave having a voice like Barry White. Instead, she heard hints of Winnie the Pooh, about an octave too high. After further assessment, she determined he couldn't be her guy. Her Dave lived alone; no "mother" bought his groceries. As she recalled their conversations, she'd never heard anyone in his house, and they'd spoken late at night until early in the morning, every day, for nearly a month.

She started to explain, in more detail, the reason for her visit but decided against it. If she'd been talking to Destiny-Dave, she sure didn't want to know.

"Actually," she turned the page upside down. "You know what? Silly, me! I'm pretty sure I've got the wrong place. Please, excuse me for disturbing you."

"No problem at all. You, uh, think you'd like to have lunch sometime? Mom's making meatloaf."

In her mind, she replied, *Not even if Idris Elba was serving.*

Instead, she lied. "I'm vegetarian."

He shrugged, grunted a "hmph," and slammed the door.

All that build up to achieve a heaping bowl of nada. Could she endure the disappointment of potentially eleven more Richard-Daves? Was any man worth the disappointment, suffering, and humiliation?

Gabby pulled her phone from her pocket and scrolled through his texts. She toyed with the idea calculating the likelihood of meeting another wonderful man due to a Shakespearian quote sent via a stray text. Then, from that group, determining the number of men who would ever type or speak the word "waspish."

She didn't need math to count the results; fingers would probably do the job. Less than five of them.

She'd been persnickety when it came to her dating choices, a limited pool to begin with. She'd only been genuinely attracted to a small number of men, the number among those who were both funny and quirky even smaller still. She'd served as a prime example of a woman too picky to be too picky. The realization helped her shore up her courage (and her patience) and march to the other end of the building to tap on the door of possibility number two.

Dave Thompson.

He lived in 232, a two-bedroom. Over her initial trepidation, Gabby knocked on the door and waited, preparing her speech before he arrived. The words seemed locked in her throat, but she'd grown bound and determined to barrel through the fear. Only beyond her comfort zone could she grow, find something, or someone, she'd never found before. She took a deep breath. This time she felt bold, ready to meet her destiny on the other side of the door, no misgivings, no turning tail down the hall, no choking on her fears.

She tapped on the door and waited. And waited. And waited. Pressed her ear against the door and knocked again. Not a sound. Not even a peep of a whisper or bump. No one was home—she'd psyched herself up for nothing.

"Really?" She peered down the end of the hall and spotted the "Exit" sign. She'd use the staircase to trek up to the third floor. Only one Dave on her list lived there. His last name was Patterson.

She trotted up the steps full of hope. This would be the time she'd meet the Dave she'd been seeking. She had a good feeling. After two very wrong Daves, this one would spare her the humiliation of going door to door like a vacuum cleaner salesman praying for the right customer.

She exited the stairway into the main hallway and, to her surprise, her destination was only four doors away. She closed her eyes and released a small wish that this guy would be the complete opposite of Richard-Dave in 202.

She knocked on the door twice, and he finally answered. "Hello," he said with a smile that could blind her faster than a solar eclipse."

Wish granted!

This man was so fine that the word required a new definition. Not quite the ultra-gorgeousness of the man she'd bumped into in the lobby, but he'd most certainly serve as a highly-qualified substitute in a pinch.

Have mercy! she thought. *Homina, Homina, Homina.*

"Hello?" he repeated, only this time as if to ask whether she still had all of her faculties.

With so many thoughts running through her mind, including a few dirty ones, she forgot to speak.

This had to be "the one." *Please be Dave.*

He appeared in every way exactly as she'd imagined. So tall he'd have to reach down to put a star on a Christmas tree. His body bulged with muscles, and she noticed boxes stacked in the living room. He must've just moved in. And to top it off, his black T-shirt read, "Be not afraid of greatness." Shakespeare.

"Uh, hi!" She stared at him with a steady eye and flirtatiously twirled a long strand of a curl between her fingers. "I'm, uh, sorry to interrupt, but I'm looking for David? David Patterson?"

She questioned where she'd gotten that hair twirling thing from. She never twisted her hair or stared at anyone with such a simpering grin. Her innocent twirl took a darker turn when she leaned into him as if trying to expose the cleavage hidden beneath her winter coat. His widened smile slowed her blinking; she didn't want to miss one second of him.

He gestured his arm as if presenting himself. "It's your lucky day. I am he. How can I help you?"

Good question; she prepared to offer a list of answers. Kiss me now. Wrap me in your arms...take me now. Marry me. Allow me to birth ten of your babies. A "yes" to any of the above would be acceptable.

"Well, you see it's funny because I'm actually Gabby—"

"Honey!" a woman called out, reaching up from the depths of hell to destroy all of her hopes and dreams. "Who's at the door?"

Oh, no!

Hubby-Dave.

"I'm still trying to find out, dear. One second, please," he said, before turning back to her. "You were saying?"

"Oh, I'm sorry...I think I've got the wrong..." She tried to conceal her disbelief and disappointment.

His eyebrows scrunched. "Are you sure? I am David Patterson."

She glanced down at her list trying to think of an excuse but none came to mind. There was only one way to get out of this situation with a modicum of grace and dignity—running as fast as possible. "No, I definitely have the wrong David. I misread…everything. Sorry to interrupt."

She was half way down the hall when she heard him say, "Okay. Good luck."

The door shut. On her hopes. On her dreams. On everything.

Darn you, Hubby-Dave.

She glanced down at the next three Davids on her list—Williams, Fletcher, and Coleman. They'd take her to the fourth floor—first Unit 413 and then Unit 430. She stepped on the elevator, but her finger skipped over the fourth-floor button, instead opting to push the seven. Gabby conceded the fight for the day. She'd suffered enough disappointment, couldn't stomach another flub.

A minute later, the doors opened and she was surprised to see Victoria heading her way.

"Hey! I pulled out my phone to text you. Any luck?"

"Zilch. Three Daves. All complete busts," she said, expelling a deep sigh. "One wasn't home. Another was married."

"And number three?"

She pursed her lips and tilted her head to the side. "Vic. You know how Richard Simmons shows the before and after pictures?"

"Yeah."

"Well, this guy is the before. Literally, the split image of Richard—if he were a big black man snacking on a Twinkie to carb load for his workout. He invited me to lunch; his mom's making meatloaf."

They locked eyes in silence and then burst out laughing.

"It's not funny! It's pathetic. I'm pathetic."

"You're not. No, the heart wants what the heart wants," she said.

"This heart doesn't want Twinkies and meatloaf."

"I'll tell you what. I'll treat for pizza and beer and you psych yourself up to try again tomorrow."

"I'm giving up. This was a dumb idea."

"Oh, no. I'm not having that. You've only got nine Daves left, well ten if you don't count the one who wasn't home. Seven days before Christmas. Have patience. The next one could be 'the one.' And if you chicken out now, it'd eat you up forever."

Chapter 13

6 Days to Christmas

Dave stretched out on his bed, paralyzed by exhaustion and the ongoing germ warfare from "the bug" trying to take his body hostage. He'd spent the entire morning moving living room piles into his bedroom, the closets, and even a few into the basement storage. He'd deal with the mountains of mess cluttering the living space before emptying the storage pod where the rest of his things were stored.

He wished an organization-decorator fairy would pop out of the sky to arrange and beautify the new space which was now a disaster and in total disarray. His kids deserved a comfortable Christmas haven, and the mere thought of unraveling this labyrinth of clutter sent him spinning into a minor panic.

The sound of the closed bedroom door echoed as he crawled under his blanket. Charlie Brown and The Muppets served as his vacation babysitter for short napping sprints. He turned onto his back and stared at the ceiling light fixture, even as his kids thumped and bumped in the living room and hall. He closed his eyes and tried to drift asleep. After thirty fruitless minutes, a light tap startled him fully awake. The door opened and the sound of tiptoeing feet crept toward his bed. He didn't even need to look up.

The culprit was D.J. Dr. Hannah had entered a skipping phase, her preferred mode of foot transportation, recently downgraded from sprinting after a firm scolding. He blamed Robbie who'd bought her a kiddie Fitbit the previous Christmas. She claimed one skip was equivalent to two walking steps.

D.J. tapped him lightly and whispered, "Dad?"

"Yes, D.J.," he replied, matching his son's tone.

"I know you told me not to wake you, so I promise I'm not waking you. Well maybe just a little bit."

"Okay," Dave replied, still not raising his voice. "Why are you in my room not waking me?"

"Dr. Hannah keeps trying to be the boss of me," he said, his doe-eyed stare and stern expression causing Dave to prop himself up on his elbows.

"She kinda is the boss of you. She's your big sister."

"It's not fair, Dad. It's not."

"What's not fair?"

"I wanna watch the Muppets first because Fozzie. But she wants to watch Charlie Brown. And she said she gets to decide because she's older, but that I can decide when I'm older."

"Sounds like a good compromise. What's the problem?"

"C'mon, dad. That worked when I was six. I know the deal now that I'm seven. I'm never gonna be older."

He struggled to stifle his laugh. Among the many traits she'd inherited from her mother, Hannah's sense of humor remained chief among them. "How about this? Watch Charlie Brown first. It's only a half hour. The Muppets lasts a whole hour and a half. So, even though she gets to watch her movie first, you'll get to watch yours for the longest."

He pondered the compromise for a moment. "Hmm. I see whatcha did there, Dad. Good idea. You can go back to sleep now."

D.J. tipped out and, once again, the room quieted.

Settling down his mind proved more difficult. He couldn't get Gabrielle off of it. She'd become a habit he had no desire to break. He'd gotten used to falling asleep and waking to the sound of her voice. To be truthful, he missed her, more than he ever realized.

He missed the way she texted him for no reason at all except that he crossed her mind. He missed that she needed to hear his voice as much as he wanted to hear hers. He missed sharing random thoughts with her throughout the day, and he doubted he'd ever meet another woman who would laugh so heartily at his corny jokes because she actually found them as funny as he.

In the short time that they'd been chatting with one another, they'd become intertwined in the fabric of each other's lives. Short of summoning up all the powers in heaven, he had no way to find her at the moment. Once he wrapped his mind around that thought, he drifted off to sleep for a second time. Then a new knock, preceded by a skipping sound, came at his door.

Hannah didn't bother to wait for an answer, just barged in and poked him in the belly, eliciting a giggle. He'd always been ticklish. "Dad? You almost done with your nap?"

"No, Hannah. For two strange reasons, I haven't started yet. What is it, Cookie?"

"It's D.J. He's being incorrigible again." Her mother's word. Since Tina passed away, Hannah had become D.J.'s smotherer, despite the fact that they'd been born barely two years apart. Dave relied on her, probably more than he should've. She schooled him on Tina's way of running the house; he'd been absent for the daily routine due to work commitments. Since their foursome had been reduced to three, he'd learned the hard way that if you gave Hannah a little power, she'd seize it all like a drunken dictator.

"Incorrigible, huh? What's he done now?"

"I started pulling out the ingredients to make Mom's famous hot chocolate because—"

"It's tradition. Yeah, I know. What happened?"

"D.J. swiped the bag of marshmallows. One for Buddy, ten for him. He stuffed them in his mouth. All at once. You remember last time he ate that many? He turned into a human volcano, like the marshmallow man exploding on *Ghostbusters*."

"Ugh." He sniffled and grabbed some Kleenex to wipe his runny nose. "Okay, okay. You guys win. Nap over. I'm up. I'm up. Tell him to spit them out, and I'll be out in a minute. I need a second to splash my face, so I can wake up a bit."

"Too late. He swallowed them already. I give it thirty minutes before we're breaking out the mop and bucket," she said, easing toward the door. "I recommend we administer two CCs of the pink stuff and twenty ounces of ginger ale," she said, citing her mother's cure-all, Pepto Bismol.

"Dr. Hannah!"

"I'm going. I'm going."

Dave couldn't help but laugh. The kids drove him crazy, but they made life worth living.

Ice-cold and refreshing, the water splashed against his skin jolted his system into gear. He gave his cheeks a firm pat to wake himself up and dried off with a towel before checking on Mount St. D.J. before he blew.

Buddy, who'd been out cold and calling hogs in his dog bed, awakened amidst the increased activity. He met Dave with a running leap that nearly knocked him off his feet the second he stepped out into the hallway.

"Hey, boy! You missed me?" Dave had been out of sight for little more than an hour; Buddy greeted him as if he'd returned from war. They'd trained him not to lick so much, but there was one skill they hadn't worked on nearly enough.

"We really need to work on the jumping thing," Dr. Hannah said, poking her head around the corner from the kitchen. "He's gonna flatten somebody one day."

"D.J.? How you feeling, man?"

"Great...so far," he replied. "Did Hannah tell ya I squeezed ten of the big marshmallows in at once. It's a new record."

"Yeah? Well, let's just hope you don't break any eruption records before the day is out. Go drink some ginger ale to help settle your stomach."

Hannah had already beat him to it, meeting D.J. in front of the kitchen with a cup.

Dave watched D.J. drink it halfway down, then with a clap, he announced, "Okay, here's the decorating plan for the day. First, we'll detangle and string the lights."

"But, Dad, our new place is still kind of a mess," Hannah whined.

"I'm trying my best, Cookie."

"You're doing a great job, Dad. Really," she said with a quick change of tune.

"We're just going to have to make do with the way things are until I can muster up a little more energy to unpack."

She gave him two thumbs up. Never in this lifetime would she know how much he needed that small acknowledgment.

"After we finish putting up the lights, we'll take Buddy for a long walk, help him burn up some energy. There's a corner store not far from here. We'll cross our fingers and hope that they carry marshmallows."

"We should get the mini ones this time."

"Yes, the mini ones. Then we'll return home and finish decorating the tree. Put up the ornaments and the star."

"And drink hot cocoa?"

"Yes, drink hot cocoa," he replied, muttering, "along with a shot of Nyquil for me."

"But, Dad, that's not how we did things at our old house," D.J. said. "It doesn't feel the same."

"Come here." He grabbed a seat on the couch and opened his arms to receive his children, who joined him, one under each. "Listen, I know the holidays are difficult for all of us, and we've made some enormous changes over the past few months. The move to D.C. is second-biggest one so far."

"Yeah, this is pretty huge," Hannah chimed in.

"The thing is, with Mom gone, our lives will never be the same again. It's a hard thing to accept. Sometimes, even me, as a grown-up, I still have trouble with it. But we all have to understand that everything can't be the same as it used to be. Some things are going to be scary, some exciting, others difficult. The cool thing about starting over is we can make up new rules if we want. We can celebrate old traditions in new ways, go to new places. The sky is the limit."

The enthusiastic nods and smiling eyes signaled the message had hit home.

"What's important is that we're together, we've got family and friends who love us, and, bonus—for the first time in ages, I'm on vacation for the entire holiday. So, for now, let's focus on decorating in whatever way is fun for us today. Deal?"

They offered hugs to signal their agreement.

"Hands in!" He held out his hand palm-down in front of them. The kids piled theirs on top of his. "Let's go Williams!" they chanted in unison three times before breaking.

Within minutes, the tree trimming frenzy began. Dave opened the box of lights and commenced the arduous detangling process. The bright strands lit up as he plugged them in to check for blown bulbs, kicking his spirit into high gear. That's when he heard a silence begging to be filled. He walked over to his iPod, selected the Stevie Wonder's Christmas album, and played on repeat the up-tempo Motown sound of "What Christmas Means to Me." They danced around and tapped their feet as the song boomed through the Bluetooth speaker. Before the tune's end, a knock came at the door. They all froze in their steps and peered at one another before Dave said, "Hannah, grab Buddy's collar, so he doesn't take off."

He opened the door and to his shock, "Diane?"

"Surprise!" She smiled so wide he could see all thirty-two of her teeth.

She appeared apprehensive when Buddy greeted her with his deep, unwelcoming bark. "Hannah, take him in the back, please."

"Sure." She tugged Buddy's collar and sang, "Come on, boy," as she led him down the hall.

Diane looked casually fine with her long, thick hair trailing down the shoulders of her hip-length wool coat. She wore black leather calf-length boots and blue jeans that clung to her shapely thighs; usually, she wore skirts, so he didn't even know she owned pants. She tugged the designer sunglasses down to the tip of her nose and looked over the top rim, exposing the gorgeous hazel eyes that might hypnotize him if he weren't so disenchanted with her attitude. In her hand she carried a large shopping bag, containing at least three professionally wrapped presents.

He stammered before saying, "What...what are you doing here?"

"Aren't you going to invite me inside?"

"Oh, I'm sorry!" He stepped aside and allowed her to enter as she sized up his apartment...and his dog and kids, including Hannah who'd returned. "Please, excuse the mess. We're still getting settled in."

"You've got a beautiful place here," she said, scanning the place from ceiling to floor. "It's spacious...yet, cozy and homey." She spun on the ball of her foot and locked eyes with him. "Not exactly what I'd expect from my star architect, but sweet nonetheless."

"A house is such a major investment. I'd rather wait for the perfect place than make a hasty decision I'll regret. This place will do nicely, and I'll rent it out when we move," he said. His kids both looked at her with wrinkled noses; their expressions were similar to their reactions to Buddy's gaseous fumes after he'd gotten into some bad milk.

"Something tells me you'll design and build it," she added.

"Perhaps I will. Let me introduce you to my kids, D.J. and Hannah." He gestured to each respectively. "Diane is a former client with my old firm in the city."

"And friend," she said. "I hope, friend."

"Of course," he replied, lying like a rug.

Without removing her leather gloves, she shook their hands offering only the tips of her fingers. Hannah looked at the interloper as if she'd grown a unicorn horn, demonstrating one of the many reasons why he had zero attraction to Diane. She'd been and always would be a snob. Moreover, with two kids and dog, his life left no room for a high maintenance woman. Diane's visit may have been intended to ensure she'd stay in the forefront of his memory, but she'd only managed to remind him of the many reasons why he so missed Gabrielle.

"Oh, no. Looks like I'm interrupting," she said.

"Yeah, you are." Miss Bossy Pants piped up without a hint of hesitation, crossing her arms over her chest. Dave shot her the stink eye but, in this case, he appreciated her lack of filter. She'd always been straight-no-chaser, and he hoped she stayed that way, especially when dealing with the male species...after she turned thirty.

"Kids, you mind heading back to your bedrooms so Ms. Diane and I can talk? I promise we'll finish decorating in a few minutes."

They conceded with maximum attitude as they disappeared down the hall. Meanwhile, Dave cleared the Christmas clutter off the couch and offered her a seat. "So..." he began, allowing her to fill in the blank.

"You're wondering why I'm here."

He nodded and tightened his lips. "The thought had crossed my mind."

"Don't be mad at Lexi," she said. "You know how I am when I want something. Relentless. I pretty much hounded her until she forked over your address, but I came bearing gifts for your family. After all your years of service to me and mine, it's the least I could do."

He reached out and grabbed the bag filled with presents. "Well, I certainly appreciate your generosity," he replied. "Um, is that all?"

"No, I confess," she said. "You see, I'm in town for a few weeks to attend a few charity events and I'm dateless. I'd hoped to convince you to accompany me...maybe not to all of them, but one or two? Maybe?"

"I don't kn—"

"I realize attending functions with me while you were in my employ would've been inappropriate and awkward, but I was hoping now, since you've left the firm and moved, maybe..."

Dave released a sigh. Forward and tenacious, that's how he'd always described her. A woman who refused to understand or accept the word 'no.' Accepting her invitation would be dishonest to himself and lead her on, but rejecting her would only make her persist. She'd only quit trying when she received the reply to which she felt entitled. He needed to find a middle ground.

"I appreciate your kind and thoughtful gesture," he said. "I'm just not quite ready to get back *out there*. I'm sure you can understand."

"Oh, I see." Her dejected expression tugged at his heart. He didn't want to hurt her feelings; he just wanted her to go away.

"Give me a little time? Honestly, I'm overwhelmed with the move, the kids, the dog, trying to set up everything and acclimate everyone."

She exposed the tiniest flash of a smile. "A slow yes is better than a fast no any day." By now the corners of her lips lifted to expose her even row of teeth. She glanced down at her watch. "I've got to run soon, but I'd love to get the grand tour before I leave."

"Probably not the best idea. I haven't had much time to...the place is a big mess."

"Please? Can't be any worse than one of your in-progress renovations," she said. "Plus, I've got an idea for a housewarming gift, but I need to check out the lay of the land to select it."

"Really, you don't have to—"

She gave him "the hand." "Not another word about it. I'll follow you."

He conceded and escorted her down the main hall. They passed the kitchen and the first bathroom; she peered inside taking it in, the travertine tile and tumbled marble were among the high-end design choices that attracted him to the space. They proceeded to the first bedroom, replete with beige-yellow walls and a princess canopy bed; it served as Hannah's space and was the larger of the kids' rooms. He knocked on the door and opened it. She'd put on her lab coat and stethoscope and was checking Buddy's heartbeat as he sat patiently and allowed her; he had the patience of Job when it came to D.J. and Hannah. He'd also spotted a couple of Band-Aids on Buddy's ears. He fully expected the number to increase.

"Looks like we've got a future doctor on board," Diane said to Hannah as she scanned her room. Hannah, in turn, offered a smirk which Diane ignored. When Buddy let out a deep bark, she quickly shut the door.

"I don't think Buddy cares much for me," she said.

"He likes everyone," Dave lied.

They reached D.J.'s room, and Dave tapped on the door and grabbed the knob, but it pulled out of his hand. D.J. stood bent over phasing from green to greener.

"What a lovely room!" Diane said, oblivious to the child's discoloration which would explain why she took no steps to get out of the way.

"Are you okay?" Dave said to his son.

D.J. shook his head and said, "I don't feel so—"

That's when the contents of his stomach exploded into a projectile stream that coated Diane from the waist down to her red-bottom boots. One solid toss emptied him of the marshmallow-laced sludge in his gut; he appeared mortified when it finished. D.J. and Dave covered their mouths in shock. Her jaw hit the floor in utter horror.

"Ohmigosh," D.J. said. "I'm sooooo sorry."

Before Dave could speak a word of apology or offer to help her clean-up, a series of knocks came at the door.

Who could be visiting now?

"I'm so sorry, Diane. We'll get you squared away. Follow me," Dave said to Diane. He called out to Hannah. "Cookie, can you answer the door? We've had a marshmallow incident."

"Mount D.J. finally erupted. Got it, Dad," she said, skipping down the hall with Buddy barking and galloping behind her. He noticed Hannah hadn't grabbed him by the collar but he'd gotten too preoccupied with Diane to remind her.

By now Diane was beside herself and dripping of sludge as Dave escorted her to the bathroom in his bedroom. "D.J., get some towels to wipe up your mess. I'll run the rug machine when you're done."

Before he could remind Hannah to hold the dog, the front door opened, Buddy barked, and a thud emitted from something large crashing against the floor.

He clenched his eyes shut as he waited for Hannah's advisory notice. "Dad! Some lady was asking for a David, but I think Buddy broke her."

Chapter 14

Gabrielle studied herself in the bathroom mirror, brushing her lips with bronze gloss before making her way to upper northwest for the second day. Her Dave awaited...she hoped.

The wind pounded against her bedroom window, promising a brisk, gusty day. She wouldn't stress, even though she'd rather be sitting next to a warm fireplace, sipping on hot cocoa, reading one of her favorite books. Instead, she'd bundle up and prepare to battle through it.

The air was thick with holiday cheer, and with only six days to go until Christmas, and ten Daves remaining on her list, meeting the man of her dreams may only be a few knocks away. The day's quest began with a short prayer that she'd find him at the first stop, sparing her the previous day's humiliation. She hoped the moment she finally laid eyes on him, the moment she met the man who'd left such an indelible impression on her, would prove him worth every second of trouble she'd endured to find him.

Gabby missed Dave. He made her laugh, happy. He filled a void she'd ignored for months, maybe years. He appeared in her life as an answer to one of her life's many questions, and he brought emotional substance, something far more important to her than the physical intimacy. Every day he cheered her on, included her in his thoughts and prayers, and cared for her in so many ways she now realized had always been absent in her relationship with Leo. Dave's actions manifested themselves in not only how she felt about herself, but also lifted her mood when she spent time with others.

She tugged on her pant waist and then down on the hem of her bulky sweater. She'd greet the icy blister with a reinvigorated hope to find this angel guy who helped resuscitate her spirit, allowed her to relive the excitement and wonder of her teen crush days once again. She picked up her phone and stared at the screen for a few minutes, hoping for a text from Dave, but the boisterous ringtone startled her. It was the song she'd selected for Reggie—"Cry Me a River" by Justin Timberlake. Previously assigned to Leo, the tone freed up when she blocked her nagging ex, thus freeing it up for the next deserving bonehead—her brother-in-law.

She answered the phone and didn't even bother saying hello, just pressed her lips together and hummed "Mmmm hmmm," with all the attitude she could muster.

"Gabby, is she there? I've tried calling and texting her a thousand times. She quit responding to me; she won't speak to me. She refuses to see me. What am I gonna do?"

"Call a good lawyer?" she replied.

The 12 Daves of Christmas

He paused. "Really, Gabby? This is no time for jokes."

"Who's joking?" she said, before cutting straight to the heart of the problem. Some issues required surgical preciseness; this one required a bludgeoning. "Who's the chick?"

"She's not a mistress if that's what you're thinking."

"What I think doesn't matter. Be most concerned about what your wife thinks. You lied to her, and she doesn't trust you."

"It's all a misunderstanding, a really big, stupid mistake."

"Big, yes. Stupid, yes. Misunderstanding? She's not convinced."

A silence fell between them.

"For the record, I don't, for a second, believe you've been sleeping around. I mean you're married to Vic. Quite frankly, you suck at lying, and you're not smart enough to pull one over on her. That's what I always liked about you. However, I do believe you've been incredibly stupid, inconsiderate, thoughtless, self-centered, and stupid."

"You said stupid twice."

"The point bears repeating. With that said, any guy who's spent so many of his Saturdays delivering open house flyers and hanging for-sale signs for his wife's listings when he could've been home watching his beloved Aggies cannot be a *total* douche bag."

"I appreciate you saying that."

"Your wife is on my couch crying as we speak. She's the strongest person in my life; I didn't realize she had tears until you screwed up. Understand, I don't ever want to see them again. I'm not a violent woman, but I do make enough money to hire people to hurt people for me. You get where I'm going with this?"

"Yes, as long as you understand that I'm treading a thin line here. If I respect her space, she thinks I don't care enough. If I camp outside your window..."

"She'll file a restraining order. I know."

"If she would just give me a chance to explain."

"I've tried, without success, to convince her to talk. How long have you two been married again? Seven years?"

"Almost eight. Next Valentine's Day."

She rolled her eyes. Both she and Vic needed to quit attaching relationship milestones to major holidays. Nothing worse than being reminded of your relationship failures while binge-eating a Whitman sampler.

"And you guys still haven't figured out how to communicate a misunderstanding?"

"It's complicated."

"No, you're just afraid of the truth."

"No, I thought she'd be gone a couple of days, not a month."

"I committed to not interfering for both of your sakes, especially after seeing what Aunt Helen's meddling did to mom and dad's relationship. But if she sees your face before she's ready, there's a distinct possibility it'll look much different when you leave than when you arrived. You can't push her. You'll have to wait this out."

"She's the love of my life, and I can't lose her."

"Trust me, she wouldn't be drenching my sofa pillows if she felt otherwise about you. Give her more time. And a word to the wise—a gesture wouldn't hurt. I'm talking big, big gesture...not a gift. In general, your gifts should never leave the store."

"Ouch! I'm calling a foul, here. She loved that Calphalon set I bought her last year. I saw her eyeing it in Macy's. She had no clue I was looking."

"See? This is proof you still haven't learned a thing. On average, how many days would you say *you* cook in, say, a week?"

"I dunno. Probably four days, breakfast and dinner."

"And what about *Vic*?"

"She usually cooks on Mondays. It's her only day off because she's always out working, and she shows houses all weekend."

"Are you picking up what I'm putting down here?" she asked. Then she answered her own question when he didn't. "She wasn't looking at the Calphalon for herself; she was looking at it for you. She's always thinking about you, caring for you, working hard for you. I don't know what happened that day except she invited you to lunch to make time for you and you rejected the invitation...only to turn up in the same restaurant with another woman."

"But that's not what it..."

"Stop. Don't explain it to me; tell her. But first, a gesture. Remind her of that guy who used to skip football and basketball games. No flowers or jewelry. If you show up here, she may weaponize them. She's not swayed by cliché presents. Use a few brain cells, capiche? They'll appreciate the exercise."

Gabby hung up and took one last glance in the mirror as the sound of sniffles emerged from the living room. Victoria had been gutted over Reggie. No matter how many airs she put on or pretended everything would be okay, her heart had broken and neither Gabby nor Reggie knew how to fix it. She needed to console her sister. And no matter how much she wanted to defend him against the worst accusations, all Vic really needed was a nonjudgmental ear.

She cracked open the door and saw Vic sprawled out on the sofa, her face smothered in a pillow in a fruitless effort to conceal her sobs.

With Vic's face concealed Gabby walked over and rubbed her sister's back.

"Hey. You okay?"

"No," she said in the midst of a string of dramatic moans and sniffles. "I could kill him for doing this to us. At Christmastime, too. Jerk. I mean what kind of husband is he? He knows this is my favorite time of the year."

"I don't mean any harm, but I doubt you would've reacted any better on President's Day."

She chuckled for a minute fooling Gabby into believing she'd successfully cheered her up. Within in seconds, she'd resumed her blubbering. Gabrielle hated to see her hurt.

"He called me," Gabby said in a soft voice. "He's a wreck, wants to talk."

"Hmph. He can talk to this," she barked, holding up her palm. Thankfully, she didn't single out her special finger.

Some wives gave their spouses the silent treatment because they wanted to watch their husbands suffer and beg. Not true for Vic. If she said she didn't want to talk, she meant it. She could hold a grudge forever and never budge an inch. The puddle of a woman sitting before her was not ready to engage in a rational conversation, but she finally released her face from the pillow.

"I can't believe he did this to us," Vic said.

"But what has he done, what has he really done?"

"He lied. That's what he did. Say what you want about me. I have my faults, but I never lied to him."

"Oh, no? What about when you bought the Hermes bag?"

"So, I fudged a little on my commission calculation."

"And the gym membership...which is actually a wine club membership?"

"Neither of those involved another man. So, what's your point?"

"Just this: Nobody's perfect." She locked her eyes on Vic's and watched for a sign that she'd received a message.

Vic looked away and dropped her chin.

"Did you make coffee? I need something warm before I head out to into the frozen tundra. It'd probably do you well to get out and inhale some fresh air. How about driving me to Foxhall?"

"Did you hear that wind out there? Not a chance. I'm not budging, but you should get a move on. The days are short, and your Destiny-Dave awaits."

Destiny-Dave.

Gabby questioned her sanity once again before trudging into the cold, but she never for a moment questioned how much Dave mattered to her; she only hoped he felt the same way about her. She couldn't allow what they shared to dissipate as if it never happened, as if the bit of magic that sparked between them was nothing more than an illusion.

Every bus ride through the D.C. streets renewed Gabby's interest in testing for her driver's license. There wasn't a nutball in the city who didn't take up residence in the empty seats beside her. She boarded the number 36 Friendly bus to upper northwest and selected a free spot next to the most reasonably sane woman she could find.

The lady wore a tabby cat pom-pom hat while reading "How to Tell if Your Cat is Plotting to Kill You." Two stops later, she departed, and a certifiable spaceship hunter replaced her. He wore aluminum foil, six layers of wool, and smelled of a whiskey so strong it burned her eyes, making for the longest bus ride ever. After almost an hour of suffering, she finally arrived at Foxhall in desperate need of a sobering cup of coffee.

She walked up to the guard's desk and thanked the heavens for small favors—the same one from the previous day was on duty and remembered her. Showing her a tiny sliver of heaven's grace, the sour-faced woman

The 12 Daves of Christmas

didn't stop Gabby, just exposed a tight grin and waved her through.

Once inside the lobby, she breathed deeply and pulled the Dave list from her coat pocket. First, she'd revisit the second floor to see whether MIA-Dave had returned home. He'd been missing the day before.

No sooner than she stepped off the elevator did she run into Richard-Dave. He wore an almost identical outfit, except this one was Sunkist orange Lycra. He looked like the sun...if the sun ate the sun.

"Morning!" she said brightly.

"Well, hello," he said. "You sure I'm not the one you're looking for?"

"Ninety-nine-point-nine, nine, nine percent sure." She slipped out of the elevator and double-timed it down the hall. "Too bad for me!" she called over her shoulder as she booked it to MIA-Dave's apartment in the opposite direction.

She reached his door and knocked once, twice. Waited. Nothing. As she headed upstairs, she hypothesized about where he could be? She envisioned him on some extravagant holiday trip, wasting away in the Maldives, soaking up sun in an overwater bungalow. Or perhaps he stayed at his girlfriend's house after buying her an engagement ring, the more sobering theory.

She groaned as the elevator dinged. *Ugh.*

Traveling up to the fourth floor, she played her script in her mind again and again.

First stop Unit 413. Unlucky thirteen. She didn't hold out much hope for Dave number four, but gathered up the nerve to knock.

The sound of heavy steps drew closer. She turned her eyes upward, thinking those footsteps must belong to a tall man. When the door opened, no one's face appeared in the empty space in front of her. She jerked back her head in surprise before a tiny voice called up from below…way below. "Hello."

Her eyes fell down and there he stood. A little man. He looked like a black, clean-shaven Tyrion Lannister with an afro. She couldn't be more surprised if Peter Dinklage himself had answered. His voice, which sounded as if he'd been sucking on helium balloons, lacked Dave's deep tenor, sounding nothing at all like the man she'd sought.

He'd been disqualified before they exchanged a word. Improvising had never been a strength, but she needed to make a graceful exit.

"Well, aren't you a sight for sore eyes?" she said, exaggerating a Southern twang. "Do you know who you are?"

"I know who I am," Mini-Dave said. "Do you?"

"George!" she said. "It's so wonderful to see you…again. I hardly recognized you. Did you grow? You're taller than I remember, and you shaved. What didya do with your beard?"

"Taller? Um, I'm afraid you have the wrong house. I'm Dave."

"You sure?"

"Positive."

"Oh, no, please excuse my intrusion."

He said nothing more, just glared at her as if she'd forgotten her meds. Then he eased the door shut as if afraid she'd snap. Her head to fell back in frustration and she muttered to the heavens, "Two more and I'm outta here. I can't do much more of this."

The successive disappointments had drained her emotions, more so than lying on her couch watching her sister cry over her broken marriage. The crescendo of excitement one minute and plummet of disappointment the next had gotten old pretty quickly. Now she just wanted to end the nightmare.

Besides, Vic needed her.

She slogged to the other end of the building. David Williams in Unit 430 was next. On the way, she tried to come up with alternatives to this method—perhaps slipping flyers under the Daves' doors and requesting they gather in the lobby for a lottery drawing so she could assess them all at once and get it over with.

"Ridiculous idea," she muttered as if trying to convince herself. "Don't be absurd."

The sound of Stevie Wonder's muffled voice boomed and the bass put a little dance in her step and boogie in her hips as she approached Unit 430. "What Christmas Means to Me"—her favorite song. It was a sign. This Dave could be "the one." She knocked several times and waited for someone to answer. After a brief silence, she heard the deep bark of a husky dog.

When she got the wrong place, she really got the wrong place.

Kids? A dog? Her hopes were dashed in an instant.

Her Dave was single—no kids, no dog. Otherwise, she may not be standing there looking for him. His home had always been stone quiet during their late-night conversations. She'd knocked on the wrong door, literally and figuratively.

When no one answered right away, she turned to leave. That's when the door opened. A large, golden, furry mass covered in Band-Aids crashed through the door. He lifted up his front paws, planted them against her chest, and sent her crashing into the floor, her head pounding in a loud thunk.

A girl cried out "Buddy!" Then everything went dark.

Chapter 15

Dave had pictured a calmer less frantic start to the day. By now he'd expected to be watching the lights twinkle on the Christmas tree, following his dog walk, as he sipped on hot cocoa and watched his favorite claymation stories, including Rudolph and the Heat Miser. Instead, his son had projectile vomited on his ex-client, a multi-millionaire heiress and, according to his mildly amused daughter (judging by her snickering), his Marmaduke of a dog had "broken" some woman who'd dared to knock at his front door.

First, he rushed Diane into the bathroom and pointed her to the linens to help her get cleaned up. "I'm so sorry, Diane. There's towels and washcloths in the pantry, feel free to use as many as you need. Also, I placed some hand soap and sanitizer on the counter. Will you be okay?"

"I'm...I'll be fine. Please, go check on the woman your dog broke. How ever I'm doing, I'm certain I'm better than her."

He chuckled and pressed his way up the hall with a determined pace. He turned the corner where he glimpsed the profile of a woman attempting to sit up.

Buddy tried to apologize with a tongue bath which seemed to overwhelm the poor lady who was already dazed.

"Buddy! Come here, boy!" Dave said in an all-business voice. Buddy lifted his head and met Dave's glare with guilty eyes; he'd gotten himself into a heap of trouble, and he knew it. The only thing missing from his pitiful expression was a dog-shaming sign that read: "I tackle friendly visitors and lick them into submission." He trotted back toward Dave, his head drooped as much as his eyes.

"Go to bed, boy! Now!"

He hadn't learned to keep his paws on the floor in time to save the young woman, but he most certainly knew "go to bed" meant he needed to find his dog bed and stay in it until Dave gave him permission to move. More than likely, one of the kids would take sympathy on him, give him a "get out of jail free" card, and hide him in their rooms. He whimpered in shame as he took slow steps down the hall and disappeared.

Dave rushed over to Buddy's victim and kneeled by her side. Her face came fully into view. From that moment forward, time and space moved in slow motion.

"Are you okay?" he asked before sneezing into the bend of his elbow. His voice still sounded froggy.

As he waited for her reply, his gaze lingered on her deep smoky brown eyes, luscious pouty lips, and the mass of thick, kinky-curly hair falling across her shoulders, protruding from a floppy hat. Her porcelain-smooth skin appeared golden-brown, gently kissed by the sun. His eyes traveled down the soft curve of her shoulder to the toned thighs accented by her black skinny jeans.

"I'm...I'm okay, I—" She locked eyes with him, and her words seemed to stick in her throat. He worried until the spark of a smile began to emerge on those lips, those beautiful lips. He recognized them...her. She was the woman he'd bumped into at the train station. Without a glint of recognition in her expression, she clearly hadn't noticed him, but he'd never forget her.

"Here." He stood and offered his hand. "Let me help you up."

She slid her hand into his palm and a powerful jolt coursed through him, first through his arm then through his entire body. He tightened his grip and pulled her up. "Thank you. I, uhhh..."

"You sure you're okay?" he asked again without releasing the hand back to its owner.

Finally, forced to tug it away, she brushed off her clothes, still appearing a bit wobbly.

"Please, come in for a few minutes and sit down. Get your bearings. I promise we're harmless...mostly."

At first, he thought she might refuse, but her tense expression relaxed with Dr. Hannah in her sights; she followed him inside. Few could resist the powers of his daughter's sweet innocence...and his sectional sofa.

"I think our patient may have a concussion. I'll grab her some ice and ten CCs of Kool-Aid."

"Oh, thank you," the stranger said, her eyes softened with Hannah's smile. Then she all but collapsed on the couch, let out a deep breath, and rubbed the back of her head.

"Can I get you anything else? Aspirin? A good attorney?" He laughed and waited for her to join him.

"No, I think the ten CCs of Kool-Aid should suffice." She managed a giggle, and her lips edged up into a half smile. "Really, I'm fine, I promise. And don't worry, I'm won't sue. I'm Gabby, by the way."

They gawked at one another in an awkward silence, frozen in each other's eyes. After a few uncomfortable seconds, he finally found his words. "I'm…Dave. Is there something I can help you with? You knocked on my door?"

Both of their heads snapped toward the kitchen as Hannah thumped and bumped, and a glass fell, but no sound of broken glass followed.

"You all right in there, Dr. Hannah?" he called out.

"Got it. I'm working without my surgical gloves. Slippery."

"Dr. Hannah, huh? She's positively adorable."

"A handful. You were saying? The reason for your visit."

"Oh, I'm sorry. Yes," she said, hesitating in her reply. "You, see, uh, I'm looking for a man…named Dave."

He jerked his head back, and his eyes widened.

"You…you're looking for a Dave?" he said. As he turned over her voice in his mind, there was something familiar about it, about her. If he wasn't crazy, he'd almost believe she sounded like…no, it couldn't be. He blew off the notion as ridiculous, absurd. How could it be? "I take it I'm not the one."

"I'm afraid you couldn't possibly...I mean, he doesn't have kids...or a dog. And there's no boxes, so you obviously didn't just move in."

He thanked the heavens he'd spent the night moving the boxes into hiding.

She tightened her lips, pinching them together. Then she fidgeted with her fingers before grabbing a sofa pillow. She appeared to want to say something but second guessed herself. Finally, she conceded her silence with a half roll of her eyes and an airy snort. "Be forewarned. When I tell this, you'll believe I've gone completely insane, but I don't know...I guess...what harm can it do?"

"No harm whatsoever. Go ahead. Promise, I won't judge...at least not to your face."

"You're funny," she said, wagging her finger before she lowered her voice to a whisper. "Well, I met this guy. Craziest thing. He sent me this totally random text message. We got to know one another but never exchanged any information other than our names. We were supposed to meet last night, and he stood me up."

He tried to contain the excitement filling him so completely it threatened to bubble out of his pores. Her words answered his every wish, every dream. He forced a calm into his voice. "Stood you up? I can't believe that."

"Okay, I arrived late. So it's possible he left thinking I didn't show up. I dunno. All I know is that his name is Dave—and I'm reasonably certain he lives somewhere in this building."

"Wow...that's pretty...wow." He couldn't have conjured up a more perfect woman to be his Gabrielle. It was her. In the flesh. He'd touched her hands, looked into her eyes, felt her buttery soft skin. She was perfect in every way. He couldn't ask for more, except it was clear she was overwhelmed by the dog...and the one child she'd seen so far.

"Whatever happens or doesn't happen, I couldn't part ways with him believing I chickened out or bailed. So, I'm here on a quest, of sorts."

"Quest," he repeated with a nod.

"Some might call it a fool's errand. My sister's a real estate agent, and she gave me a list of all the Daves in this building. I've been going door to door trying to find him. There are twelve. You're number five." She reached into her pocket and pulled out a list. "Don't ask me why I'm telling you this. Despair, maybe? Insanity?"

"I'm easy to talk to. I'm told I've got one of those faces. What's your name again?"

"Gabrielle, but everyone calls me Gabby. Gabby Garrett." She smiled and glanced over at the bookshelves and grinned. "Good selection."

The only books he'd managed to stack on the built-in shelves so far were his kids' boy wizard books and his own hardcover volume of the Complete Works of Shakespeare.

Hannah returned with the Kool-Aid. "One concussion remedy, coming up."

"Thank you, Dr. Hannah," Gabby said. "I'll be a good patient and drink it all up." She tilted the cup and tossed back the drink, her eyes widening with every swallow. She finished the last drop, turned to Hannah, and asked, "Ummm…how much sugar did you put in it, Sweetie?"

"Two tablespoons extra. It'll work faster."

She coughed. "Well, I appreciate the extra care. You've got the perfect bedside manner." She stood to her feet and scanned the room.

"You've got a beautiful place here."

"Thank you. Trying to organize but…you know how it is."

"I'm really good at design and organization." She rubbed her head again. "But I wouldn't want to encroach on your *wife's* territory. Anyway, I should go. She'll probably be home soon."

"Oh, I'm not married," he said. Her smile told him everything he wanted to know. For a moment, a flicker of a second, he thought they'd connected, but even if they hadn't, she deserved to know the truth. So, he decided to confess his true identity. "Listen, there's something I'd like to—"

"Hi, I think I'm all cleaned up now." Diane appeared out of nowhere and at the worst possible time. She exposed a tight grin toward Gabby. "Ah, you must be the lady Buddy broke."

"Guilty as charged," Gabby replied, raising her hand.

Both ladies pasted on fake smiles, but he could tell Gabby was suppressing her disappointment.

"I hope I wasn't interrupting anything."

"No, we were just giving Gabby here a moment to collect herself." Dave had been so taken with Buddy's victim that he didn't even hear Diane's footsteps or remember that he'd left her in the back to clean up.

What would Gabby think about seeing Diane here? He needed to correct any wrong assumptions sooner than later.

"I really shouldn't take up any more of your time," Gabrielle responded, moving toward the door. "But I appreciate the hospitality...and the Kool-Aid."

Dave began to ramble trying to stall her departure and explain to Diane at the same time. "Gabrielle knocked on the wrong door, searching for a resident in the building. Buddy welcomed her."

"Yes, he brings quite the welcome wagon," Diane replied, her voice flat, cold. She had no use for Buddy...or any animals, confirming yet another reason she was wrong for him in almost every way.

He studied Hannah's expression, which lit up as she looked at Gabrielle. His sweet daughter saw something good in her as had Dave. "You aren't leaving already, are you?" she asked, her voice high pitched and sweet. She even added the puppy eyes, the same move she'd used on him every time they visited Target's toy section. "Buddy wants to say he's sorry. He didn't mean to hurt you."

"I'm afraid I must go, but thank you so much for coming to my rescue. And you tell Buddy that I have no ill will toward him. He seems like a nice pup."

"Happy to help, and yes Buddy's a great dog. My mom got him before she...anyway. He weighs over two-hundred pounds, but he bounces around like he's still a puppy."

"Well, it's clear he's a sweet one," she said, which made Dave smile inside. "I only feared he might lick me to death." She chuckled and grabbed the doorknob.

Diane glanced at her watch. "Actually, I'm running late for my next appointment and I need to change clothes. I'll follow you to the elevator," Diane said to Gabrielle, all business, clearly ensuring she didn't leave another woman in her "territory."

"Actually, I'm taking the stairs. I've got a couple more places to check, but I'll walk out with you."

They each said their goodbyes and Dave escorted Diane to the elevators. Gabrielle, to his dismay, had disappeared down the hall in the opposite direction and into the stairwell.

When the elevator dinged, and the door opened, Diane pressed her hand against his chest and allowed it to linger there. "Promise you'll give some thought to the ball?"

"Sure," he replied, grabbing her hand and shaking it to put a halt to her less-than-subtle flirtation. "Talk to you soon."

"Yes, you will." She offered a seductive glance and wave before the doors shut. The heat in her look could've set him on fire. The only thing she didn't do is lick her lips and growl like a tiger.

He turned around to go home and ran smack into Gabrielle who, judging from her uncomfortable expression and inability to look him in the eyes, had witnessed the entire scene.

"I'm sorry," she said. "I'm not creepy or anything. Forgot my list."

"Oh, yes. For your quest." He smiled inside, thankful he'd have an opportunity to correct any misperceptions around Diane. "Follow me. And feel free to stalk me any time."

He opened the door and took a glance around but didn't see it. "You sure you left it here?"

She patted both of her coat pockets and her pants and shrugged. "Yeah, it's gone but I don't see it on the couch. I think it was the butler, in the library, with a candlestick."

He chuckled. "Funny." Then he tightened his lips. "Hmmm. I suspect three cute gremlins may have had something to do with its disappearance. D.J.? Hannah, Buddy?"

"D.J.?" she said. "You have another daughter?"

"No, a son. Dave, Junior."

"Two kids. Wow."

They all appeared in the living room moments later, and Dave introduced D.J. to Gabby. The kids bore sheepish expressions, and Buddy circled the room with a soggy sheet of paper hanging from his mouth.

"I think we've found the culprit."

Dave removed the paper and winced when it soaked his fingers. "Blech!" He started to hand it to Gabby and instead handed it to Hannah. "Go blow dry this until it's not so..."

"Slobbery?" she said.

"Yeah, and take your brother with you."

"Please, take a seat for a few minutes," Dave said to Gabby. She seemed happy to oblige.

"The property here is gorgeous...and, uh, so is your girlfriend."

He wanted to chuckle at her obvious attempt to find out his relationship status. Usually, he'd toy with her before revealing the truth, but his time with her was short, and he couldn't afford to waste a second.

"No, no, Diane...she's not my girlfriend and never has been. She's a former client who stopped by to drop off gifts for the kids."

"Ohhhh, okay. I understand. But I wasn't probing."

"Of course, you weren't," he said with a chuckle. "Actually, I'm a single dad."

"Wow, divorced? Widowed?"

"The latter," he said with a grim expression. "Cancer."

There it was, all over her face. The expression he hated—pity. This is the part at which women usually stopped seeing him as an eligible bachelor and instead viewed him as an emotional charity case. But, unlike the others, she made a quick shift and changed the subject as if nary a word had been spoken.

"Your home is…well, you have beautiful furniture. Very artsy."

"I'm sorry for the state of things, I, uhh, work a lot of hours and haven't had much time to do any proper decorating."

"No, I get it. With two kids and a dog, it's good you can walk through the door without bulldozing your way in." She glanced at her watch and then back at him; she seemed rushed to leave. He couldn't figure out if the issue stemmed from learning about his wife or personal reasons. "I wish I could hang out, but I've got to catch the bus across town." The melancholy tone of her voice betrayed a sadness she seemed eager to conceal from him and maybe even herself.

"You sure? You're welcome to stay. We can push our crap out of the way so you can make yourself more comfortable."

That's when the kids returned and gave her "the eyes." They all but begged her to hang out and help decorate and walk the dog. Even Buddy had gotten in on the action, nudging her hand with his enormous head to prompt a parting pat. Another minute and she may have given in. But they disappeared again.

"I wish I could, but my sister is at my house alone and pretty sad. I should go home and check on her."

She shifted her gaze to the bookshelf once again, probably as a distraction rather than due to any particular interest in the books.

"Kids? You finished drying the page?" Dave asked.

"Almost," they yelled back.

He studied her as she looked at his bookcase. "You seem fascinated with something over there."

"You have the boy wizard stories. I love those. I've read them all. Books five and seven twice. I'm also a fan of Shakespeare. I own everything on this shelf."

"You do!" D.J. said, sneaking up and surprising them both. "The wizard books are my favorites, too."

"Say, what? A fellow fan." She offered him a high five. "Oh my goodness. If you like the books, you've really got to play the game. It's awesometastic." Her voice was as animated as her expressions.

Dave chuckled as Hannah joined the conversation. "No way. You play the game?"

"Sure do! Level seven."

"You made it all the way to level seven?" Hannah's eyes widened with amazement.

Gabby blew her nails and brushed them against her coat. "Only took two days. Two very long days and three bags of spicy Doritos," she said with a chuckle.

"Doritos are my favorite," D.J. said.

"As much as I love playing the games. I've gotta say, the books are the best."

"Yeah, we're supposed to be reading them over the holiday but Hannah"—D.J. shot her a stink eye glare—"is taking forever and we've only got one copy."

"Oh, no. That will never do. I mean, how are you going to talk to one another about the best scenes as they happen? Tell you what. One day soon when I return to the building, I'll make sure you guys get your own copies, so you can read at the same time. Reading's even more awesome when you've got someone to share the story with. How's that sound?"

They both jumped and cheered. "Yay."

Buddy returned, curious about the reason for the noise. He walked straight to her and put his head under her hand, nudging her to pat him and forgive him for his transgressions. She was happy to oblige.

She turned to Dave after looking outside. "I'm really going to miss my bus if I stay any longer; I've got a long hike across town."

"You sure? You're welcome to stay…or I could drive you home."

"No, please. I couldn't accept. Besides, looks like you've got a lot of work on your hands, and I don't want to be in the way." She gave Buddy one last pat on the head before heading for the door.

"O—kaaaay," the choir moaned in unison.

He opened the door, and she exited into the hall, once again heading in the direction of the stairwell, this time with her list in hand.

"Well, if you need help with anything the next time you visit, I'm on vacation, and I'd be happy to help."

She stopped in her tracks and walked back. "You know, I really could use your assistance. How about we exchange services?" she pitched. "I'll help you organize, and you get me through the security gates. It's only a matter of time before I catch the guard on an off day."

"Marsha? She looks— "

"Hostile," Gabby finished.

"Fair enough. Hostile. But she's a total creampuff. It's Burt you need to beware of. He may look like Santa, but he's got the soul of the Grinch."

She chuckled.

"See you tomorrow?" he asked.

"I sure hope so."

He opened the door to the unit and returned inside. He had no desire to watch her leave. He sat on the couch and pulled a pillow into his grasp before he realizing he'd been smiling from ear to ear. He tried to stop but couldn't. For once, it seemed fate had worked in his favor. He'd seen her, met her, and fallen in love with her all over again.

"You like her don't you, Dad?" Hannah asked, eyeing his goofy smile.

He shrugged. "Don't be silly, Cookie. We just met. But she seems nice enough."

"Mmm hmm," D.J. said. "Nice try."

"You two little rascals mind your business and find the boxes with the ornaments. We'll start loading up the tree in a few minutes, but first I'm going to give Uncle Brian a call."

"You're gonna tell him about your new *girl—friend*," Hannah teased.

He rolled his eyes and shook his head as he hoofed it down the hall, concealing himself in his room as he made the call. By the second ring, Brian picked up and Dave blurted out, "I've met her."

"Who?"

"Gabrielle. Gabby. The woman I've been texting for weeks. The one I was supposed to meet last night. The one I feared I'd never see again. She came here."

"Wait...wait. You said she stood you up."

"She did," Dave replied. "Or at least I thought she did. I was mistaken; she never used the easy out clause. Turns out she ran into problems and showed up late. Today, she appeared at my condo door looking for Dave."

"Well, how about that! I'm happy for you, bro," he said. "So, all those fears for nothing. She's good with the dogs, the kids?"

"I think so. She behaved pretty well toward them, to be honest. A pure natural. Hannah seems enamored with her, and we know how Hannah is with women. She doesn't like many, certainly not Diane."

"That's my niece," Brian said with pride. "Let me find out Dave's got a girlfriend."

"Uh, well, not exactly."

"What do you mean? You said you met her. You said she met Buddy and the kids. Everything's everything, right?"

"Yes, she met a Dave. She didn't meet her Dave."

"So, wait. You didn't tell her?"

"In so many words—no."

"Coward."

"Truth-teller," he replied, his expression pained. "Listen, don't think for a moment that I don't feel terrible about the situation because I do. It's just when I saw her connecting with the kids, I didn't want to ruin it. But I'm going to tell her. When the time is right."

"Oh, what a tangled web we weave," Brian warned. "You're going to find out the hard way that there is no right time to tell the truth after a lie. Put on your big boy pants and spill it before this blows up in your face."

Dave paused to consider his options.

"Bro, if you want this to work long-term, there is no other option."

"Fine, the next time I see her I'll confess."

Chapter 16

Gabrielle had never spent much time fantasizing about her future mate, even before Leo. Seemed pointless, and she'd been too busy pursuing her dreams and aspirations, the ones she had before she settled into the stability and routine of her good government job. Her present mundane existence didn't leave much room for the imagination or dreams.

On the rare occasion she invested more than a few seconds to imagine what her ideal "the one" would be like, she pictured a man of reasonable height (taller than she), a conservative, borderline nerdy dresser (the khaki and button-up look), and dorky eyeglasses (as opposed to the sleek rimless ones). She pictured someone who'd spent hours debating sci-fi movies and comic books. Someone who lived a quiet, settled life.

She never visualized anyone as delicious as Dad-Dave, the sexy, single father. She never envisioned his deep piercing eyes, cleft chin, nor his wickedly dreamy smile. The strapping broad shoulders, toned athletic body, and power thighs never entered her view. Not that she'd paid attention to him or anything, but only the blind couldn't notice his scrumptiousness. However, Dad-Dave came with a few additional accessories she'd also never pictured, including a dog as big as the dining room table and two, living, breathing, eating kids, even as adorable as they were. A ready-made family never entered her realm of thought, nor had any of the responsibility included in such a package deal.

She'd struggled to keep her Beta fish alive for more than three months, mourning for two weeks when little Sparky died. He sunk to the bottom of the tank instead of floated. Took her three days to gather up the nerve to call Vic so she could come over and flush him. All of this for a fish.

She could barely conceive the depth of connection and bond she might build with Hannah and D.J. They not only required regular feeding and care, but also promised an unquiet life with glorious chaos, the opposite of everything she'd imagined. Everything about Dad-Dave rested outside of her comfort zone, way into an outer rim, the never-me, nuh-uh zone.

The mere thought overwhelmed her, just in time to find out whether Dave number six would be "the one." While part of her hoped to put this search to an end as soon as possible, another hoped to prolong the quest for a little while longer now. Long enough to see Dad-Dave once more and deliver the books to the kids.

The beautiful brood lingered in her mind and lifted her lips into a smile. Regaining consciousness in the midst of Buddy's tongue bath, opening her eyes to find a family of angels hovering around and tending to her, they'd brought her an unexpected gladness. But the reality was she'd connected with another man, her heart was with Dave, and she owed it to the possibility of what they could become to keep her mind focused on finding him.

Now sitting in new Dad-Dave's living room again for the second time, waiting for his curly-haired cuties to return from the back with her dried list of Daves while conversing with him, she couldn't deny the attraction radiating between them. The longer she lingered in their presence, the more danger they posed to her mission to find him…"the one."

After swapping services with Dad-Dave, she stepped into the fifth-floor hallway and allowed her eyes to follow the numbers in both directions until she found the unit belonging to Dave Simpson. Number six. He lived a couple of doors to the right of where she stood. She knocked and waited for an answer. Didn't take long for the door to open and her eyes to nearly bulge from their sockets.

"Well, hello," she said to the gorgeous mass of muscles lurking in the doorway. Her eyes traveled up and down his scantily clad body as she attempted to speak. "I'm, uh, looking for...ahem, David Simpson."

That's when he smiled, and she stopped herself from shrieking in an embarrassingly loud volume. Spinach. Chewed and coating the entire right side of his mouth. A little bile crept up from her intestines and made her stomach jerk.

"You found him!" he said. "And you are?"

"Gabrielle. Gabby Garrett? Name ring a bell at all?"

Please don't ring a bell. Please don't ring a bell.

He considered the question for a few moments longer than necessary. If he didn't know her name off the bat, he wasn't the guy. Unfortunately, she'd need to wait for him to draw the same conclusion.

"I'm sorry," he said. "The name doesn't ring any bells." With every "S" spoken, his prominent lisp caused spinach-laced spittle to fly into her face.

"I suspected that may be the case. I'll let you get back to your meal."

For a moment, he appeared as if he'd planned to make a pass at her, giving her a come-hither look she'd rather see from Richard-Dave than Spinach-Dave. She'd take hard pass and shut it down in the gentlest way possible.

"By the way, you have an *entire bushel* of spinach all up here." She bore her own pearly whites and gestured her pinky over the offending row. He quickly covered his mouth and disappeared inside the unit. Another Dave had bitten the dust, and this one gave her more relief than all the others put together.

She trucked it toward the stairwell and sucked in a deep breath. Only six more Daves to go, but her head started aching again. She rubbed it and veered away from the stairs and toward the elevator. She thought it best to head home, get an ice pack on her bruise. Maybe try again tomorrow.

An hour later, Gabby joined Vic at home. Her sister had exited the confusion stage and entered the binge-eating stage in her transition through the phases of her marriage time-out. An open bag of lemon Oreos and two half-eaten pints of Ben and Jerry's—strawberry cheesecake and everything but the kitchen sink—rested on the coffee table.

Reveling in her sugar high, Vic turned to Gabby bearing a cheesy grin as if she'd just polished off a bottle of vino. "Well, how'd it go? You find him yet?"

"No," she replied. "No luck so far. However, the visit did prove to be quite interesting."

Vic bolted upright and positioned herself to dish. As Gabby removed her winter garb and headed to the kitchen to make herself a tall, warm drink, she recounted her afternoon in all the detail Vic would require.

"So, Dave Thompson still didn't answer the door. I've concluded that he's either vacationing or he's bought a ring for his fiancée and has decided to camp at her place."

She responded with an eye roll. "You and that imagination."

"Anyway, so I get to the unit of the next Dave, and he can't reach the peephole."

Vic crinkled her brow. "Can't reach the—I'm almost afraid to ask. Is that code for something?"

"I wish; it's not code. He literally cannot reach the peephole," she said, attempting to suppress her laughter. "He's a little person—Mini-Dave. I could plop him in the front seat of a grocery basket and still have room for two loaves of bread and a carton of eggs."

Vic cracked up laughing. "Well, I mean, I'm sure you were surprised to see him, but little people are in. They've got a show on cable and everything, have you seen it?"

"No, and it's not about the attraction, it's about the shock. That's not something you conceal after you've been talking for weeks. That'd be as bad as hiding...kids or something. You know what I'm saying?"

She tightened her lips and nodded. "True, very true. So, what'd you say? What'd you do?"

She brought her cup of coffee to the end table, set it down, and then collapsed on the couch. "I handled it as the courageous and mature woman I was raised to be. Knowing his name was Dave, I asked for George, and then hauled my butt out of there so fast I left skid marks on the carpet."

Vic reached out and patted her hand. "Please tell me the day got better. One of them's got to be the guy."

"Actually, yes, it did. Much better, in fact." She began to describe her visit with Dad-Dave, deep diving into every event, every emotion. A half hour later, she found herself still blathering about how handsome he was and how cute the kids were and how the adorable dog nearly knocked her unconscious.

Vic's face lit up, which Gabby imagined served as a mirror to her own. She talked about them loving her favorite books as much as she, and their gracious invitation to decorate and walk Buddy. After emptying her soul of the day's events, she sat there quietly and waited for Vic's reaction. Her sister had always been the reasonable one; she'd talk her down from cloud nine and list every practical reason why no union between them would work.

In response to Gabrielle's impatient expression, she said, "What do you expect me to say? The guy seems pretty amazing. You should've seen your face when you were talking about them. We could save money on electricity because you lit up brighter than that tree over there"—she jutted her head toward the Douglas Fir in the corner—"I hope you don't think I'm pouring sand on *this* fire."

"Yes, that's exactly what I expect you to do. It's your job. I mean, really. What good are you to me if you can't talk me out of this?"

"Gabby, you've been hibernating here in your chick-cave for almost two years, subsisting on TV, snacks, and books alone. No flirting. No dating. No nothing. Suddenly, the universe thrusts two men into your life, two Daves who by all accounts are single, smart, at least one is gorgeous, and you've rejoined the land of the living. And for some weird reason, they're both interested in *you*."

Gabby hurled a pillow at Vic's face; she blocked it.

"I'm not interfering in any way, shape, or form. "

"But Dad-Dave's got kids," she said. "You remember what happened to Sparky?"

"Really, Gabby? It was a fish, not Baby New Year. I'd like to think you'd be a little more responsible a with human. Besides, as long as they're old enough to speak, they'll never starve or overeat."

"And what about Diane Wealthy vonPageant Barbie? I caught her palming his chest in the hall. If he's attracted to her, he'd never be interested in me."

"Well, he invited you to return, did he invite her?"

Gabby shook her head no.

"Listen, I don't know if this guy is *the guy*. But, like you said, for all that you know your Dave could be four feet tall or proposing to his girlfriend. He could have a wife...or he could be cheating on his wife with his girlfriend. He could be a meth dealer on the run from the cops."

"Really?"

"The point is you could do worse than a nice guy with two kids and a dog—much worse. Exhibit one: Leo."

Gabby grabbed the remote and turned off the TV. "No more 'Breaking Bad' for you."

"I'm just saying, he's cute, seems like a good dad. Maybe you should quit while you're ahead. There could be more Spinach-Daves in your future."

Gabrielle considered Vic's plea. She opened up her phone and glanced down at Dave's texts. No matter what Vic said, Destiny-Dave was worth the effort. Moreover, as valid as her sister's reasoning may be, Gabby was unprepared to accept Dad-Dave's package deal. Besides, Diane had made it abundantly clear that she'd set her sights on him. For all Gabby knew, her claws had long been embedded in the fabric of that family.

No, she needed to find the man who told her she had him at waspish, even if only to close that door so she'd feel free to open another.

Two more days, she declared in her mind.

If she hadn't found her Dave by then, she'd give up this quest and maybe explore this Dad-Dave thing. Perhaps life with him would be nothing she could've ever imagined...in the best way.

Chapter 17

5 Days to Christmas

The next morning, Gabrielle practically bounced out of bed and flitted around her bedroom as she dressed, eager for the day's adventure. She lingered in the mirror a little longer than usual, flat ironing her coiled locks. Vic always said the style better framed her face, and she wanted to put her best foot forward, not for Dad-Dave as Vic would tease, rather for Destiny-Dave. Of course there was no point in straightening her hair if she didn't spend more time on her make-up. Vic had bought her a contouring kit which she hadn't bothered to touch since it'd been gifted last Christmas. The only considerate thing to do was to wear it and put her hard-earned money to use. Gabby's usual half-hour routine stretched on for more than an hour before Vic called her.

"Hey, what are you doing in there? Coffee's ready. I made a pot this morning."

She took one last look at her handiwork and tugged her clothes straight before opening the door. She strutted into the living room, presenting herself before Vic's suspicious eyes.

"Well, well, well. Lookie here, lookie here. Don't you look particularly fetching this morning?" Vic revealed her full even row of teeth as she spun her index finger in small circles, gesturing for Gabrielle to turn around.

Gabby flashed a sheepish smile and obliged. "Did I do okay?"

Vic returned her gaze to her sister's and the pride in her expression and approving nod told her everything Vic didn't say. "Cute outfit. Flat ironing. Contouring. Something to make me go, hmmmm. Me thinks someone's trying to look hot for Dad-Dave."

"Am not! It's just that when Destiny-Dave sees me, I want a *wow*, not a *meh*." The sweet scent of hazelnut crème yanked her into the kitchen for a cup of java. She pulled open the mahogany-colored cabinet door and retrieved her favorite jumbo mug with Snoopy and a stack of books pictured. She filled it to the brim and took a seat on the couch. The butterflies flapping around in her stomach left little room for food. "I've got a good feeling that fate's on my side again. I'll find him…and also, I may be late. Thought I might offer Dad-Dave a hand with getting his place organized and decorated."

"Is that so? Sounds like someone's drifting on the River Denial."

"I could say the same."

"What do you mean?"

The 12 Daves of Christmas

"What's going on with you and Reggie? Yesterday? The snack fest? I mean come on, Vic, this isn't like you. I haven't witnessed you gobbling down Gluten and carbs like that since you found out the Spice Girls broke up. You don't run from problems, and you certainly don't eat them. You always face them head-on. So why the departure here? Something else is wrong. Reggie may be part of the problem but he's not all of it. You can lie to yourself, but you can't lie to me. Not anymore."

Vic locked her gaze on Gabby, her eyes bleary from sleeplessness. She fidgeted with a pillow in her hand, another tell-tale sign that she was suppressing a secret.

"I'm a horrible person."

Gabby looked at her appearing in shock, total disbelief. "What in the world would make you say such a thing? You're the best person in my universe."

"What if I'm not sure whether I want to be married anymore?"

"Don't want to be—Vic, what are you talking about?"

Tears pooled in her eyes. "For a couple of years now, I've been evolving into this woman I barely recognize anymore, inside and out. I look in the mirror, and I don't know who's looking back at me. I used to have fun, wake up excited to face the day and all its possibilities. There was no routine, no sameness. Every day was different, and I couldn't predict my life from one minute to the next. I packed a bag, jumped in the Jag, and drove wherever the wind on my bumper carried me. I discovered new things, new places, new restaurants, new people. I used to explore, eat gluten and carbs, happy carbs. Then my Jag was totaled and Reggie bought me a Volvo; my entire life went from Jag to Volvo."

"Yes, you've changed, Vic. But that's all a part of growing up."

"There's a difference between maturing and losing yourself. I've lost myself, and I want her back, but I don't know how to get her back." She stood and paced the room. "For many months now I've been holding my life together by a thin thread. Struggling through the sameness of this routine every single freaking day. I'd reached the end of my rope, found myself standing at the edge of a cliff waiting to fall over, maybe a small part of me hoped Reggie would bless me with the final shove. But I didn't allow myself to fall, rather I tried to change things, you know? I honored my vows and tried to be a part of the solution. That's when I surprised Reggie for lunch, and I caught him with the other woman."

"Geez. If that doesn't send you into a free-fall, nothing will."

She nodded. "And what scared me more than anything is that I should've been angry, furious. I should've felt betrayed, tried to kill him…or at the very least scratch out his eyes. I did none of those things. I felt none of those things."

"What did you feel?"

"A lifted burden. Relief." Her expression was now filled with guilt and anguish. "He presented me with an excuse. Was it the one I'd been hoping for? Had I asked for it? Had I willed it through my inner thoughts and wishes?"

Gabby shook her head. "You couldn't predict this would happen. You had nothing to do with his decision to reject your invitation and have lunch with another woman that day."

"Still, it was as if I'd been standing inside a dark tunnel for years and, all at once, a light presented itself, a small glimmer of hope. I gravitated toward it, sought freedom inside of it. It was in that moment that I realized I no longer wanted to fix my marriage—I wanted to escape it."

"Oh, Vic." Gabby set her mug on the table, stood, and opened her arms to her sister; Vic quickly fell into them.

"I'm a rotten person, a horrible wife," she said into Gabby's shoulder as her body shuddered. Finally, tears flowed, washing down her face like a sweet cleansing rain. Gabby led her to the couch.

"You're not horrible, Vic, you're human," Gabby said. "You think you're the first wife to experience this? Well, you're not and you won't be the last. You and Reggie got hitched right out of college. You were so young, much different people. Whether or not you join your life with that of another person, change is inevitable."

"But neither of us changed for the better."

"Says who?" Gabby said. "Who's to say that you and he won't come out on the other side of this happier and with a deeper understanding of one another? Who's to say you won't learn more about what you both want and need to be happy and find a way to commit to making it happen?"

"Somehow it doesn't feel that way. As a matter of fact, the exact opposite seems most possible."

"Sister. Dear, sister, you won't have any real idea about how this is going to turn out until you talk to him," Gabrielle said. "Com-mun-i-cate."

"How can I call him when I'm still not certain about how I want this to turn out? Right now I can't say."

Gabrielle had advised Reggie to make a gesture—she just didn't realize at the time how big it needed to be. If he didn't hurry up and do something to remind her of all the things she loved about him, and there truly were many, he may be wifeless before the holiday's end. When Gabby returned from the day's quest, she may try to grease the skids in his favor, but the first move was his to make. He's the one who fed this beast, lunching with another woman in the first place.

She offered Victoria a peck on the cheek. "I've got to get out of here. I don't want to wait until the middle of the afternoon to get started. The wind chill's gonna be sub-zero after dark."

"Well, get a move on, then. Bundle up and don't forget the bag of books you left by the door. I'd drive you, but the way my depression is set up..."

"Actually, today, you need to stay home. Consider giving Reggie a ring...or at least answer his calls. The man's bugged you thirty times a day since you got here."

"He knows where I am."

"Really? You've made it clear you don't want to see him."

"I don't," she said. "But if he were really so desperate to reconcile, it wouldn't make a difference...would it?"

Women sure knew how to send out confusing signals. On the other hand, too often there was a direct link between a woman's crazy and a ridiculous choice made by a man.

An hour a later, Gabby arrived at Foxhall toting her book bag filled with the boy wizard books as promised. She'd practically hummed during the entire bus ride, didn't even bother shoving headphones in her ears or pretending to ignore the eclectic bunch of riders. Indeed, she happily entertained a lengthy conversation with a man who believed the government had bugged his crockpot in an effort to steal his chili recipe and sell it to the Russians. What his conspiracy theory lacked in lucidity, it more than made up for in creativity.

Thankfully, Gabby exited the bus before he reached the sequel. She strolled up to the guard's booth, waiting for the usual duty cop to wave her inside. Instead, a cantankerous Santa-looking dude "greeted" her with a snarly expression and a Grinch-ish disposition. The cold winter winds had nothing on him. She didn't even attempt to explain that Marsha had allowed her to enter.

"Good morning!" she said cheerily.

"What's good about it?" he barked back. "Your driver's license and the number of the unit you're going to visit?"

She thought about diffusing the situation with a little levity, but the old man appeared to have zero interest in pleasure or laughter. So, she reached into her purse and complied without comment.

Gabby handed him her identification card.

"What unit are you going to?"

She froze for a moment, and in the silence, he said, "You don't know which unit you're going to?"

She replied, "Four-thirty. Dave...Williams."

He checked the tenant list and found his name. "Okay, I need to call for verification."

The wind whistled past her ear as she waited for him to do his security thing. She hoped Dad-Dave would honor their deal. The guard returned moments later. "Proceed to the lobby. Enjoy the rest of the day." The tone in his voice said he couldn't care less.

After deciding to save her trip to Dad-Dave's place for last, she arrived on the sixth floor and proceeded to knock on the first door.

Dave Coleman.

Would he be the one she'd been looking for?

When his door opened, she became engulfed in a ball of thick, pungent smoke that called to mind a couple of the spiff-lovers from her roommate's artsy set during Gabby's second-pancake New York summer. Apparently, the smog had been gathering at the door waiting to make its escape. It burned her eyes and made her cough. Through it, she heard a voice say, "Hello."

"Is Dave here? Dave Coleman?" she said through intermittent coughs.

A thirty-ish, curly-haired, bronze colored man dressed in a black jogging suit emerged from the smoke with a full beam on his thin face. Hookah-Dave.

He looked as happy as he smelled. "I'm Dave Coleman," he said, sounding like a displaced surfer. Gabrielle had no idea what kind of twisted expression into which her face had contorted, but he responded by adding, "Medical marijuana. Rheumatoid arthritis."

"Ah," she replied with an understanding nod. Although he was mildly attractive, the thought of spending more than thirty seconds in a condo where you could get a contact high from sitting on a sofa in no way fit her picture of an ideal mate. "You wouldn't by any chance know a Gabrielle, would you?"

He jerked his head back. "Why, yes? I know a Gabrielle very well. She's one of the best people I know," he replied.

In the brief silence, her stomach plummeted to the floor. *Nooooooo*, she screamed in her mind. This can't be him. That's when he said, "She's my mother. What about her?"

After her heart returned to the cavity, she said, "Oh, I'm sorry to disturb you. The Gabrielle I'm looking for would be in her thirties; she couldn't possibly be your mother. I apologize for the disruption."

A huge sense of relief washed over her as she made her way to the next two doors. The first belonged to Dave Wallace, a tall, wiggy blonde, wearing a little black dress, stilettos, and flamingo pink lipstick. Apparently, he was a drag queen preparing to perform as Christina Aguilera. Gabby named him Barbie-Dave. Definitely not her guy. She didn't even bother to ask his name; just told him she'd knocked on the wrong door.

The outlook took a turn for the worst from there.

Her last try before heading back to Dad-Dave was a total and complete bust, and she knew it from the moment he opened the door...supported by his walker.

AARP-Dave wasn't the guy, either.

She'd arrived with such hope for the day, all for naught. She started to continue her quest and head to the next floor, but decided to stop while she was behind. Besides a growing reticence to endure the disappointment, she wanted an excuse to return to Dad-Dave and the kids again, whether or not she'd admit it to herself. Of all the places she could go in that moment, beside him is the one place she truly wanted to be.

Chapter 18

"Bundle up, kids. It's going to be a chilly night. Make sure you put on your thermal underwear, you hear me?"

Not one single reply filled the silence. Funny how their hearing seemed much improved during any discussions of gifts or shopping.

"You hear me?"

"Yeeeeees!" the choir sang a few moments later.

Dave had wrangled up the kids and prepared to head downtown knowing Gabby had returned to the building. He'd authorized her entry and expected her to drop by and at least say a quick hello before setting off to find…well, him. To his disappointment, she'd skipped the morning greeting, at least for the time being, leaving him no opportunity to invite her on their outing. Now he risked missing a key opportunity to spend quality time in her presence.

Earlier that morning, he'd spent hours and hours working up the nerve to tell her the truth, to divulge his true identity. He demanded that he do the right thing, warned himself that he'd concealed too much for far too long, conceded he should've told her the entire truth from the beginning. But his fear remained greater than his courage. What if she'd grown fond of D.J., Hannah, and Buddy but still wasn't ready to take on the complexities of dealing with a single dad? The busyness, the noisiness, the confusion of their daily existence might overwhelm someone content with a quiet, solitary one, as he knew her to be from their phone calls. He couldn't trick a woman, a potential mate, into joining him on this journey. His ideal partner must willingly accept him and everything he had to offer.

Enter Plan B.

He'd planted an idea in the kids' heads—a visit to the National Christmas Tree. It'd been an annual family tradition during his formative years in Washington, but he'd not visited the grounds since he and Tina moved to New York. A trip to his childhood holiday haunt could spark the beginning new traditions. His greatest hope was that if Gabrielle joined them, if she experienced a fun outing with the family then maybe she'd embrace the life he had to offer.

But his plan remained contingent on her showing up, something she hadn't done yet, something he'd begun to wonder whether she'd do. He considered wandering through the halls to find her, but he didn't want to come off like a stalker. So, he impatiently waited for her, staving off his anxious kids the entire day as he struggled to disguise the number of times he stared at the door.

A glance at the pink evening sky signaled that the night and expected frigid winds were settling in, promising to be too chilly if he stalled much later. So he gave in to their protestations and dressed to go.

"Okay, who's ready?" he called out as he exited his bedroom, "I am."

"Almost, Dad!" Hannah replied. "Looking for my Rudolph earmuffs. Can't find them anywhere."

"I unpacked them yesterday. Check the closet," he replied.

"Dad, can I take my Nintendo?" D.J. asked. "I'm going to need something to keep me entertained while we look at the Christmas displays."

"Really, D.J.? That's the purpose of the trees."

"But it's just gonna be standing there."

"No video games. However, I will allow you to bring a great attitude and leave the whining at home."

"Really, Dad?" he replied.

He chuckled to himself and walked to the hall closet to grab their coats. Just as he removed them from the hangers, a knock came at the door.

His heart fluttered, Gabrielle had completed her mission for the day. Unfortunately, now they were ready to leave, and her timing couldn't be worse...or could it?

"Looks like my Christmas present came early," he said, attempting to subdue her with his charm after he had swung the door open.

"Hi, Dave." Her smile spread as wide as the doorway. She offered a wiggly finger wave and seemed as happy to see him as he did her. "I came to help you get your place in order, organize and arrange as we agreed. You buzzed me in as promised"—she gave him a once-over—"but it looks like I've come at a bad time."

"Au contraire. Your timing couldn't be more perfect," Dave said. "Please, come in. The kids are getting dressed. They'll be out in a second."

She stepped inside and inhaled the scent of Dave's apple cinnamon candles. He burned them hoping the warm smell, if not the mess, might make her linger a little longer.

"It's kind of late in the day, isn't it?" She dropped her purse on the coffee table and glanced at the discombobulation.

"Hannah? D.J.? Someone's here to visit," he yelled down the hall to the kids. He made quicksteps back to her. "They aren't dressing for the day; they're preparing to face the cold."

"Oh, you guys are heading out?"

"Yes, as a matter of fact. We're going to see the National Tree."

"Oh, I so love it. One of my favorite D.C. traditions. It's funny, I live on Capitol Hill and haven't visited in, oh, I can't even remember. You guys will have fun."

"Care to join us? It's last minute, but we'd love to have you." He wanted to plead with her, find a way to convince her without appearing psycho. With the sound of footsteps trampling toward them, he decided his accomplices may prove far more convincing.

"Yeah, yeah. Pleeeeeeease," Hannah pled as she skipped in from the beyond, dressed in winter boots, corduroy pants, a pink sweater with white embroidered flowers and Rudolph earmuffs.

D.J., following tight on her heels, echoed the sentiment. "Yeah, pleeeeeeease." In contrast to Hannah's more coordinated outfit, he appeared as if he dived into his laundry hamper and emerged from his bedroom in whatever stuck.

Pressed for time, Dave didn't balk about his sloppiness as he usually would. D.J.'s coat would mask the mess beneath, and they weren't going any place else.

With two sets of sad puppy dog eyes yanking on her heartstrings, she'd have to be an ice queen to resist the power of their "force." For him, she could not. Her heart was as warm and as pliable as he'd believed.

"How can I say no to these two?" she said with a chuckle. "You two must really empty your dad's wallet around this time of the year, huh?"

"We try," Hannah replied with D.J. briskly nodding in agreement. Gabby folded over with laughter.

The family gathered near the door, all bundled up and ready to go, and her face bore a distressed expression. "I'm afraid I didn't dress warmly enough. I don't want to cut in on your fun when I need to leave because I get too cold, too soon."

"Oh, no, you don't have to worry about that," Dave said. "I promise I'll protect you. I'll keep you warm." He looked her in the eye and didn't flinch. He wanted her to understand he meant every syllable of every spoken and unspoken word.

"Yeah, we'll keep you warm," D.J. piped in, breaking their gazes.

"Besides, it wouldn't be any fun at all without you," Hannah added.

"Awwww," Gabby sang, stopping when she caught herself. Too late, he'd already spotted it. The look. He couldn't explain it. Some women did it, and others did not. He'd not seen the doting smile flash in a woman's eyes while she looked at his children since Tina. It was a look filled with delight and adoration, a look of acceptance and patience. No heavy coat would keep him as warm in these frigid temperatures as his memory of that moment, of that look ... of her.

By the time they climbed up from the subway's bowels near the White House, the sky had turned a violet-blue except for a dark pink streak that trailed across the horizon. In one direction, Dave noticed the red lights, bows, and sparkly ornaments hanging from a towering tree circled by smaller ones; the South Lawn stood further in the distance. The Washington Monument stood the opposite way, soaring into the night under glaring spotlights surrounded by a circle of flags billowing in the cold night. Gabrielle shuddered in the wind's wake, but he pulled her close to him and helped wrap her scarf a little tighter. Then he handed her his extra set of gloves.

"Oh, no, I couldn't," she said. "You need them."

"No, I need you...I mean, to be warm. You know, so we don't have to cut the night short. I'm giving them *to you,* but really they're for the kids...*and me.*"

The smile that followed was girlish and shy. Gabby glanced down and then up at him, her eyes twinkling like the stars.

"Pink at night, sailors delight," Hannah said.

"Pink in the morning, sailors take warning," D.J. followed.

"Looks like we're gonna have some good weather," she continued.

Gabrielle looked at Dave with a quizzical expression. "What's that about? The pink?"

"Brian, my brother, he used to work for NOAA, the National Oceanic something or other. He teaches them random things. As long as doesn't involve fire or drugs, I just roll with it."

"Ah," she replied. "Okay, where to first. This is your party. I'm just along for the ride...walk."

"Pathway of Peace!" Dave said. "Everybody hold hands, so we don't get lost."

Hannah and D.J. obliged. As he held out his hand to Gabrielle, a clueless D.J. grabbed it before their fingers could touch. Hannah, who caught on to the disruption, rolled her eyes and gripped her brother's free hand... along with Gabby's. They strolled the Ellipse, beaming brightly in the glow of the Pathway's Christmas lights.

"We need a song. Who gets to pick?" D.J. asked.

"I think we should let Gabrielle pick," Dave's sly smirk hijacked his face. He sensed she did not like to sing but would if coaxed from their conversation.

"No, no," she replied. "I promise you, you do not want me to howl."

After Gabrielle refused to give in, Hannah offered a compromise. "Okay, how about we all sing, but you get to pick the song?"

"That's a deal I can live with. 'Grandma Got Run Over by a Reindeer'? Everybody knows that one? No?" she said responding to their blank expressions.

They all flashed her a sideways glance and then burst out laughing.

"Ohhh-kaaay. I'll definitely take that as a no," she said. "'How about 'Up on a Housetop'? Everybody's got to know that one."

"It's Hannah's favorite," D.J. said.

Hannah only smiled. As the choir began to harmonize, Dave could feel the Christmas spirit breathing life back into his weary family. It'd been so long since they felt the true sense of wonderment that the holidays bring, a gift delivered to him by a funny girl and a stray text.

As they strolled Presidential Park, the kids and Gabrielle couldn't take their eyes off all of the trees, ornaments, and bright bulbs, but Dave focused elsewhere. He couldn't take his eyes off her. Watching this Christmas moment through her eyes made everything new for him. She gleamed as much as his children, as if they'd all experienced Christmas for the first time together. He wanted to grab her, hold her, and thank her for the gift of happiness, of her, but he resisted under the watchful eyes of two nosy witnesses.

Every feeling was instinctive, as the universe had intended. He needed only lean into the flow. As they approached Santa's Workshop, the kids begged to go inside without adult supervision. After a short debate, Dave relented.

"Fine, you can go," he said. "But we're right here."

"Really, Dad," Hannah said. "It's not like we're gonna disappear. It's one room. We're either in or out. We know where to find you."

"Okay, Dr. Hannah. Go."

He chuckled and shooed them away, then turned his attention to Gabrielle.

"So, you enjoying yourself?"

"A little chilly, but I'm truly having the best time. More fun than I—"

"More fun than you what?"

She hesitated for a moment then continued. "It's just...I'm surprised. I never thought I'd be so comfortable around kids."

"Well, mine seem very taken with you." He locked his gaze on hers. "And they're not alone."

The soothing melodies of an a cappella group began to fill the air. They sang as part of the nightly entertainment, local performers, invited by the park service. As "All I Want for Christmas" echoed around them, Dave took advantage of the night, the stars, and the music.

"Shall we dance?" he asked.

"Here? In front of everyone?"

He pulled her close to him and placed one of his arms around her waist. Then he grabbed her right hand and held her as they swayed to the tune.

She glanced over both shoulders, scanning the immediate area. "Everybody's staring at us."

"What everyone? Nobody's here except you and me." He pulled back and locked his eyes on hers. "Do me a favor. Close your eyes. Please. For me."

She flashed a skeptical expression before obeying his wish.

"Don't worry. I've got you." He held her close and resumed the sway. "See what I mean?"

"Yeah," she sang with a smile in her voice. "Nobody's here except you and me."

After another moment passed, he pulled away from Gabby. Her eyes remained closed and her lips puckered slightly, begging for his. He pressed his mouth gently to hers and an electric force pulsed between them. It turned from sweet to sensual before he could catch himself. The excitement was instant, thrilling.

She opened her eyes and he tried assess what she was thinking but she offered no clue, so he went the safe route. "I'm sorry," he said, afraid he might have offended her.

"Please, don't be. I'm not," she said. "You just... continue to surprise me. That's all."

"Listen, Gabrielle, there's something I want—something I need to tell you," he began. The kids dashed across the lawn yelling, "Daaaaaad!"

He shook his head and grinned at her before turning to them. "What's going on?"

"We're getting cold. Can we go home now?"

He turned to Gabrielle. "Of course."

"Aren't you getting cold?" Hannah asked Gabrielle.

She glanced at Dave. "No, not even close."

"We'll ride the train with you since we're close to your home," he said. "There's no way I'll allow you to catch the Metro alone on a night like this."

"Good," Hannah said. "Then we'll know where to pick her up for breakfast in the morning."

Dave bore a quizzical expression.

"You forgot, didn't you? Tomorrow is merry berry pancake day," she turned to Gabrielle. "Dad makes the best pancakes."

"Well, I'm not sure if I'm officially invited," she said. "You should probably make sure it's okay with your dad."

They all looked at him and waited for an answer.

"Of course, it's okay with me. You in?"

Chapter 19

"So, let's start from the beginning," Victoria said, grilling Gabby who'd started making a cup of hot cocoa after returning from her evening at the National Christmas tree. "You went looking for Destiny-Dave and found three more busts."

"Yep."

"And you returned home, but not before spending a romantic evening with Dad-Dave and his kids."

"Yep."

"And you two—"

Gabby nodded. "He kissed me."

"But then you—"

Her face bore a cheesy grin. "He's pretty amazing...and it's killing me."

"Killing you? Why?"

"After two years of this self-imposed love drought, my life is all of a sudden raining men. What are the chances that within a single month I would meet two amazing guys, both named Dave and living in the same building?"

"Slim and none," she said. "You sure they're not the same guy?"

"Impossible." Gabby pinched her lips and shot Vic a sideways glance. "He never said a word about kids or a dog. We talked all times of the day and night, and I never heard a peep. If by some miracle he could hide the kids, he'd never hide Buddy. He's gargantuan." Her expression turned distant as if she'd gotten lost in her memories.

"The thing is...I had a real connection with the Dave I met via that wonderful, stray text message. He woke me up out of my hibernation, brought me back to life, made me feel again. If Destiny-Dave hadn't come into my life, I probably wouldn't have been open to this...whatever's happening with Dad-Dave. I can't forget the things we shared...nor him."

"Of course, you can't. No one expects that. But maybe Destiny-Dave came into your life to open up your heart for business so that you'd consider Dad-Dave. Maybe he came into your life for a specific reason and not a season," she said. "You've got to face the possibility that Destiny-Dave has served his purpose."

"Yeah, you may be right. I guess. I don't know."

"Where'd you guys leave things? I presume you're going back to finish up your list tomorrow, right?"

"Well, that and I'm helping him organize and straighten up his house. The Williams bunch is picking me up in the morning. I had the vision. His house will be amazing when I'm finished."

Vic's expression asked, "Why?" but her mouth didn't.

Gabrielle responded, "They've invited me to breakfast."

"My, my, my. This could be a good thing. A man who offers to cook?" Her face lit up as brightly as the Christmas tree and then dimmed almost fast. "Please, God, just don't let him make pancakes."

"It's a pancake breakfast. The fifth annual merry berry pancake breakfast."

Vic emitted a groan so loud it filled the room. She walked over to Gabby and grabbed her by the shoulders. "You listen to me. All that second-pancake nonsense, you leave it at this doorway," she said, pointing to Gabby's front door. "Do not take that baggage with you. It's not fair to him...or to you. Or to any of us for that matter."

"Okay, I won't," she lied. Her sister stared at her with a lingering skeptical glare to which Gabby responded with a sheepish shrug. "What? I promise I won't hold it against him, but, for the record, I think we both know what's coming."

She and Victoria knew the truth. Gabby could no more ignore the first pancake than she could the nose on her face. She could try to deny it, overlook it, but one fact remained: when he lopped it on her plate, the swelling excitement consuming her before, during, and after that amazing first kiss would dissipate into nothing. Then she'd resume her quest to find the other Dave, Destiny-Dave, the one without the adorable kids and the lump of a beautiful golden dog.

For tonight, in the dwindling time she and Dad-Dave had left, she'd revel in the warmth of that spine-tingling kiss. She'd recall the electricity coursing through her as his lips pressed against hers, the feel the touch of his palm against her cheeks as he caressed her.

She'd remember the butterflies in her stomach and how they flipped twisted and turned, how her heart skipped a beat, and her hands trembled with anxiousness. She'd remember her thankfulness that, for once in her life, reality had risen up to meet the vision and bring her imagination to life.

The moment delivered, restored her faith for the hundreds of moments that had failed her.

She allowed herself to indulge in the glory of what they shared, and she'd never regret it, no matter what came of their relationship or how it drew to its inevitable end.

4 Days to Christmas

Gabrielle bustled around the house in a flurry the next morning, trying to find the perfect outfit to wear, think of the right words to say, and practice in her mind the right things to do. Part of her realized this day would mark the beginning of the end for her and Dad-Dave which made her a little gloomy, but she fought off the negative thoughts by focusing on special time they'd spend in each other's presence before the day went south. She'd reverted back to her teen years, hoping he'd sneak and hold her hand or kiss her cheek. Perhaps they'd steal a kiss while the kids played in their rooms. She thought to get mistletoe too late; he'd be there any minute.

A horn honked as she put on her wool coat and spun the pashmina around her neck. Gabby pushed the curtain aside and stood in the window, her red scarf visible to passersby, and peered outside. Dave's eyes scrolled until he spotted her; he waved, and she returned the favor.

"Vic! I'm leaving," she yelled, hoping beyond hope that her sister would confine herself to the guest room and allow Gabby to make her escape without embarrassment.

T'was not to be.

No, Miss Nosy Pants flew out of the bedroom wearing pajamas, a robe, and jumbo pink curlers stacked on her head. "You didn't actually think I'd let you get away without snooping first. Where is he? I want to see him."

"Really, Vic?" she said. "You're like the mom who shows up to school in her pajamas. You at least could've taken out the rollers."

"He's not even going to see me. Is he out there?"

She peered out and, of course, he'd pulled up, caught a glance at her, and waved. Gabby winced and rolled her eyes.

"Hey, now! Cutie on duty! You know he's a special kind of fine when you can see it clearly from three floors up. If you don't want him, I'll take him."

"You're married."

"That's debatable."

"What am I going to do with you?" Gabby said. "I'm leaving now before either of us gets into more trouble. Oh, and thanks for the embarrassment."

Vic laughed. "Can't say I never gave you anything! Merry berry pancake day!"

Within the hour, they'd arrived at Dave's condo. Gabby hovered around the breakfast bar watching Dave pull out the bowls and mix as he heated up the griddle and the kids played in their rooms. Pancake time. Usually an innocuous activity, she couldn't help but feel any potential future hinged on this moment, causing Gabby's heart to race and fingers to fidget.

On any other day, in the presence of any other guy, she'd play a "perfect moment" in her mind like a movie and watch as things fell apart spectacularly in reality. She expected the same result this time, but for a change, she'd adequately prepared herself to handle the disappointment.

From the moment he lopped the first pancake on her plate, she'd never see him the same way again. Gabby now believed, with all of her heart, that her ideal would believe her worthy of the best things life had to offer. Just as she believed Dad-Dave worthy of a perfectly organized home, she needed someone who believed her worthy of a second pancake. Yes, they were small gestures, but they spoke volumes.

After looping his "My Cooking Is So Good Even the Fire Alarm Cheers Me On" apron around his neck, he made small talk as he added ingredients and whipped the batter.

"Cool apron," Gabby said. "Is it accurate?"

"Unfortunately, I got very little practice before Tina, you know." His eyes shifted away from hers. He still grew emotional when talking about his wife. She imagined he always would. It was no surprise that he changed the subject.

"So, you and your sister...you guys close?" She eyed the package of multigrain pancake mix—healthy; a bottle of real maple syrup sat on the counter behind him—perfect.

She chuckled. "Yeah, probably too much so. She's my best friend, my confidant, my matchmaker, sometimes she's a second mother. Don't know what I'd do without her."

"That's nice. My brother Brian and I are close too. You said she's staying with you for the holidays?"

Gabrielle expelled a deep sigh. "Sort of. She lives in Potomac, Maryland. Let's say she's on sabbatical from her marriage."

He flashed a quizzical look.

"She and her husband...they're going through a rough patch. An affair. His affair. Well, his alleged affair. I dunno."

"Wow. That's sucks. Christmastime, too. You think they'll work it out?"

"It's hard to say. It's the gamble of marriage, right? When you put two individuals of independent mind and thought into such a major commitment, and they both grow as humans tend to, they run the risk of growing apart."

"True. It's a constant give and take that requires understanding and a deep, abiding friendship at the core. Not every couple can lay such a strong foundation."

"No, but they'll find their way back together once they make it to the other side of this. It's just, Vic. Let's just say my sister can be stubborn."

"I hope that's not genetic."

"Oh, I can promise you it is hereditary— one hundred percent. No question about it." She chuckled as he poured batter onto the grill. "Looks like it's pancake time."

"Almost. Kids! Breakfast is on."

They thundered back into kitchen and took up seats next to her. She watched him expertly flip the first one without a mess. Her mom and dad always splattered; he'd performed like a regular pro, except his first pancake looked like, well, the first pancake. That much he'd not perfected.

"Yum!" D.J. said. "But, dad, you didn't put the blueberries in."

"I'll put them in the next batch."

"Okay," he replied.

By now, Dave had almost finished cooking it. Gabrielle glanced to the left and right at the kids' eager, hungry faces. No way would she allow him to serve the first one to them. She refused. They may not understand the difference; they may not care. But she did. She'd sacrifice herself on the skillet, so to speak.

"First pancake's up!" Dave said.

He lifted it up with the spatula. Gabrielle took a deep breath and held up her plate to accept her fate.

"Oh, no, no, no," Dave said, refusing her plate and pushing it back toward the counter. "Gabrielle is a guest, so we have to teach her. What do we do with the first pancake, kids?"

"Pancake toss!" they yelled in unison.

D.J. walked over to the trash can and pressed his foot on the lever to open the lid, while Hannah grabbed the spatula loaded with the reject and batted it inside. Then everyone except Gabby yelled, "Score!"

Gabrielle's mouth fell open, and she batted her eyes in slow succession before the reality hit her. A burst of happiness, of elation overcame her.

"What?" He shrugged. Dave appeared confused by her reaction. "It's rule number one for berry pancake day. No one in this house ever eats the first one."

"We never like the first ones," Hannah said. "They're pretty homely. Nobody wants to eat a homely pancake."

"So, dad said we shouldn't have to eat it," D.J. continued. "We're special, and we deserve the best."

"Well, as the youngest, I always got stuck with it," Gabrielle said. "So, personally, that's one of the best rules I've ever heard."

"Stick with us," Hannah said. "You'll never eat a first pancake again."

She savored this moment, surprised breakfast had taken such a beautiful turn. She'd prepared herself for the worst, imagined the worst, and the reality turned out so much better.

The beginning of a new trend, she hoped.

"You coming over for first gifts?" D.J. asked Gabby.

She tilted her head and narrowed one eye. "What's that?"

"Every Christmas we stay up until midnight and open one gift. Not the ones Santa brings us. My favorite is always the one from Dad. Promise you'll come," Hanna said.

"Sounds like heaps of fun. If it's okay with your dad, how can I refuse?"

"Consider yourself officially invited then," Dave responded. "There's also cookies and hot cocoa involved. Doesn't get much better than this?"

Gabby's eyes smiled as she looked at Dave. The house felt warmer. She'd found something amazing there in the cozy (even if disorganized) condo—a family, a place that felt like home. With every passing second, she drifted more deeply into unfamiliar territory, a confusing space in which she simultaneously hoped and feared she might find Destiny-Dave.

In her heart, Gabby declared this the last day of her quest. Should today's search end as all the others, she'd release the promise of what might've been, of what could be, and embrace this unexpected blessing—what is.

After breakfast, they rallied to clean the kitchen. D.J. and Hannah retreated to their bedrooms to play while Buddy found his dog bed and laid down for his mid-morning nap. Dave and Gabby tackled the disorder within the living and dining rooms only. Dave's orders. Within a few short hours, her magic touch had turned dysfunction into beauty, comfort, and harmony. Dave smiled as he surveyed her handiwork.

"I can only hope my pancakes were as good as your decorating."

"They were better. The best," she replied. "I think you missed your calling. You sure your name isn't Jack? Hungry Jack?"

He chuckled, and his eye shined when he looked at her. Perhaps the fault lie with the lights on the tree. Maybe there was more. "You're a big hit with my kids, you know. D.J. and Hannah haven't warmed up to anyone this way."

"Not even Diane?"

"Especially not Diane. I hope you can come back tomorrow for Merry Movie Night. All Christmas movies, all the time."

"Depends on how things go today. Your pancakes have got me stuffed up to here," she said, motioning her hand over her head. "After I check these last three Daves, I'm going to need a nap. I can't believe I'm almost done." Despite the enthusiasm in Gabby's voice, the thought of finding Destiny-Dave put a knot in her stomach.

He patted the sofa. "You'd be amazed. I've got the best napping couch ever. You can stay, even use my favorite quilt. It's heavy. My grandmother sewed each patch with her own hands."

"I appreciate the offer but—"

"You can stop looking for him whenever you get ready, you know."

She shook her head. "No, I can't. Not really. I mean, it's possible, but it'd be a mistake."

"Why?"

"Because this guy...he meant something to me. He's not just some random person off the streets. We connected on a real level. He made me..." she caught herself and stopped speaking. She didn't want to hurt his feelings, but she didn't want to lie.

"No, go ahead."

"I don't want to—"

"No, please," he said. "I can handle the truth."

"For better or worse, I've placed him high on a pedestal. In my mind, he's perfect for me...in every way. And I may be mistaken. Who am I kidding? I'm most likely mistaken. With my track record, there's a miniscule chance he's this great, relatively normal guy who's waiting with open arms. He even may be upset that I searched for him."

Dave chuckled, cleared his throat, and bit his bottom lip.

"But the thing is, if I don't find him, I'll always wonder what I left behind. There'll always be this ghost haunting us…and by us, I mean you and me."

"Perfect pedestal guy."

"And what might've been."

"Yeah, I get it."

"Do you? Do you really? I need you to understand."

He nodded.

"You, the kids, Buddy...you're all so amazing. Especially you. I mean, you're really wonderful, smart, fun....gorgeous."

"I hope that last one is reserved for me."

"Actually, I was referring to Buddy, but you'll do in a pinch."

They both fell back laughing before her expression phased from happy to serious. "Honestly, you're nothing I imagined and everything that feels like home me. If I didn't know the other Dave existed, if I'd only met you a few weeks earlier, we'd be engaged in a different conversation right now."

"There's something I want to say," he said.

She glanced down at her watch. "And believe me I want to listen, but I don't want to knock on doors too late. How about this? I'll stop by after I'm done for the day, and we'll talk about whatever you want, for as long as you want. That's how certain I am that this will be over today, once and for all."

"Deal." He twisted his lips to the side. "Please, don't forget."

"I won't. I promise," she said. "Besides, you're my ride home."

Chapter 20

Gabrielle floated out of Dave's condo, high on everything about him, the night before, and breakfast that morning. The euphoria didn't emerge following the digestion of carbs. His presence filled her with an overflowing joyfulness that made her bubble out of his unit.

The way he looked at her, his eyes begged her to stay, to forget about this quest for Destiny-Dave. She couldn't deny, at least not to her heart, that she wanted to oblige, cuddle up beside him under grandma's heavy quilt, and watch Christmas movies all day. But when she told him she needed to complete her mission as much for his peace of mind as for hers, she'd meant every word. Neither of them needed the shadow of Destiny-Dave looming over their relationship, threatening to disrupt whatever they managed to build together.

So, she pressed forward. Only four Daves and three floors to go. The next two lived on the ninth and tenth, respectively. Then she'd make her way back to the second floor one final time to see whether or not MIA-Dave had reemerged. After that, she'd end this quest once and for all. This would be Destiny-Dave's last stand.

She reached the ninth floor and trekked halfway down the hallway to 917. She winced as she rapped her knuckles, and then banged the knocker, part of her hoping he'd be "the one," and a bigger part of her hoping he'd turn out to be another Richard-Dave or Tyrion-Dave, two people she couldn't force herself to date, even on her worst day.

Seconds later, the sounds of sniffling caused her eyebrows to scrunch and blinks to increase in speed. She shouldn't be surprised with the weather. Half the city had the flu. The knob twisted, the door opened, and they stood eye to eye. Neither seemed impressed with the other. He was her height with a stocky build. She could tell he lifted weights. Apparently, he lifted something else, too—boxes of Kleenex. She eliminated the flu theory as the steady streams of tears poured down his cheeks; he could barely gain enough composure to speak.

Her heart broke for him. Had someone in his family died? Had he suffered a major break up? The questions hung in the air as he struggled to speak. His breath stuttered as he said, "Hi, can I help you?"

"I'm sorry I've come at a bad time. Are you okay?"

"Yes, I'm fine," he said, realizing he'd been crumbling in the doorway. "Oh, this. Sorry. This movie gets me every time. *Toy Story 3.*"

Toy Story 3?

Weepy-Dave.

The man blubbered as if the Ebola virus had taken out half of his family...and all this sobbing was over *a cartoon?*

The 12 Daves of Christmas

Gabby didn't know whether to join him with a Kleenex or laugh until she cried. One thing was for certain: one wish had been granted. She felt more attraction to a head of lettuce than to this mawkish guy. Still part of her hoped he was Destiny-Dave. She'd run back to Dad-Dave as fast as her feet would carry her.

"I apologize for interrupting your movie. I'm looking for Dave Madison?"

"That's me. Do I know you?" he asked right before taking a long, snotty sniff. Then he blew his nose into a pink Kleenex.

"I don't think so, but may I ask...do you know a woman named Gabrielle? Gabby?"

He took a moment to think about it, as it turned out a moment longer than necessary. The fact that he couldn't recall her name sent up a red flag. He wasn't the guy.

"No, ma'am. I can't say that I do."

She really wanted to exhale a big breath of relief and say *Phew*! "I'm sorry again for interrupting you. Thank you for your time."

"No problem," he said with a quizzical expression. He didn't know what had just happened, but she did.

She left Weepy-Dave and proceeded to the tenth floor for the next two — Daves Brown and Wallace. She tapped on the first door, and Biker-Dave answered. He wore a cowboy hat and so many tattoos, it took her a minute to figure out his ethnicity. His skin was coated from his neck, down his arms. She couldn't see any more beyond that. But, then again, she'd seen plenty enough.

He spoke with a raspy gruff voice that sounded as if he'd been smoking Marlboros since his mother had weaned him off of breast milk; she knew without question he wasn't her Dave. She quickly disappeared from his doorstep.

Trekkie-Dave answered the door at her next. He wore a Dr. Spock uniform and ended their brief conversation with a Vulcan salute and a mandate to "Live long and prosper." She wondered if he slept with that thing on as she sprinted to the elevator with the swiftness of an Olympic runner.

On the ride down to the second floor to check on MIA-Dave one final time, she clenched her eyes shut and made a wish to the universe to make this last visit quick if not painless.

She crept past Richard-Dave's house until she made it Dave Thompson's unit. She felt certain he'd not reappeared. More than ever, she'd resigned herself to give up for good. Dad-Dave and she would live happily ever after.

She took a deep breath but the door opened before her knuckles even touched it. In the threshold stood the Adonis she'd bumped in the lobby on the first day of her search, a man so gorgeous he left her breathless. Now standing in front of her shirtless, he wore little more than a big smile and track pants, with his Michael Eaton eyes, Idris Elba height and build, and Jason Mamoa's skin. His gorgeousness paralyzed her. His white smile blinded her. She struggled to find her words. Turned out she didn't need to.

"It's you! I was hoping I'd find you." He remembered her. She couldn't believe someone like him would even retain an accidental bump from someone like her.

Oh. My. God represented the only words that came to Gabby's mind. After all this time, she'd finally found the Dave she'd been looking for...at least she hoped.

"You're Dave? Dave Thompson?"

"Yes, it's me," he said. "And you're—"

"It's me, Gabrielle!" she interrupted. "I'm Gabby." She looked at him and over his shoulder.

"Somehow I knew I'd find you again." He gave himself the once-over. "Although I think it's clear I wasn't prepared for it to happen this moment. I'm sorry about my attire."

I'm not, she thought to herself.

"Would you care to come inside, maybe for a minute? I've got nosy neighbors, and I should finish dressing."

"Sure," she said. "I'd love to."

By now her thoughts fogged, so she operated on autopilot, not really thinking straight, just allowing him to guide her into the house to sit down. She couldn't believe after all of her searching, after all of the anticipation, she'd finally arrived. She'd found him.

His home qualified a bachelor pad, decorated with a minimalist approach with three anchoring pieces in the room, two of them a few grand worth of electronics and the other a large sofa. His place was pristine, sterile almost. She'd imagined Destiny-Dave living in a homier place, like Dad-Dave's, complete with the comfortable sofa you could sink into. His couch was cold and black, covered in rich, top-grain leather, with cushions so tight you could bounce a quarter on them. She felt more likely to slide off of it than to nap on it. On the plus side, there was no sign of kids or a dog. A few packed boxes littered the floor.

This must be Destiny-Dave.

"Gabrielle. Of course, you're Gabrielle," he called from the bedroom. "How'd you find me?"

"Long story. I can't believe it's really you."

"Me, neither," he replied, his voice closer now. He emerged from around the corner fully dressed. "I'd like to...can I give you a hug?"

"That would be nice...fine." She practically fell into his open arms, melting into him like ice cream on a hot chocolate chip cookie. His solid body had spent many hours in the gym to produce the strong biceps that wrapped her up in a powerful but gentle grip. Her heart pounded in his chest as she inhaled his scent of sandalwood, leather...and Douglas fir sap. She attributed the latter to the fresh-cut tree resting in the corner. Its empty branches begged for lights and decorations.

The hug ended and Destiny-Dave and Gabby stepped back and gazed at one another, both bright-eyed and amazed that this moment had finally arrived.

With all of her senses heightened, taking in everything at once, she struggled to absorb what happened. An awkwardness in the lingering silence increased their distance, even while they stood closer to one another than ever. He'd become a stranger to her now. Even still, a palpable attraction pulsed between them. The softness in his gaze told Gabby he thought her beautiful. Perhaps they'd close the discomforting distance in time.

"I can't believe you're...here," He fidgeted, didn't quite know what to do with his hands. "Can I offer you something to drink?"

"Uh, sure, what do you have? Any eggnog?" *Spiked preferably*, she said in her head.

"Oh, no! Too many calories," he said.

She scrunched her face in confusion. *Dave? Worried about calories?* She played back the image of his six-pack and shut down the urge to grouse.

"But I just finished making a berry-spinach smoothie." He shuffled items in the refrigerator. "I've got some freshly made carrot-beet-celery juice. It's delicious."

She frowned and winced. "Ummm, water's fine, thank you."

Whatever flames ignited at the sight of his shirtless body standing at the door had been thoroughly doused by the mere mention of carrot, celery, and beet juice. Had he suffered a heart attack since they last spoke? What dreadful, mind-altering, mutation had transfigured him from meat buffets to vegetable smoothies?

He reappeared and handed her a tall glass of water with orb-shaped ice cubes floating in them. Very rich looking. She almost didn't want to drink it.

"Well," he said. "Here we are."

"Here we are," she repeated. "I guess it's a little strange...you know, finally meeting one another. Like this."

"It is," he said. "And just in time for Christmas, it seems."

"Just in time," she said. "I'm a little nervous. Can you tell?"

"To be honest, so am I. Never expected us to meet like this. I pictured it differently in my mind."

"Me, too," she replied. "I hope I haven't ruined it by showing up on your doorstep like this."

"Ruin?" he said. "Impossible."

She grinned on the outside and melted on the inside.

"I've actually got to cut this short because I have an appointment, but I've got an idea," he said. "Maybe we could meet for dinner? A date. A real date. And I'll let you pick the spot."

"That sounds amazing. When?"

"How about tomorrow night?"

"Perfect." Gabby glanced down at her watch. "Well, I should be…I need to, uh, go. But I'll see you tomorrow." She wrote her number on a scratch pad sitting on the living room table then stood and walked to the door. He followed and offered her a kiss on the cheek as her receipt that the moment had happened.

In a dreamy haze, she flitted and skipped up the stairwell to the Dad-Dave's place, pressing her hand against the spot where Destiny-Dave's lips had been.

He wouldn't believe what had just transpired.

She knocked on his door and waited for him to answer. Within seconds it swung open, and he stood there with an amorous smile.

"Gabby! You're back. Come in. I've got something to talk to you about."

"No, first, I've got something to tell you! You will never in a million years guess what happened."

The 12 Daves of Christmas

He began to speak and stopped himself. "What is it?" he asked, taking in her excited expression.

"I've found him!"

He jerked back his head. "Excuse me? Define found."

Chapter 21

For nearly an hour, Dave had paced steady rows of footstep tracks into his plush carpeting. He waited for Gabby to return so he could confess, tell her the whole truth, at last. Spending the past few days with her had convinced him of two things: one, she was the right woman for him and his family; and two, he'd begun to fall in love with her.

Truly in love.

He never dreamed his heart could open this way for anyone again, yet here he stood, in the thick of his intensifying emotions, ready to profess the truth. Her voice was the song he'd eagerly waited to greet him in the mornings and the lullaby he'd fallen asleep listening to every night for those short but beautiful weeks. He was the man whose texts ignited her journey to Foxhall, and he hoped they could now pick up where they left off.

Since witnessing her affection for his brood and theirs for her, he believed she could join them, love them. Now he felt secure enough to explain that she'd been looking for him all along and trust that her initial sense of betrayal would subside…in time.

With the suitable passage of time, she'd spend this, and maybe every Christmas with them.

He'd checked the wall clock every thirty seconds, anticipating her return, wondering what had kept her. After all, it shouldn't take this long for her to visit the final three units and listen to them tell her they weren't the man she'd been looking for. Yet, there still had been no knock at his door, so a sense of worry crept in.

He felt certain she was physically safe but he wondered if, in her disappointment, she went home instead of returning to him. Didn't matter. Tonight, the deception would end. He'd camp out in front of her place and explain everything there if necessary.

Dave took determined paces toward his bedroom to grab his shoes and summoned the kids when a knock came at the door. He told them to standby as he dashed to answer. Peering through the peephole, he saw her standing there, smiling from ear to ear. Her mission had ended unsuccessfully, but she was still smiling. Perhaps, now that she'd eliminated the possibility finding this guy in her texts, she'd be ready to embrace her feelings for the one standing in front of her, the flesh and blood dad with children and a dog. A wave of nausea overcame him as he opened the door. The moment of reckoning had arrived.

"I'm so glad you're back," he said. "Come in. I've got something to tell—"

"No, I've got something to tell you! You won't believe it."

She cut him off before he could utter the words he needed to speak. The split second turned out to be just enough time for him to second-guess his decision. He started to confess but stopped himself and took in her expression. "What is it?"

Either she'd given up her search and finally decided to acknowledge they shared something real, or...

"I've found him!"

"Excuse me? Define found." Was she intimating that she'd discovered his own true identity? If so, why did she appear so thrilled about it?

"I located the Dave I've been searching for, silly. He's downstairs on the second floor. Unreal, isn't it?"

All sound dissipated and air barely escaped his lungs. His eyes bulged, and he took a step backward.

"You're right," he said. "*Un*-real."

She appeared astounded by his stunned reaction. Did she really believe he'd be happy for her? More than that, whoever she'd "found" was a stone-cold liar perpetrating to be a man he was not. He should end the charade here, reveal the truth. But now the only way to expose the fraud was to out himself in the same breath, destroy her happiness, and make her feel like a complete fool.

"He, uhhh...he's the one, huh?" He refused to smile. It took every ounce of his energy not to storm off in a rage, find the weasel who'd pretended to be him, and introduce the phony to his knuckles. "Are you sure? How'd you...are you sure he's the guy?"

"What do you mean am I sure? You're not trying to suggest that someone would lie to me about his identity, are you? What kind of creep would do something so vile? Besides, he didn't seek me out, I'm the one who knocked on his door."

She waited for Dave to respond but he offered silence. He questioned why this con man would participate in this farce, but one need only look at Gabby to see why. She was the best and worst kind of beautiful—oblivious to her gorgeousness, inside and out. She didn't realize her powers of attraction. Perhaps, the fake would game her, trick her into falling for him, then confess his true identity when they'd invested too much in the relationship to walk away.

Dave never meant any harm or hurtful deception. His only goal had been to assess whether she and his children could get along. What he'd done was different, but the result might appear the same to Gabby.

He wanted to scream, shake her by the shoulders, ask her how she could believe the charlatan. Then his own role in this surreal turn of events smacked him squarely in the face: She believed the other guy because Dave had failed to confess truth. She filled the awkward silence between them, breaking his thoughts.

"The past few days with you and your family have been amazing—the breakfast and the National Christmas tree, everything. So this, me finding Dave, it doesn't change anything between us."

The edges of his lips curled upward. "It doesn't?"

She shook her head. "Of course not. No matter what happens, you and I will always be *friends*."

Friends. The words hit him sledge-hammer hard. The friend zone was one place he had no desire to be. His smile disappeared, and he tightened his lips. "So where did you find this...*Destiny-Dave*?"

"Unit 213. Remember, I told you about it. I thought he was off marrying his girlfriend or maybe vacationing in Bora Bora. Turns out he was traveling. You may have seen him around. Looks like he spends *a lot* of time in the gym. Tall black guy." She gestured her hand above her head to demonstrate his height. "Caramel skin, greenish eyes. Body for days."

"Hmmm," he nodded.

"Yep. Single, no kids or anything. And packed boxes scattered around his floor. It appeared as if he'd just moved."

"Wait a minute I think I've seen that guy downstairs. The gym-rat." Dave jerked back his head. "He told you he moved from New York?"

"Yes," she replied, before giving the thought more careful consideration. "Well, actually, now that I think about it, no. Not exactly. We were so surprised to find one another that honestly, I think we were too much in shock to exchange any real details."

"I see."

"Not to worry. We'll talk about everything soon. Very soon. As a matter of fact, he invited me to dinner."

"Sounds nice." He noticed a shift in her expression. "What's with the face?"

"I dunno. Nothing, I suppose. Everything's…fine. Anyway, can I trouble you for a ride home? Or should I catch the bus?"

"Oh, I'm in the friend zone now—you can catch the Metro."

Her mouth fell open.

"I'm kidding. Just jokes." He chuckled as she play-punched him in the arm. "Let me grab the kids and my coat."

After dropping off Gabrielle, Dave sunk his depressed body into the couch and draped his arm across his face, lamenting his every bad decision, every deception. If he had only confessed sooner. If he'd only told her everything during their first text exchanges, as he should've, then maybe she wouldn't be with him, but then she also wouldn't be preparing to go on a dinner date with The Imposter. The thought of her falling for the guy nauseated him, but any effort to protect her would only hurt her more.

The world had snatched the magic carpet from beneath his feet mid-flight.

He sucked in a deep breath and exhaled in despair when the sound of footsteps and a small voice materialized in the formerly empty floor space beside him. Suppressing his groan, Dave removed his forearm from his eyes and turned to face Dr. Hannah. With her toy stethoscope plugged in her ears and medical bag dangling from her arm, she'd arrived to save him from himself, his thoughts. Her partner in crime arrived on her heels seconds later.

"Dr. Hannah and my humble assistant, Dr. D.J., at your service. You don't look so good, Daddy. Can I help?"

He smiled the biggest one he could muster. It barely lifted the corners of his mouth upward, but it was better than nothing, he supposed. Hannah opened her bag and commenced with her examination. "Sit up."

Dave obeyed, allowing his daughter to breathe life back into his weary soul. The only other choice was to never leave the couch again...ever.

"Time for a check-up, Mr. Williams. What's bothering you besides your cold?"

"I'm not sure," he lied. Then he shrugged.

"Let me investigate," she said. "Open wide and say 'ah.'"

He did as asked and she stuck a tongue depressor so far down his throat it nearly gagged him. Then she tapped the reflex hammer on his kneecap until he bolted his leg upward with a fake kick. D.J. marked the results on his clipboard. Finally, she pressed the stethoscope against his chest and listened. "Hmmm...interesting," she said.

"What is it?" He faked some concern.

"I think I've found the problem," she said. "It's your heart."

Little did she know she'd hit the nail on the head. It'd been broken by every fault of his own.

Dr. Hannah held out her palm, opened upward. "Dr. D.J. Bandage, please."

He reached into her medical bag and pulled out a Band-Aid, a small one. She unwrapped it and taped it to his shirt, right over his heart, then offered D.J. her hand again. "Medication, please."

Again, he reached in the bag once more, this time pulling out two Hershey's kisses. Hannah grabbed them and handed them to her father. "Take two of these and call me in the morning."

The smile he forced earlier came naturally now. A Band-Aid on his broken heart and chocolate kisses. Amazingly, he did feel better. What would he do without his munchkins to bring him back to life when he felt as if he could barely hang on?

"Thank you. I'm on the mend already." He opened his arms to invite a group hug. "I appreciate you two. I'm going to rest now before I take my medication. Then we'll walk Buddy. How's that sound?"

"Okay, lie down. You need plenty of sleep." She turned to D.J. "We'll come check on our patient later. Love you, Dad."

He pressed his hand against his heart and replied in kind. They disappeared down the hall, and he laid there, his despair washing over him like a wave, but his daughter's adorableness renewed his desire to untangle this mess of a web. His mind processed through a list of potential solutions. His best countermove might be to allow Gabby to live this lie, in the short term. The Imposter could be many things but never Dave Williams. Once she realized The Fraud wasn't the man who'd texted her for all those weeks, she'd return to the one who loved her, she'd return to him…if she could ever forgive him.

Before he could get lost in his misery again, the phone rang. He groaned as he pulled his cell from his pocket.

"Hey," he said, unable to disguise his distress.

"What's wrong with you?" Brian asked.

"It's over."

"What's over?"

"Gabrielle. Everything. It's over."

"Slow down and tell me everything that happened."

Dave obliged, revealing the details of Gabrielle's visit, the good, the bad, and the sad.

"I'm so...*bummed*. First time I've connected with anyone since Tina, and I've ruined any possibility of a future. Women like her don't appear every day. I don't want to lose her, but I don't have a choice."

"So, what are you saying? You're...you're just gonna give up? You're not even going to try and fight for her? Even worse, you'd surrender to a con?"

Dave snapped to attention. He'd not viewed the situation from that perspective. He not only owed it to Gabrielle to prevent the scoundrel from taking advantage of her, but he also owed it to himself and his happiness to convince her that he was the one for her, and they could bounce back from his transgression, even if she resisted.

He put Brian on speaker before tapping his screen, pulling up his photos, and scrolling through his pictures until he found the one Hannah took during their visit to at the National Tree Lighting. He texted it to Brian.

"I sent you something. Check it out."

A second later, Brian's phone sounded. "Man, she is hot! Wow. No wonder you've lost your mind."

"Gabby's totally hot and, get this, she has zero idea about how incredible she is."

"Now that I see this picture, I suppose I understand why you hesitated."

"I hesitated before I ever laid eyes on her. I mean there I was falling in love with her mind, and she was walking around looking like this."

"For whatever reason, you made this choice—the wrong one. You messed up when you decided against telling her about the kids. Now you've got to man-up, dude. Confess everything or someone else may wind up marrying your future wife. You want to see her spend the rest of her life with a con man? Do you want to sit in a pew on the bride's side with the kids and buy crystal champagne glasses for two to celebrate her new marriage?"

He gulped hard.

"The way I see it," Brian said. "Confessing is your only way out...except."

"Except what?"

"Well, it's possible she may realize she's more in love with you than this other 'Dave,' despite the kids. If that happens, none of this matters. I mean, don't get it twisted, she'll probably get angry and quit speaking to you for some time. But after she's had time to think and cool off, she just may forgive you. Then you'll have everything you ever wanted."

Dave quieted and smiled.

"Or—she'll disappear from your life forever."

"Really?"

"The difference is, if she realizes that she's fallen for you, you have a fighting chance. If she doesn't realize it, you're screwed either way. So, for you, it's really a win-win."

"How do I do that? How do I make her fall in love with me?"

"If I knew that, I'd be universally acknowledged as the genius I am, and we both know that hasn't happened yet. However, based on what you've told me, she loves

Christmas, and she hasn't celebrated one in a long time. Help make the holiday special."

"Mmmm, I dunno. We've done some of the holiday thing. If it were going to work, seems like it would've worked by now," he said. "But there's also another option. What if I can sandbag him? Do something or say something to scare him into walking away? That way I can get rid of him without making her feel like a fool. Nothing like commitment-talk to make a man bolt."

"Well, judging from her picture, that plan could backfire," he said. "But *there is* something else that may do the trick."

"What?"

"You remember Belinda McDonald? Sophomore year?"

"Yeah, she stalked you for two years. Nice looking girl, but she was definitely a little…off," he said, twirling his finger around his ear as if his brother could see.

"I paid her no mind because I was into Liz, remember? But Liz wouldn't give me the time of day. Then Belinda got ultra-aggressive, and I figured, what the heck?"

"Yeah, you took Belinda to homecoming, right?"

"Sure did. I needed a date. She was there. Liz showed up with that football player, what-his-face, the running back. But she couldn't take her eyes off of me. One year of watching Belinda take interest in me and she had a sudden change of heart, remember that? It took Belinda to make Liz truly appreciate what she had…and what she'd be missing out on. We got married after graduation and the rest, as they say, is history."

"So, what are you saying?"

"In my experience, nothing makes a woman realize how much she cares about a man than jealousy over another woman. What you need is a double date."

"That's ridiculous. She'd never fall for that." He rubbed the scruff of hair on his chin while he considered the proposition. "But who do you have in mind?"

Brian paused, and Dave's curiosity piqued in the silence. "How about Liz's sister, Mindy?"

"Didn't she pour sugar into her boyfriend's gas tank? And then cut all the tongues out of his two-hundred-dollar tennis shoes?"

"She's an actress. She can act like your girlfriend. That's all that matters."

"Nah, I'm gonna take a hard pass on that one. She's insane. Crazy trumps beauty and actress. I'm not even going there."

"What about that Diane woman, the cougar from New York? Didn't you tell me she's in town...and that Gabrielle actually thinks you're in a relationship?"

"Yeah, but I told her, in no uncertain terms, there was nothing between Diane and me except business."

"Well, now that she's with this other Dave, tell her differently. Or better yet, *show her*. Pick the perfect dining location, preferably some place that you and she would love and they would hate."

"Yeah, show her how much we have in common," Dave added.

"Exactly. Then once you find a place, give Gabby a call and offer to double…say you understand it may be awkward going out with a stranger. If her goal is to find

Mr. Right by Christmas, you've only got a couple of days left to prove you're her guy. Make it fast, and make it count."

Brian gave Dave the gift of hope. A double date with Gabrielle wouldn't be enough to put an end to this nightmare if the night didn't work in his favor. He needed inside information, and there was only one way to find out in time.

Chapter 22

3 Days to Christmas

Dave embraced his new mission: Sabotage.

After wallowing in self-pity, he decided that the relationship between he and Gabby may end, but not this day and not due to some fraud. Brian had breathed new life into him, infused him with a renewed energy. When Gabby described The Imposter, he immediately knew to whom she'd been referring. Months ago, when Dave arrived in D.C. to scout new places, he toured his new building from top to bottom, including the workout room.

The gentleman in question, an obnoxious gym-rat, and was present at the time. He wasn't just loud, he was loud and rude. Thoughtless, inconsiderate of everyone around him. He seemed to think the world revolved around him, and made himself the focus of narrowed eyes and annoyed looks. He worked out on the leg machine, blustering as he talked into his Bluetooth, meanwhile failing to notice a line had formed, showing blatant inconsideration to everyone standing around him. He didn't care, just yapped about meetings, urgent ones, with *his people*. Apparently, he was in great demand.

God forbid he should leave his phone turned off for an hour; imagine a world the that could bear the burden of his silence in the exercise room while his neighbors blew off steam from their stressful days.

Dave owed it to himself and Gabby to save her from that fate that was "him," even if her eyes were so full of his pecs and biceps that she couldn't see the obvious—he'd never be the right man for her.

"Kids?" he yelled. "Throw on your workout clothes. We're going downstairs to the gym."

They responded to him with silence. That didn't mean they didn't hear him. Somehow, they'd gotten the idea that when he called them, audible responses were optional.

"Kids! Send up a flare if you hear me."

Still not a word was spoken, but he did hear bumps and thumps.

"Five minutes. Anyone who's not ready to go has to wait until the day after Christmas to open presents."

Still, no answer but the muffled noises had quickened to a frenetic pace. As he disappeared into his bedroom to change into his Underarmor, the patter of feet tamped across the floor.

Dave hadn't yet learned everything he wanted to know about Gabrielle, but she was well worth fighting for. He'd give her his all, something he failed to do for Tina—his biggest mistake.

Tina gave him everything, and in return, he, too often, gave her his leftovers, the pieces that remained after the firm and needy clients, like Diane, zapped him of his energy and ability to form full sentences. He remembered with regret responding to her with his signature grunts.

She didn't mind; she never minded.

She'd learned to decipher what each one meant. Sometimes she'd asked him to reach down and find more to give to his family that loved him; most of the time she allowed him the space to disengage until he found his own way. All part of her charm, really. She'd gifted him with an understanding and unconditional love he'd not fully reciprocated; time stole his second chance.

But maybe Gabrielle's emergence into his life offered him the second chance he didn't deserve.

With the kids in tow, Dave peered into the gym door window. He located his target sitting in his usual spot, doing his annoying jackass thing. He pumped iron on the weight bench, no less than three hundred pounds. His obnoxious grunting and groaning was audible through the door.

"Okay, guys. To the Kids Club, you go."

"Dad, please don't take too long. This place is for babies, and we want to watch Charlie Brown."

"I promise. I won't take long at all. You'll be back in plenty of time to see your movie. But we do own it, and you watched it the other day."

"It's different on TV. Everybody's watching it. And there are no commercials on the DVD," Hannah said. She'd been fascinated with the two minutes and two seconds between shows since she was a toddler. She'd dance through an entire show and freeze with captivated wonder during commercial breaks. She glanced down and tapped the face of her watch. "You've got one hour."

Dave skulked across the threshold, and his surreptitious entry was met with a crush of sound—a woman's feet padding at a steady pace on the treadmill, the airy hydraulics from the stair stepper, and heavy plates clinking against each other as the Imposter switched out weights on the barbell. Sitting on the edge of the bench, he yammered on about a bunch of nothing at someone on the other end of his earpiece. So engrossed in conversation, he didn't notice the new arrival. Dave found a spot on the ab machine, out of the imposter's direct line of sight, someplace quiet so he could eavesdrop.

"Yeah, I'm still juicing," he crowed. "This vegan diet is tough, but I can handle it. Never thought I'd give up animal protein, but I do feel better."

Dave smiled inside. *Strike One.* Both he and Gabby loved meat and avoided anything green if at all possible. Dave listened on, hoping for another tidbit, one which came faster than he expected.

"Hey, speaking of which, what's a good vegan restaurant? I've got a date tomorrow with that Rachel girl I told you about. She's supposed to pick the restaurant, but I'm going to choose if I don't hear from her soon. You know how women are. Indecisive."

He lifted the curl bar to his chest.

"I told you about her earlier, remember? The one who magically appeared on my doorstep after I bumped into her in the lobby a few days ago."

He lowered the bar and raised it again. "Yeah, that's what I said. Gabrielle."

Dave frowned; the man didn't even remember Gabby's name. Dave, on the other hand, would never forget it. He listened and watched the Imposter take a few more reps and set the bar on the rack.

"You should see her. I couldn't believe she showed up at my place, although I should've figured she'd hunt me down eventually. The ladies can't get enough of me. It was a small miracle…*for her*."

Dave rolled his eyes so hard he thought the sound was audible.

"She was confused, maybe? I'm not sure and to be truthful, I don't care. I may not be the one she was looking for, but that doesn't mean I'm not the one she wants. I guarantee you, whoever he is, he can't hold a candle to *The Dave*."

The Dave? Narcissistic much? He choked back the sourness gurgling in the back of his throat.

"One night out with me and she'll forget the other— I know. I know. I'll tell her, eventually. Who knows? We may not even hit it off. For now, tis the season for giving, and what woman wouldn't want to receive the *gift of me*."

The Imposter scanned the room, looking for witnesses to his shadiness.

Dave avoided his stare, shifting his position to look in the opposite direction. As the Imposter slithered over to the cardio section, Dave grinned. He'd struck gold. Moments later, he made his escape without notice, collected the kids, and returned home to plot his next move.

Let the games begin.

Chapter 23

Despite his joke to the contrary, Dave graciously dropped off Gabby at home. She always hesitated when getting out of his car, never feeling quite ready to leave. Standing on her stoop, she waved until they pulled off and watched until his taillights disappeared into the distance. Then she glanced up into the night sky and allowed a snowflake to greet the tip of her nose. Everything about the day made her happy, made her smile, except her return home. She couldn't deny the source of her bliss.

It should've been Destiny-Dave, but it wasn't.

No, instead, Dad-Dave had delivered in spades.

He'd given her what no other man had yet to offer, not just *the hope* of a second pancake life, but *the promise* of one. To him, she was worthy of the best the world had to offer. Even with Destiny-Dave now firmly in the picture, still only one person occupied her mind, a fact she couldn't deny.

However, she believed she owed it to whatever she hoped to build with Dad-Dave to see this Destiny-Dave thing through until its end, an end she believed would come sooner than any of them anticipated.

She turned her attention back to the snow. She enjoyed watching the flakes fall, and the idea that snowflakes built on one another; they didn't destroy one another. Maybe the newness appealed to her. Or perhaps it was the fact that the snowflakes helped cover the disunity in the world, quieted down distracting thoughts so she could find music in the silence. She only hoped it didn't hamper tomorrow's plans — dinner with Destiny-Dave.

Gabby grinned and hummed as she held out her hand to catch a frozen treasure in her palm and then flounced up the steps and into her row house door. Her smile vanished at the sight of Vic's waterworks as she clasped the phone to her ear. Her sister gave her "the hand," quashing Gabby's impulse to run to her side.

"I was there for you. I went there like a fool, trying to breathe some life into the dry bones of this relationship, and there I find you. Sitting in our restaurant, at our table, with your little Fi-Fi. If you wanted to make our marriage work, you would've invited your wife. So, what's this crying all about, Reggie? Really? Are you trying to fix this because you want *us to be right*? Or because *you don't want to be wrong*? And, yes, there is a difference." She stood and paced toward the window.

Gabby started toward her, to stand by her side, to hold her hand, but Vic avoided Gabby's gaze, channeling her frustration into her fingers as she scraped her scalp. She decided it was better for Vic to scrape her scalp than her little sister, so she conceded her space and kept a safe distance.

"To be honest with you, Reginald"—calling him Reginald was never a good sign—"I don't know how or what I feel. I'm numb, paralyzed. What scares me most is that I'm not sure if I feel anything at all."

Vic flapped her hand toward the box of tissues sitting on her slate end table. Gabby started to pull a couple out but hesitated. Vic could get irritated easily when distressed so she just placed the box within reach.

"No, don't do that. Don't come here. I need a little more time, more space...so I can figure this out. If I could tell you how much time I'll need, I would, but I…can't say."

She snatched a fistful of tissues and dabbed them beneath her eyes.

"I realize Christmas is only a couple days away, and we've never been apart. Maybe you should've thought of that at the restaurant. We'll try again in a few days."

She walked back over to the couch and collapsed into what had become her favorite seat.

"I've got to go. Gabby's home. She needs to talk," she said with a long pause. "Yeah, me, too."

Gabby stood there dumbfounded. She'd believed, perhaps naively, that Vic and Reggie would've worked out their problems by now. They'd served as her beacon of matrimonial hope, the only truly happy couple she'd ever known, aside from her parents. They were the living and breathing happily ever after.

Now, Victoria's heart had hardened toward him, a condition that grew more severe with each day apart. Part of her thought Vic's reaction bordered on the extreme. *A cozy lunch?*

Yes, bad. Very bad. It could've been worse, much worse, though. A sin, perhaps, but not an unforgivable one. So Gabby thought.

The idea that the separation had been less about Reggie's indiscretion and more about a change in Vic's perspective began to congeal in her mind. While Gabby muddled through life, Vic immersed herself in it. She'd always possessed the freer spirit between the two sisters. She lived every moment to the fullest, within the confines of her relationship boundaries and her budget. Gabby never questioned Vic's love for Reggie, but from the day she found out they'd become engaged she'd wondered whether Vic would ever be content living a life tethered to another being, her freedom constrained by her spouse's feelings, his love.

"Me, too? You've demoted him to pronouns and prepositions? We're just going to pretend you don't even tell him you love him anymore?" Gabby asked her.

"I'll tell him when I mean it. Right now, I can't say that I do. I'm not certain how much longer we can go on this way. Maybe if he had shown up."

"But you told him not to come."

"If he wanted to make this work, he'd show up anyway. That's what being married is about. Showing up anyway, but I'm done with this topic for the day," she said, releasing a deep sigh. "You were practically glowing when you came in the door. Good news?"

"Mmm hmm. Diverting the conversation. I see what you did there. Lucky for you I'm anxious to share my news, the best news...I found him."

Vic perked up. "Details. I want!"

"You've got to see him. He's beautiful. Perfect. Where to start? Where to start?"

"How about at the beginning?"

Gabby got comfortable; this story would take minute. "Okay, well, Dave, Dad-Dave, picked me up this morning, as you well know, and he made the most delicious breakfast."

"Merry berry pancakes or something, right?"

Gabby nodded.

"And you're still smiling?"

She nodded again. "I'm sitting there watching him flip pancakes. He's so good he could be a chef. But this pit is brewing in my stomach. Part from hunger, part from anticipating the absolute worst. When he slid the first pancake onto my plate, he'd ruin everything, and he'd have no idea how or why. That's when he did it."

"Darn it, Dad-Dave I was rooting for you!" she snapped her fingers in disappointment.

Gabby shook her head and suppressed a grin.

Meanwhile, Vic cocked her head to the side. "What?"

"He threw away the first pancake. Tossed it. Declared that nobody eats the first one in his house. Then he gave me the perfect second pancake. Without question the best one I've ever eaten."

Gabby prattled on, spending the next few minutes incessantly chattering about her morning and the kids, about how wonderful and sweet they were, about how much she loved the mammoth dog. She marveled at how she'd rediscovered her love of Christmas, how Dad-Dave made her remember the best and forget the worst of it, how the universe conspired to deliver the most wonderful holiday ever, how even the falling snowflakes seemed to dance for her in their descent.

"I've discovered the magic of the season again, and it's all thanks to that Dad-Dave...and the two precious kids...and a dog. Who would've thunk it? I sure as heck didn't see this coming."

Victoria stared at Gabby in silence, her dead-eye stare interrupted by a series of slow blinks.

"What?" Gabby asked.

"This story was supposed to be about the Dave you found, Destiny-Dave?"

She flashed a sheepish expression and winced. "Oh, that's right. Him."

"Yeah...him." Victoria narrowed her eyes and shot her a glare.

"After breakfast, I told Dave I needed to complete my journey. He said he wanted to talk to me about something, he had something to say." She seemed unaware of the smile stretching her mouth. "Honestly, I'd almost decided to give up the search. With Dave and the kids and my feelings, I don't know. Part of me wanted to stay there, but I owed to him and myself to finish. Otherwise, there'd always be *this thing* hanging out there. After all, the other Dave meant...*means* something to me. I kept thinking, what if he texts 'you had me at waspish' while I spent time with Dad- Dave? What if he offered a reasonable explanation as to his disappearance? All of my feelings might come rushing back and then where would Dad-Dave and I be?"

"That's a valid, well-reasoned argument. The heart usually inspires the opposite. Anyway, go on," she said. "You were on your way to find Mr. Magic."

"Oh, yeah, I hit a couple of other places and saved the best for last. He opened the door, and my jaw hit the floor." She practically drooled at the memory of him. "Remember I told you about the gorgeous guy I bumped into in the lobby?"

Vic nodded.

"Him!" she said. "Have you ever seen a man so good-looking you forget how to speak? Think? He's like a Rock knock-off. Homina. Homina."

"Ho-ly. So, what happened next?"

"Well, I'm standing in his doorway staring, as if the heat from his body's burned off my brain cells, when he finally breaks my trance. In my mind, I'm swooning like a thirteen-year-old at a Justin Bieber concert, so I barely hear a word he says. But I kind of peered over his shoulder and noticed two things: no kids and unpacked moving boxes everywhere. I figured it must be him, had to be the right guy."

"So, what happened next?"

"I introduced myself, and he knew who I was. He'd been looking for me or at least he suggested he had. He invited me in to talk, which neither of us could seem to do. The moment was awkward. I'll admit, we lost the familiarity we had in our texts and phone calls. Being with him was nothing like being with..."

"Dad-Dave?"

"Yeah, exactly. And there's another problem. Major. One I hadn't anticipated given our frequent messages and previous expressions of great affection for..."

"Each other?"

"No, meat. We're carnivores, but he offered me a vegetable smoothie...or juice or something. *Blech*!"

"You didn't tell him you repelled all things green...except money?"

"I'm pretty certain the subject came up in texts, but I may be wrong. We laughed and joked so much about everything and nothing during our phone calls that the critical detail may have slipped my mind."

"Just because he drinks vegetable juice doesn't mean he doesn't eat meat."

"Yeah, true. I suppose I'll find out soon enough."

Victoria's left eyebrow arched.

"We've got an opportunity to rediscover the magic tomorrow. He invited me to dinner. Said I can choose any place I want."

"See? He can't be a vegetarian. He's allowing you to pick the restaurant. Where ya going?"

Gabby shrugged. "I haven't had two seconds together to think about it. Everything's just been turned upside-down."

"Or maybe you don't want to think about it. You sure you know what you're doing?"

Before Gabby could answer Vic's question, her cell phone rang. She'd already given him, Dad-Dave, his own ringtone.

She held up a finger to Victoria as she answered.

"Hey!" The tone of her voice mirrored her excitement in anticipating the sound of his.

"Gabrielle," Dad-Dave replied.

She couldn't explain why at that moment but lilt of his tenor forced the butterflies in her stomach into full flight.

"I just wanted to make sure you're okay. You seemed unlike yourself this afternoon. You sure everything went well with ... Dave? The other one?"

"All is well...I think," she said. "Well, it's just that texting was easy, natural. Then we met. *Awk-ward*." She shrugged her shoulders as if he could see. "He invited me to dinner, but I can't deny I'm a bit nervous. Scared I'll spend half the conversation convincing myself I'm not insane for thinking what we shared in a few texts and phone calls was real."

"It was," he said and fell silent as fast. "I've no doubt what you felt was real. You don't strike me as a capricious person," he said with a cough. "Just an idea, but what if you didn't go to dinner alone with him? At least not on the first date."

"What are you suggesting? I'd feel uncomfortable with you sitting there alone."

"Oh, no. Three's a crowd. It'd be a date...a double date. You, Dave, me and—"

"Double date?" she snapped. "What do you mean?"

The twinge of annoyance in her voice startled her. Some irrational sense of possessiveness crept up from a darkness in her heart that she didn't know existed. An uncontrollable flash of jealousy rushed through her, and the speed and intensity proved surprising. She contemplated accepting his offer, more so as an excuse to spend a romantic moment with Dad-Dave than Destiny-Dave. Her own tables had turned on her, and the unexpected shift in her emotions took her in a new direction, one she'd only begun to anticipate.

Her response had apparently taken him back, too. "I realize my single-dadness makes dating a bit more of a challenge, but bigger miracles have happened. Even with kids, and the dog. Some women find me attractive, believe it or not. Shocker, but true."

"No, no. Honestly, I didn't mean it that way. It's just with this being last minute and all. I thought it might be tough to schedule a sitter."

"You're forgiven," he said with a chuckle. "So, what do you say? Are we gonna double?"

The thought scared her enough for her to respond, "Um, okay?"

"You say that as if I'm intruding. I don't have to…"

"No, it's not you. It's…nothing. I'm actually grateful you asked." She forced herself to be gracious. "How could I refuse such a generous offer? Who, uh, who do you plan to bring?" The words tasted like venom in her mouth.

"Diane's in town. She'd invited me out, but I'd been spending so much time with you I hadn't had the opportunity to take her up on her offer."

"*Diane*," she said with an airy, exasperated, huff. "Okay. We're on."

The 12 Daves of Christmas

"And I have an idea for the restaurant, too. How about Fogo de Chão? All of the meat we can eat. My former administrative assistant gave me gift cards for Christmas. It'll be my treat."

"Oh, I couldn't allow you to—"

"I absolutely insist."

She pondered her answer for a second and only a second. "All right, then. Tomorrow. Fogo. Is six okay?"

"Perfect. *We'll* see you then."

We'll?

Ouch.

Chapter 24

2 Days to Christmas

Armed with a Swiffer duster, Dave had removed unwanted particles from every piece of furniture in his newly reorganized house—twice. He'd rearranged the pots, pans, and dishes in the kitchen for the third time. And now he'd returned to the mirror to continue the unending debate — tie or no tie.

He took it off.
Put it on again.
Changed his shirt...again.

Of course, he liked quality clothes, but no one would ever accuse him of being metrosexual. He'd never been fashion forward. For these reasons, he understood that his indecisiveness had less to do with his clothing selections than his destination and the special person he'd meet there, the only one he cared about.

"Hannah? Can you come here for a second?" He turned away from the mirror and toward the door. Hannah appeared seconds later wearing her lab coat, reflector, and rubber dishwashing gloves from the sink.

Between her forefinger and thumb, she clasped a needle and thread.

"Hey, dad. We gotta make it quick. I'm in the middle of surgery. Benji lost an eye. I'm reattaching it." Benji, her favorite teddy bear, was almost as old as she. Tina bought him as a present for her third birthday, and no matter how much his condition deteriorated, she'd refused to allow him to fall apart. He hoped someday to marry someone who cared for him that well.

"I need your opinion. Tie or no tie?" he asked with the silken strip in his hand, offering views of his shirt with and without it.

"Hmmm, you're going out on a date with Diane, right?"

"Sort of."

"No tie."

"Why do you say that?"

"Because if you wear one, Diane will think you're wearing it for her, not for Gabrielle. So, no tie."

Sometimes he hated how astute she could be. She noticed things oblivious kids couldn't grasp until they grew much older. But sometimes he felt thankful she was wise beyond her years. He smiled and laid the tie on the dresser.

"You really like her don't you, dad?"

"Who, Diane?"

"No, Gabrielle."

His lips raised at the corners answering her question before he could speak. "Why do you ask that?"

"I see the way you look at her," she said, before taking a seat on the edge of his bed. "We never told you this, but sometimes when you thought we were in bed, D.J. and I used to sneak into the living room and just watch you and mom. You'd sit in front of the fireplace at Christmas, wrap gifts, sing, have food fights with the popcorn you were supposed to be stringing for the tree."

"Really? You little rascals."

"We saw the way that you looked at her and her at you. Never thought we'd see that again, with anyone...until Gabrielle."

"What do you think about her?"

"She's pretty great, right?" she asked and answered.

"Yeah, pretty great." He picked up the tie again and held it up to his collar. "What do you think? Tie or no tie?"

"Dad, we're trying to win over Gabrielle, not Diane. No tie."

"Right. No tie," he repeated.

The knock on the door came as he laid the tie on the bed. "That's your uncle. Grab D.J. and Buddy, and I'll answer the door."

"Can I have a few minutes to finish my surgery?"

"Oh, my bad. Yes, please. We wouldn't want Benji to be without his good eye."

She chuckled and disappeared; he ran to the door and opened it.

Brian gave him the once-over. "Look at you! Dapper Dave. Maybe you should wear a tie."

He laughed as he stepped aside and allowed his brother inside. He fingered his collar to straighten it. "You think?"

"No, Brian," he said with a chuckle, laughing at Dave with a hint of pity in his eyes. "You look fine, but how many times have you gone back and forth on the tie?"

"Once...hundred. At least. I finally deferred to my nine-year-old daughter. Pathetic, right? How'd you know?"

"I was there for your first date with Tina, remember? Back then, you deferred to me. I told you to wear a tie, but you were going out with Tina not the Grand Duchess of Scroogeville."

"She's not a Scrooge. She's just...Diane."

Brian's wry smile made Dave shake his head. "What's the look for?"

"You know for what. Or should I say, for whom?" he said. "Just try not to stammer too much, and don't do that thing with the fork."

"What thing?"

"You know the thing."

Dave rolled his eyes and called out for his brood. "Hannah, D.J., Buddy. Uncle Brian's here."

Sounding like a herd of cows, they rushed in and smothered Brian with hugs and greetings. Buddy offered a few deep barks and nuzzled against Brian's leg, nearly knocking him off balance.

"Okay. Everyone get your coats." He turned to Buddy and said, "Not you. You're wearing yours."

Minutes later, they were heading out the door. As the kids ran to push the elevator button, Brian turned back to Dave. "Don't forget, we want you to win over Gabrielle. Not Diane. I can't be responsible for anything that might happen to her if she should ever show up to my house with Liz there; she may not make it out alive."

"If I know Liz, I wouldn't make it *inside* alive if I showed up with Diane."

Dave chuckled as he watched his brother and kiddos disappear. Then he checked the clock for the billionth time in a row and rolled his eyes. Time to pick up Diane and head to the restaurant.

He gave himself a final once over in the bathroom mirror, put on his coat and shoes. He started to leave but stopped in his steps and ran back to his bedroom. He grabbed his tie and tucked it into his jacket pocket. Just in case.

Dave and Diane rounded the corner at tenth and Pennsylvania Avenue, and the Brazilian meat factory stood directly in their sights. Snow flurries signaled the arrival of the front-edge of the expected Christmas showers. For kids who'd wished for a white holiday, it appeared as if Santa would bring more than presents under the tree. It'd been years, three to be exact, since he'd done any more than spend the season with his head buried under a pillow, counting the hours, minutes, seconds until the dreaded time passed. At this moment, he felt thankful for his renewed spirit.

Diane stunned in her little black dress, which had a small split revealing her thigh above the knee. She wore leather boots with a heel that made her tall enough to look him straight in the chin.

If only her inner beauty matched the outer.

He checked in with the maître de and returned to Diane. "He says we can't be seated until our full party arrives. I wonder what's keeping them."

"Who knows? But I'm starved."

Dave scanned the swanky, well-appointed dining room, its walls covered in rich, dark woods. Tables concealed under white linen had been strategically spaced to allow the servers carrying meat skewers to maneuver through the crowds. The attendants smiled and nodded as they cut slices of seasoned, juicy goodness onto the plates of happy diners.

Poinsettias capped the buffet where bouquets of lilies normally sat; white Christmas lights intertwined with pine tinsel had been wrapped around the ledges and stair rails. And an expansive Christmas tree decorated in red and gold ribbons and shiny balls served as the restaurant's centerpiece.

"Looks great in here, don't you think? The decorations aren't overdone. Just enough."

She shrugged. "I didn't notice, to be honest. Decorating's not my thing. For me, tis the season for fundraising. I've set records five straight years in a row, and I'm well on the way to making it six," she said with hardly a blink.

He sensed she'd been motivated more by the competition than the actual giving.

Diane turned to him with hunger in her eyes, as if she'd arrived with an appetite for more than the meat on spits; she allowed her palm to linger against his chest and leaned forward to fill the space between them, breathe in his scent. "Did I tell you how intoxicating your cologne smells? And you look amazing."

"Thank you. It's relaxing not to have to wear a suit."

"You hang a suit quite well," she said. "But I have to admit, I'm loving the casual look on you. You seem more comfortable in Washington. Or maybe it's the holidays."

"Definitely the holidays," he lied. It was Gabby, all Gabby.

Dave eyed her thoughtfully, hard-pressed to recall an occasion during which Diane had been kind to or considerate of others, a time when Christmas had meant any more to her than a boost to her social schedule and a valid excuse to break out the formal wear. He wondered if she could ever appreciate drifting through a crowded tree lot to pick out the holiday centerpiece or snuggling in the corner of the sectional with a bowl of Orville Redenbacher's to watch *A Christmas Story* for the thousandth time. Or if she had the capacity to value a gift's sentiment over its cost. She'd never shown him any hint of willingness to change and to be this woman for him or anyone else.

But he'd met a woman who possessed every quality he'd have been lucky to find once in a single lifetime, let alone twice. As he turned to check the doorway for her, Gabby's sorry excuse for a date entered first along with his Christmas angel trailing behind. Dave offered a nod when he saw Gabrielle; and she returned the favor.

Dave couldn't help but notice the general reaction to The Imposter's arrival. The eyes of every woman in the vicinity (and those of a few men) zeroed in on him the moment he stepped through the door. Like it or not, the guy had charisma if one liked that sort of thing. Dave could never compete with this guy's off-the-charts testosterone levels, even though in height and build, they were comparable.

He took a second to size up his competition, who sauntered in with a smug confidence wearing slacks with a button up—and a tie. He groaned to himself. He should've worn the blue one.

"Well, you guys made it. We began to wonder if you were going to show up?" Looking at Gabrielle in her signature red scarf, leather jacket, and skirt, an appreciative smile took his face hostage. His mind drifted back to the memory of their kiss before she broke his concentration by making the introductions.

Gabby locked her eyes with Dave's. "The gang's all here. Nowhere I'd rather be…than with this delicious food and all." She immediately shifted her gaze toward Diane. "It's good to see you again. You look marvelous." Gabrielle gave Diane the once-over and pasted on a phony smile.

Diane responded with a cold greeting and an equally fake one, at least until she set her eyes on The Imposter. They exchanged brief heated gazes until Dave and Gabrielle shared a huggy glance, a gesture not overlooked by Diane. When she spotted Gabrielle's eyeballing, she pounced on Dave like a lion on a baby goat, leaning against him, grabbing his hand, and all but attaching herself to his arm.

Territory claimed.

A hostess arrived and broke the tension. "Your table is ready. Follow me this way, please."

They arrived at their spot and took their seats shortly thereafter. Each placed their drink orders with the waiter before engaging in small talk as they examined their meat cards. One side red, the other green. Green welcomed waiters to the table where they'd slice meat from a slab onto a plate. The red side stopped the waiter while you ate or when your stomach became sufficiently stuffed.

Gabrielle noticed the shift in Diane's attitude. Instead of paying more attention to Destiny-Dave, Gabby declared Diane her rival with a piercing glare, as if Oprah had gifted Gabby a favorite thing and Diane had not only stolen it from her but also flaunted it in her face. At that point, it seemed the first shot had been fired, and the covert war commenced.

"I don't know about you guys, but I'm starved." Dave glanced across the room at the waiter passing by. "That filet mignon's gonna hit the spot."

Diane patted her stomach. "Are we ready to get started?"

Gabrielle nodded and turned to her date. "What about you?"

"Actually, I've just started a new diet. Vegan. I'm going to spend my evening at the salad bar. But you guys go ahead."

When The Imposter stood up, he took about fifty pairs of eyes with him. All except Gabrielle's whose eyes remained locked on Dave. Diane took in the imposter's rear view with her cougar vision, discreetly fanning herself with her napkin.

"All right, then let's do it," Dave said.

The first waiter stopped by with filet mignon, and they all accepted slices. Seconds later, the lamb arrived, and chicken followed after that. Gabrielle, whom he knew took no shame in eating a hearty meal, played it conservative on her portions, probably to avoid appearing greedy in front of Diane…and him.

To ease her concerns and ensure she enjoyed her meal, Dave assuaged her guilt by saying, "I love a woman with a healthy appetite."

With the *covert* war already in full swing, that's when the *overt* war between Gabrielle and Diane commenced.

Chapter 25

The Christmas before her wedding, Gabrielle ventured to surprise Leo with fresh, homemade croissants, hot from the oven. He loved all things carbs, and they'd had a rocky time in the preceding days, so she attempted to do something special for him.

The dissention emanated from her unwillingness to give up the unsuccessful interior decorator "hobby thing" and become more of a homemaker, his reliable plus-one. She capitulated with hardly a fight and never second-guessed her decision, and croissants would signal her foray into the plus-one world.

Besides, how hard could croissants be?

After all, Pillsbury sold them in cans for a couple of bucks. A little flour here, a little butter there. Some elbow grease and a rolling pin. She had one. She'd mostly used it as a makeshift hammer to secure loose nails, but she could attempt to use it for its intended purpose in an effort to make her man happy, couldn't she?

After twenty-four hours of intermittent baking, nine pounds of dense dough (including seventeen sticks of butter), two broken rulers, a missing pastry knife, and a nearly empty box of parchment paper, Gabrielle was coated with so much flour she could pass for Frosty the Snowman. She hadn't managed to make a croissant lighter than a baseball and could cut diamonds with the shells.

Croissants were hard, very hard—and yet still easier than trying to make conversation with Destiny-Dave.

He picked up Gabrielle at her condo, under Vic's watchful eyes (although he didn't get out of the car to meet her), and they drove to Fogo. The snow she'd wished for had already begun to fall. The drifting flakes took her back to the Christmas morning snowball fights she used to have with her sister and cousins when they were young. She longed for her old, carefree spirit, the one that allowed her to live free and happy.

She'd expected this night would be the beginning of something extraordinary, but straining to fill the awkward silences between her and Destiny-Dave practically sucked the oxygen out of her hopes.

"A beautiful evening, isn't it?" Gabrielle asked Destiny-Dave during their ride to the restaurant.

He shrugged. "Meh. It's all right, I guess. Typical as winter nights go, I suppose. You look amazing, though." He couldn't lift his eyes above her neck. She'd be surprised if he could tell her the color of her eyes. She ignored it, though, grinned and nodded her head in appreciation.

Then she waited for something, anything to fill the quiet. He didn't emit a single sound, didn't ask any questions. She could hear nothing except the faint hum of the engine in his 7-series BMW and Donny Hathaway crooning through the radio.

"You ready for Christmas?"

"Not much to do really. My mother forced a tree on me, as usual. It'll die, and I'll be sweeping up needles for the next year." He must've noticed her tightened expression. "I'm usually traveling and don't celebrate, that's all. I suppose I could do more to embrace the spirit, but it always seemed like a lot of trouble for one day."

One day? She repeated in her mind. *It's not one day. It's "the" day.*

"Not a fan of the holidays, huh? Wow. Perhaps that's changing. You took time off this year for vacation, right?"

"Not so much for the holiday. I wanted to get in some more time at the gym. It's hard to stick to a steady routine when I'm working. Those two-a-day workouts really bulk up the biceps. Squeeze that," he said, holding up his arm.

After clasping it with her fingertips, she said, "Ooh, solid. Impressive." She smirked on the sly and then locked her eyes on the taillights on the car in front of them to prevent them from rolling into the back of her head. Otherwise, she'd be forced to spend the evening looking at her brain which, under the circumstances, might not be the worst thing to happen this night.

That's when it returned, the deafening silence waiting to be filled. He had a way with words...a special talent for disguising his knowledge of them. This man who texted messages teeming with brilliance, could barely maintain a routine conversation about traffic and the weather, let alone Shakespeare.

He seemed more concerned with the contents of a Luna bar than what was on her mind and in her head. He showed little interest in learning about her, what she thought, what she felt.

He did, however, seem consumed with ogling her, evident from the lustful gazes he'd showered on her from the moment he collected her from her condo.

She'd lost hope for the evening's promise before it began.

The problem?

Dad-Dave would arrive with his date Diane Wealthy vonPageant Barbie who dressed in clothes more expensive than Gabby's house payments. An economist-wannabe-interior decorator couldn't compete with all that.

She tried to settle her thoughts as she entered the restaurant lobby, and there Dad-Dave stood.

A bolt of consciousness struck and she realized, too late, that she only wanted to spend her evenings with Dad-Dave. She hadn't driven to the restaurant with her true, one and only Destiny-Dave. Instead, he was standing in front of her. The sight of him trapped her lips in an instantaneous smile, one she couldn't suppress if she even cared to try. Handsome on the outside, beautiful on the inside, he stood there in living color, full of humor—and words.

Lots of words.

She loved Dad-Dave's words, his mind, both a thousand times more than the impressive but skin-deep, GQ handsomeness of the other one. When he smiled at her; she puddled. The entire world disappeared and only she and he remained. As she sauntered closer, she inhaled his scent. She knew it now; it was familiar, home.

He was her heart's true desire. And the only thing that stood between her and her dream was Diane, who'd arrived looking beautiful and chic, wearing a skirt split up to her earlobes. Diane who looked as if she'd strolled straight off of a New York Fashion Week runway and into Fogo de Chão. Diane whose endlessly long shapely legs seemed to go on for days, months, years.

Narrowed eyes and tight lips quickly displaced Gabby's smile.

Destiny-Dave wrapped his arm around her shoulder, perhaps growing a little possessive in the wake of Dad-Dave's gazes at her. They approached their dinner companions and prepared for the evening ahead.

"Looks like the gang's all here. Nowhere I'd rather be…you know, with all this food," Gabrielle said, first peering at Dave and then pasting on a smile for his date. Diane appeared to be the kind of woman who didn't need a menu or a buffet; she'd feast on Gabby's misery, chew on her jealousy and spit it back in her face. Gabby couldn't give her the pleasure. "It's good to see you again. You look marvelous!"

"You, too," she said. Her smile was fake, too. "Um, who's your guest?"

"Oh, I'm sorry, Dave," she said to Destiny-Dave. "This is the other Dave, your namesake, and his lovely date, Diane."

Diane looked at Destiny-Dave the way one looks at a box of chocolate cupcakes the day after Lent.

"It's a pleasure to meet you," she said with an emphasis on "very." "Now that our party has arrived we can get seated."

"Great. I don't know about the rest of you, but I'm starving."

Dad-Dave shook Destiny-Dave's hands and greeted him with a "Nice to meet you."

It seemed as if a decade had passed since she last celebrated the holidays and now she'd reentered civilization, the land of the living, breathing, and reveling. After a few minutes of chit chat, a hostess took them to their seats where they ordered drinks. Gabrielle took in the ambiance and festive decorations, and then eyed Diane who'd attached herself to Dad-Dave like white on rice.

Destiny-Dave bee-lined toward the salad bar, of course. God forbid he should eat anything consumed by humans. His diet was the food of the gods. Gabrielle, Dave, and Diane flipped their meat cards, and the servers began frequenting their table with slabs, slicing off slivers on their plates. First came the filet mignon, then lamb, chicken and ribs.

Gabby tried to restrain herself to avoid looking like a pig in a trough, especially since Diane's plate held perfect portions, just right for one so dainty and snobby.

That's when Dad-Dave opened up the floodgates with eight little words every girl longs to hear at the dinner table. "I love a woman with a healthy appetite."

Game. On!

The waiters couldn't serve the tables fast enough. Diane and Gabrielle went to war, waiving down waiters like airplane marshalers signaling pilots on the tarmac with the orange flags and batons. It was the *Game of Thrones* with extra meat and no dragons. Within an hour so much meat sat in front of them they could no longer see the table. Gabrielle stuffed her jaws with Brazilian culinary delights, while Diane's face had turned borderline green. Amateur.

With pity in his eyes and expression, Dad-Dave studied Diane, leaned over, and whispered, "You don't look well. Are you okay?"

She gulped hard and audibly, then covered her mouth with her napkin. "If you'll excuse me for just a moment."

She stood up and asked the nearest waiter to point her to the bathroom. Then took off running like an Olympic sprinter.

"I hope she's okay," Gabrielle said, feigning concern.

"I'm sure she'll be fine," Dad-Dave said.

"Clearly a lightweight. She should've stuck with the salad bar." Destiny-Dave said, leaning back to eye Gabby's…assets. "She should be more like our Gabrielle, here."

Dad-Dave snarled at him and smiled at her. "We all should be more like Gabrielle."

"If you say so," Destiny-Dave mumbled.

She flashed a demure smile at Dad-Dave and glanced away to see Diane taking careful steps toward them. Her coloring phased from green to red in the seconds it took her to get from the staircase to the table.

"I hate to be a bother, but I need to go. Now," she said in an attempt to whisper into Dad-Dave's ear. Probably came out louder than she intended. "I was hoping you might take me to your place. It's closer."

He bolted out of his seat and smothered her in attention; over his shoulder, she flashed a gloating expression at Gabrielle.

Faker.

"I hate to cut this short, but Diane's unwell. I should escort her home so she can lie down."

"I'd be happy to drive her home...you know, if you wanted to stay," Destiny-Dave said, drawing glares from Dad-Dave and Gabrielle. "No offense, please. This clearly isn't my scene, and you two seem to be enjoying the restaurant. As expensive as it is, somebody should get their money's worth from this joint."

Diane looked almost ready to accept his offer when Dad-Dave interceded. "I appreciate the offer, but I'll make sure she gets home okay. And don't worry about the check. It's on me. I'll take care of it on the way out."

Of course, Diane milked the moment with the adeptness of a farmer's grip on a cow's udder, draining it for all the sympathy she could get. "I'm so so sorry, but I'm not well at all. I do hope you both will enjoy the rest of your evening. You really make a very sweet couple."

If Gabrielle could audibly growl without appearing insane, she would've. Instead, she gritted her teeth and said, "Sorry to see you go. I hope you *get real*...I mean, *well*."

A slip of the tongue? She'd blame the wine.

A few minutes later, they were gone.

Gabrielle's heart broke a little, but she decided to make the best of a bad situation. In reality, she only wanted to pull a Derek Matheson: excuse herself to go to the bathroom and disappear forever.

After eating in an awkward silence, Destiny-Dave asked, "Do you want to get out of here?"

She looked up with an expression of relief. "I thought you would never ask. How about we check out the Capitol tree before you drop me off at home?"

He nodded and smiled with all the excitement of a turtle on morphine, serving as further confirmation that Destiny-Dave was not the man she hoped he'd be. In fact, she began to wonder if he was the right Dave at all. That thought stuck with her until he opened her door and helped her into his car.

"You know, I was thinking about the first time we made contact. That was a funny phone call, wasn't it? We stayed up until midnight."

"Yeah, crazy."

Her suspicions were now confirmed. She'd prepared to call him on it and give him several pieces of her mind when he fessed up.

"Listen, I have a confession to make. I'm not who you think I am."

"Oh? What do you mean?" she asked facetiously.

"I'm Dave, but I don't think I'm the one you knocked on my door looking for. In fact, I'm certain I'm not."

"Cat's out of the bag. The fact that you didn't eat meat gave me pause initially, but you confirmed my suspicions a moment ago regarding the phone call. I met *the* Dave via a stray text message. We didn't talk for a while."

"I apologize, but I'm not sorry. You're a beautiful woman, and I thought once we got to know one another that we would hit it off and it wouldn't matter. But you and I don't have a lot in common. If I had to spend another minute trying to think of the right thing to say, my head would've exploded."

She cackled and allowed her head to fall backward. "You're a great guy. You're just not Dave...well, you're Dave, you're not mine. Trust me, the only disappointing thing about this experience is...I still haven't found him."

An awkward silence filled the car as she tallied the number of streets remaining before they reached her place. "Well, now that we've got that truth crap out of the way, what do you say we go to my place? We may not have similar interests mentally, but under the covers it doesn't matter, does it?"

"Excuse me?"

"One night with me and I promise you'll forget the other guy. The only thing you'll be *searching for* is another night with *The Dave*."

"What! If you don't let me out of this car, you'll be searching for your front teeth. You must surely have bumped your head. I wouldn't go through *the next block* with you, let alone to your place. Stop the car."

"So, that's a firm no?"

"If you don't stop this car!"

Gabrielle strolled in to the sight of Vic dabbing her eyes as *It's a Wonderful Life* played on the big screen. She always cried when Clarence got his wings. After finally noticing Gabby, her eyebrows crinkled, and she glanced at her watch.

"You're home early." Vic swung her feet around to the floor and sat up. "Did you even get a chance to eat? What happened?"

Gabrielle removed her coat, kicked off her shoes, and explained her evening with Diane and the Daves, including Destiny-Dave's confession. Then she made one major revelation.

"I'm falling for Dad-Dave. Kids, dogs, and all."

"Tell me something I *didn't* know," she replied.

"I can't deny it anymore. I mean, I knew it, but until I saw him with Diane…you should've seen her pawing all over him. And the glare she shot me when she faked sick and convinced him to take her home. Even she must've sensed something between us."

"I knew you were over the moon for this guy after he fed you the second pancake. He seems like a very special person, and he makes you happy, brings out the best in you."

"All I need to do is see his face, and I light up inside. Frankly, when Destiny-Dave confessed, the sense of relief overwhelmed me more than any sense of disappointment or anger. All I wanted to do at that moment was jump on the train, ride up to Foxhall, and tell him my true feelings."

"Well, what's stopping you? Let's go."

"First—Diane. What if he's there with her? D.J. and Hannah aren't home. Do you have any idea how sick I'd be if I walked in on them… *together*? I can't even. Also, I have to wonder if I'm really ready to take on the responsibility of kids and a dog. I mean, I couldn't keep two fish alive."

"To your first point, that's why we should leave now...before he does something he'll regret, something he can't take back. Has my life taught you nothing?" Vic scrambled to her feet to put on her shoes and a coat over her pajamas. "To your second point, I don't understand the rush to have all the answers right this minute."

"What do you mean?"

"You're not planning to marry the man tomorrow. This is what the dating process is all about. You try each other on, feel each other out. Take time to decide if you're prepared for the entire package. You may not be today but who's to say that won't change in a month or a year. However long it takes you to figure it out."

"You've got a point...and a darn good one. I've got to tell him the truth."

Victoria smiled from ear to ear. "It's about time, but..." Her eyebrows furrowed and released then her lips parted slightly.

"But? What's that look for?"

"Oh, it's not about Dad-Dave; we're flying over there right now if I have to drag you by your pinky toe. I'm just curious about something, not that it matters."

"What's that?"

"If Destiny-Dave isn't the one you've been looking for, then who is?"

Chapter 26

1 Day to Christmas

Gabrielle and Vic couldn't leave the house fast enough. They made a mad dash for Vic's Volvo and put the new tires to the test. They screeched out of the parking lot and onto Pennsylvania Avenue heading toward the Rock Creek Parkway, the fastest route to Dave's place.

"Should I call him? I should call him. I don't want to catch him off guard."

"You *absolutely want* to catch him off guard. Trust me, you don't want to find out what kind of guy he is after you marry him."

Gabby stared at her phone, willing the ancient thing to ring and nothing. "You're right. But if he calls me, I'll tell him I'm on the way. Yeah, that's what I'll do."

It was late in the evening, leaving clear roads at every turn, and each light turned green as if the universe had joined in the plan and paved the way for them.

Within minutes, Vic had wrangled her way through the security gates.

"I'll sit here until you send me a text message and let me know everything's good. Then I'll leave. I'll go out on a limb and assume Dave will bring you home. Sound like a plan?"

Gabby nodded and all but dove out of the car when they reached the entryway. She whooshed through the doors and shot up the stairs as if running on wind; she didn't even bother with the elevator. When she reached his door, she lifted her knuckles to knock and hesitated. Fear struck her heart, and she was afraid of what, or better still *who*, lie on the other side of the door.

She turned to walk away and started down the hall before she shook off the fear and returned to finish her quest for good. By the time she reached the door, it had opened, and Dave was standing in the threshold with one arm in his coat.

"Gabrielle. You're here!" His eyes widened; he was surprised to see her.

"You're leaving?" She peered at him then past him to check for Diane's presence. "I can go and come back another time."

"No, no. I took Diane home if that's who you're looking for. I'm on my way to your place. Come in, please. Have a seat. I'm glad you're here."

She walked inside, and he helped her out of her coat. Then she texted Victoria as promised. "Diane all right?"

"I'm certain she's fine. Contrary to her suggestion at dinner, I dropped her off at home and told her in no uncertain terms that my romantic interests lie elsewhere."

"I was beginning to think—"

"Don't." He grabbed her hands, offered a reassuring squeeze, and then led her to the couch. "I can't tell you how happy I am to see you. I have something I really need to tell you."

"Please, me first."

"But—"

"I know what you're going to say, but please, just listen."

He nodded and stroked his finger gently against her cheek, putty in her hands.

"I realize I told you that I needed to find the other Dave, but now I believe the truth is I was just making excuses because I was afraid."

"Of what?"

She shrugged and stood. "Of you...of all of this, the kids, the dog. For my entire life, I've imagined these perfect relationships, but my reality always managed to disappoint. The men ended up being untrustworthy and eventually making a fool of me. A happy existence with kids and a dog? I never in my wildest dreams would've pictured you and D.J. and Dr. Hannah...and Buddy. You're nothing I imagined...and yet everything I needed...wanted."

"Our world can be a little overwhelming for anyone, at first."

She nodded, returned to his side, and covered his hands with hers. "But then I got to know you and the kids...and that massive hound, and I fell...all in. And that scared me even more."

He chuckled at her desperate expression.

"Don't laugh. It's not funny. I carefully tended to the lives of two Beta fish, and they died."

"You probably overfed them. You loved them too much."

"I had to get Vic to come over and flush them down the toilet, and I cried for two days."

"So, what? You think you're gonna overfeed my kids?"

She laughed. "I just never thought I had what it took to raise a family, to be a mom. I know we're not getting married tomorrow or anything…"

"Whew. Good. I was thinking more like next week."

She delivered a playful poke in his chest. "But I'm ready to give up my search for Dave. I've found the one I want…the only one I want."

"So did I," he said. "And you don't have to worry. We won't rush anything. Let's take it slow. One day at a time. I'm not going anywhere."

"Neither am I."

He leaned into her and pushed back the hair spilling over the edge of her shoulder. His deep-set eyes sparkled in the glow of the Christmas lights. She traced the curve of his sumptuous mouth with the tip of her finger and gazed upon him, studying his face, searching for the truth, the honesty, the love.

Gabby found them all in his lips when his mouth fell open, and they pressed against hers.

She surrendered to every hope, wish, and dream for this Christmas, for this life. She released her fear and pain of the past so she could embrace the future, whatever it may hold. A relief settled in her heart. The search was over, Dad-Dave filled the void in her life and gave her the greatest gift—hope for a perfect Christmas—with one day to spare.

After they separated, both still intoxicated by the passion, he kissed her once on her lips, each cheek, her forehead, and the tip of her nose.

"Mmmm," he moaned. "That was perfect. *Almost.*"

"Almost?"

"There's one more thing we could do to take it over the top. You game?"

"I'm in. All in."

Gabrielle glanced up at the wall clock. 4 am. "Oh my goodness, can you believe this? We've been at it all night."

"Right? Time flies when you're having fun. I'm just glad we got it in while the kids were away."

"Me, too." She gazed at him with adoration and then smiled. "You have a little something on your lips. Let me take care of that for you."

She walked over to him and covered her mouth with his. "Mmmmm. Taste like snickerdoodles."

He chuckled. "I was afraid you were about to say chicken. That would mean your grandmother's old recipe had taken a bad turn."

She laughed as the oven timer went off. "Last batch is done!"

"The kids will be really surprised...and jealous," Dave said.

"It'll be fine. There's plenty of dough left over in the fridge. We can make some more after you pick up the crew from Brian's house later. After all, it wouldn't be Christmas Eve if we didn't bake cookies."

Dave removed his dad-apron that read "May the Forks be with You," wrapped up Gabrielle in his arms and squeezed her into a tight embrace.

"Well, before you go, I want to show you something. It's a present I made for you. I hope you like it."

He walked over to his steel and glass drafting table and retrieved a blueprint tube from beneath. "Here. Take a look."

He pulled out the paper, stretched it until its contents were fully visible, and handed it to her.

"What is th— Oh my goodness. You didn't!"

"I did. It's the blueprint for your new and improved Barbie Dream House."

Her mouth hung open. The detail was astonishing. "Could we supersize this? Are you kidding me? A three-car garage? A Jacuzzi? A full basement? To heck with Barbie and Ken. I'm moving in."

He chuckled and stroked her hair. "Maybe someday you will."

She broke eye contact and looked at the ground.

"You sure you can't stay for a little while longer?" Dave asked.

"No, I need to go home, shower, and spend some time with my sister. I'll be back later. I promise."

He pulled back and gazed into her eyes. "You better. And bring Victoria with you. I want to get to know her."

She smiled from the inside out. With every moment that she spent with him, he felt more and more like home.

The 12 Daves of Christmas

An hour later, Gabrielle returned to Capitol Hill and walked in the door.

"Happy Christmas Eve!" she called to Victoria, who was sitting at the computer, fully dressed and dolled up. A stack of listings sat on one side of the desk and a steaming cup of coffee on the other. At the sound of Gabby's voice, she spun around in her seat.

"Ladies and gentlemen, the walk of shame!"

Gabby laughed as she kicked off her shoes, tossed her coat on the chair. She found a cozy spot on the sofa and curled into it.

"There's no shame in my walk, Missy. At least not *this morning*. We spent the night watching Christmas movies and baking cookies. Grandma's snickerdoodles."

"And you didn't bring any home?"

"No, because you're going with me to Dave's place tonight. My new boyfriend wants to spend some time with you."

"Boyfriend? Do tell..." She clapped her hands excitedly.

"Well, what had happened was...wait a minute. Why are you looking so spiffy?"

"Tired of looking like a hot sack of death. So, tell me about Mr. Dave."

"When I got there I hesitated, but I pushed through the fear. Before I knocked on the door, he opened it. Apparently, he'd dumped Diane and was on his way to see me."

"Shut the front door."

"Right? He stopped my momentum, trying to tell me something but I didn't let him. I spewed it out. Confessed everything, my hopes, my fears. And his response was pitch perfect."

Victoria hung on the silence until Gabrielle completed the thought.

"He said there's no rush. We could take it slow. He's not going anywhere. And get this—he designed a new Barbie Dream House for me."

"Man, he sounds wonderful. Can I get him in an age forty-five?"

"You've got him. In an age forty-three. Reggie. He made a mistake, Vic. But he loves you, and he's not going anywhere."

Vic didn't respond, but she went from sweet to sour in less than a blink. Her entire demeanor changed. She rolled her eyes, cranked her neck, and turned back to her work. Still wasn't ready for the truth she needed to hear—and stubborn. Always had been, always would be. "You reminded me of something I'd meant to do," she barked, her voice snippy.

"Listen, I didn't mean to set you off, Vic. I just hate to see you two apart on Christmas Eve." Gabby headed into the kitchen. "You want more coffee? You probably no longer need it."

"I'm good," she barked, her fingers tapping hard against the keys. "Looks like the tax records are back up." A few minutes later she said, "And what have we here?"

"What?" Gabby said, sucking down the hot elixir.

"Looks like I've finally found your Dave. This record says he closed on the property last month and his former residence is in New York."

"And?"

"His name is Dave Williams, and he lives in Unit 430," she snapped, still angry from the earlier sting of Gabby's defense of Reggie. But when she turned around her anger simmered down when she witnessed the pain that the discovery had caused her sister.

"Vic, are you sure? No, that can't be right. Check again, please. Check again."

Vic swept out of her seat and to her sister's side. "I'm sorry. I didn't mean to...you know how I am when I'm angry."

By now tears had begun to pool in Gabby's eyes. "He's been lying to my face...all along. Every single day we were together." Her knees weakened as if the air had been knocked out of her. She shook her head and collapsed on the couch. "This can't be right. We spoke for weeks on the phone. I never once heard a kid or a dog. I mean, it's not like you can stash them in a closet."

"I don't know what happened," Vic said, now wanting nothing more than to make her baby sister's pain go away. "Okay, I'll admit this is bad. He shouldn't have lied. But this doesn't have to be a deal breaker, does it?"

Gabby looked at Vic as if her head had detached and spun across the room. "Doesn't have to...he's been *lying* to me *for weeks*, but not only lying, concealing from me everything important about his life, everything important to who he is as a man. He made a fool of me, like all the others. Did he expect to have a little fling and dump me like yesterday's trash? Is that what this was all about?"

"No, Gabby, he probably—"

At once Gabrielle bolted out of her seat, slipped her feet into her shoes, her arms into her coat, and started buttoning it in a furious bluster.

"Where are you going?"

"Back to Dave's place."

"Maybe you should call him, instead…in an hour, after you've calmed down."

"No, I want to see his big, fat, lying, fat face when he spews his next load of bull pucky and before the kids come home. That way the next time I walk out of there, we're finished for good."

"You want me to drive you?"

She shook her head and held up her Metro card. "Of all the things, I pictured happening in our relationship, I must admit, for once, I didn't see this coming."

Chapter 27

Dave could not have architected a more perfect ending to his night. Gabby had removed all doubt about her ability to love him and all of him. Brian's prediction had come to fruition. Her subtle sparring match with Diane confirmed for her and him that her feelings were real, his single-dad package would not impact their relationship.

She'd fallen for the single guy *and the* father.

The only question remaining had been the precise moment when he'd tell her they were one in the same. The minute her face appeared in his doorway, after he dropped off Diane, he'd pledged to confess the truth, but hearing her profess her growing love for him played like Miles Davis on a snowy Saturday night.

He believed no moment in time could hold that much perfection, at least until the kiss.

The touch of her mouth on his would linger in his heart for the rest of the season, maybe the rest of his life. It sparked the beginning of the beginning. His Christmas wish had come true, and she was standing in front of him, ready for him and all he had to offer.

He completed the moment with one delicate kiss to her lips, each cheek, her forehead, and the tip of her nose; he wanted her to know how precious she was to him.

"Mmmm. That was perfect. *Almost.*"

"Almost?"

"There's one more thing we could do to take it over the top. You game?"

"I'm in. All in."

He kicked off their quasi date night with Brian's famous hot cocoa recipe, a tub of popcorn, and back to back Christmas classics—*It's a Wonderful Life* and *The Preacher's Wife*. They both had a thing for stories about angels. Apparently, she'd selected Denzel Washington as her eternal man crush, helping him to score major points by including it in his movie collection.

Once the closing credits ran on the final flick, the baking began. They made a late-evening run to Whole Foods, laughing and playing as they maneuvered through the aisles and then returned to his place to bake chocolate chip and snickerdoodle cookies.

With the sun barely over the horizon, she returned home to clean up and rest. Big dinner later. They planned to start their relationship slow, introduce Vic to the kids. Later, she'd attend a get-together at Brian's place. The mother smothering was at an all-time high during the holidays and too much to bear early on. So they'd avoid his mother's smothering.

After she left, Dave tried to rest, but it refused him.

Every time he laid down to sleep, his body practically yanked him out of bed. Christmas Eve had brought with it the gift he'd never dreamed he'd receive — love. His heart filled with so much joy over the turn his relationship with Gabrielle had taken, he could barely contain the energy. For a change, the unsettled feeling didn't derive from stress or anxiousness, rather happiness.

More and more, he realized what he felt for Gabrielle was different...because he was different. He'd abandoned that New York man who'd been so consumed with success that he left little room to enjoy his loved ones. He got back to his roots, his D.C., growing into the man who changed his job to fit his family, embracing his new existence, working to live rather than living to work. Despite Dave's lingering regrets over the past, he'd become a better man.

He stripped off his shirt to take a shower, hoping the hot water would relax him. He'd planned to grab a nap before Gabby and the kids returned when a knock came at the door. He glanced at his wrist to check the time and scrunched his eyebrows. Then he trotted up the hall and looked out the peephole.

Gabby?

His elation from her early return quickly disappeared. Her scowl accosted him as he let her inside, even as she scanned his chest with wanting eyes.

"We need to talk. Can I come in?"

He stepped out of the way. "Of course, please. Are you okay? Is something wrong?"

He closed the door, walked to her, and tried to lean in for a kiss, but she jerked back and turned her back on him.

"Were you ever going to tell me?"

"Gabby, baby, what's this about?"

"Come, come you wasp. I'faith, you are too angry."

Dave clenched his eyes shut and tightened his lips. His worst nightmare had come to life. Not that she'd found out the truth, but that she didn't find out from him. "It's not what you think."

She spun around, tears streaming down her face. "When were you going to tell me, Dave? Huh? When you left two hundred dollars by the bed and disappeared in the morning?"

"It's not like that, Gabby. You know better."

"Then what was it like, huh? We talked for weeks, and you lied to me."

"I didn't—"

"Really? Concealing the whole truth is no better than a lie. You kept the most important parts of your life hidden from me. Was that because I'm a fling? What was the plan? Meet me at Union Station, have a quickie at the local motel, and disappear from my life?"

"Listen, I know you're upset. You've got every right to be, but don't be ridiculous. Such an insinuation is insulting both to you and to me."

"Insulting? You made a complete and utter fool of me. Watching me run around this building like I'm playing Where's Waldo. And the man I'm searching for has been standing in front of me practically the entire time. Before I leave, and you never see me again, all I want to know is why?"

His head fell backward, and he grunted in frustration.

"I need you to listen, okay. Hear me out for one second."

She remained silent. She may not be listening, but at least she'd stopped snapping.

"Ever since Tina died, I've been the sad guy. I couldn't pull my life together. Few things have been more difficult than living in New York and passing the sites where I'd spent every special moment with my wife daily. I used to wear my grief like outerwear, you know. It was a hat, and sweater, and coat, sometimes a jacket, a tracksuit. It cloaked me. Couldn't shake it. No matter how much I smiled, my misery was palpable."

"I can only imagine, but—"

He gave her the hand. "So, whenever I tried to meet someone new, and they took one look at me, they immediately took pity on me. Their attraction was based on sympathy. I became a challenge, a project. Part of my mystique, I suppose. Part of the new and exciting game of 'Who's going to be the magic woman to heal Dave's broken heart?' All I wanted was someone to see me as a man again, as a guy looking to date a girl, take her to a movie, steal a kiss at the end of the night. I got sick of being Sad Dad. Right when I'd conceded the fight, I sent the wrong text to the right girl."

She struggled to contain her smile, but he caught a glimpse of it before it disappeared.

"For the first time in years, I wasn't Sad Dad. Do you have any idea how freeing that experience was? No pressure. No expectations. No judgment. I found myself again, the Dave before the pain, and I didn't want to let it go. More importantly, I didn't want to lose you. So, yes, I was selfish and didn't consider how the truth would affect you when you discovered it. Yes, you should be angry with me. But don't think for one second that I was playing you or that I only wanted a fling."

"That's a very understandable explanation. You only forgot one detail."

"What's that?"

"*You lied.* And this isn't small. This is major."

"If you want me to regret hurting you, I do. If you want me to take it back, I can't. If I confessed up front, we might not be standing here today. But this doesn't have to be the end if you can find it in your heart to forgive me."

She pressed her hand to her heart and started toward the door.

"Please, Gabrielle. Don't go."

With a teary-eyed gaze, she glanced over her shoulder. "I thought this Christmas would be different."

"I'm falling in love with you, don't you understand? It still can be."

"No, it can't," she said, wiping the tear streaming down her cheek. "You're no better than Leo."

"How can you say that?"

"He allowed me to show up at that church, with everyone in my universe there to serve as a witness to his final act of our relationship; he ditched me at the altar all because he was afraid of how I'd handle the truth. He left my family and me there to deal with the fallout."

"He was a coward."

"*You're* a coward. You allowed me to make a fool of myself because you didn't trust me with the truth. I don't know if I can ever forgive you for that."

He grabbed her gently by the shoulders. "I understand your hurt, your disappointment in me, in what happened. No, things haven't worked out the way you pictured. But that doesn't mean we can't get through this. This isn't what I imagined, either. I never dreamed that I would fall so deeply, so fast. Let this be a bump in our road, not a dead end. My motives weren't sinister, just poorly thought out. I only wanted to find out if you could love me...for me."

She pulled her arm out of his grip. "Then that is the real shame, isn't it? Now, we'll never know." She opened the door, closed it behind her, and took his heart with her. He turned to look at the Christmas tree, fell onto the couch, and let out a deep breath.

The thought of losing Gabby turned a promising holiday into an awful nightmare. Explaining to the kids that his deception is the reason she'd disappeared forever—impossible.

What would he do now?

Sulk. Groan in anguish.

He laid there in a daze for the better part of an hour before he worked up the nerve to call his best friend, Robbie. As much as he would like to wallow in a pool of self-pity and regret, as much as he wished he could turn back time and alter that single moment to reveal the complete and unhindered truth, he had to deal with the consequences.

Gripping a sofa pillow in one hand, he dialed Robbie with the other. His friend answered moments later and Dave proceeded to confess the details of the entire sordid scene. Every word he spoke burned like jagged steel jammed through his chest; losing Gabrielle was preventable, if only he'd…well, his confidante said it all and it didn't take long.

"I hate to say I told ya so—"

"Then don't."

"But I feared something like this would happen. You couldn't conceal the truth forever. It was bound to come out eventually."

"I'd planned to tell her…at some point."

"When? On your honeymoon? After the birth of your third child?"

"Really? Don't be ridiculous."

"There's only one right time to reveal that you've lied. Never."

"Thanks."

"You gambled and waited. You lost."

"So, what am I going to do now?"

"I'll tell you exactly what you're going to do. You're going to release your death grip from the pillow…"

He looked in his hands and threw the pillow to the side.

"You're gonna drag yourself off that couch."

He stood to his feet.

"You're going to put on clothes, join me at Brian's house, have some eggnog and eat a dozen of Liz's Toll House cookies, and pick up your kids. It's Christmas Eve. They've endured a lot over the past few years. It's not about you. This day and every day, really, is all about them."

"You're right. I know you're right. Give me an hour or so, and I'm on my way."

"Full of Christmas cheer."

His voice droned. "Half full. It's just as good depending on how you look at it."

"You're gonna be fine. Keep the faith. Chances are, if you have a little patience and give her time to digest what happened, she'll cool off. Don't misunderstand me, she had every right to be angry and hurt. But she'll forgive you. Love forgives idiocy. Ask Rebecca."

"What if she doesn't come around?"

"Lick your wounds, move on, and try again. It simply wasn't meant to be, but there's always Diane."

Dave chuckled before hanging up. He strolled into the kitchen, and a grin subsumed his somber expression. The moments he and Gabrielle spent in his barstool eating pancakes and baking cookies rolled through his mind in playback reels. She made him happy. No, they made each other happy. She was the perfect manifestation of his Christmas wish.

When he held her in his arms, something told him not to let her go. But he knew he had to eventually. He'd hoped for a little more time to break the news to her gently, in his own way.

Fate, as usual, had other plans.

Her most stinging rebuke was a harsh truth to his lie.

There had to be something he could do to get her, his Christmas wish, back into his life for good.

Chapter 28

Gabrielle exited Dave's apartment with streams of hurt washing down her cheeks. She dashed to the stairwell and headed toward the exit. She needed to get out.

Faltering mid-flight, she stopped, took a seat on the top step, and allowed her head to fall into her hands. She sobbed, both for the predicament she'd gotten herself into, and the reason she had no choice but to walk away.

Her outpouring of emotion surprised her.

She hadn't realized just how deeply she'd invested her emotions in him...in them. He brought her a comfort which she hadn't acknowledged. For the first time since the end of her disastrous engagement, she'd released her fears and anxieties to embrace hope. With Dave in her life, she'd finally been freed of the burden of the desperation, the endless longing to change her relationship status to "taken." She thought she could finally relax and embrace the bliss of the days to come. And now—square one. Right back to where she left off two years before.

All she wanted to do was go home, crawl under the covers, and wait for Christmas and the year to end. Her new start would begin in January.

On her sluggish bus ride to her Capitol Hill row house, she gawked at the last-minute shoppers lugging overflowing shopping bags and excess holiday glee, crowding sidewalks covered in freshly fallen snow. She questioned whether she'd made the right decision, if she could forgive and forget.

One fact she understood over all others was that happiness was most inherent in truth. Even with its potential for pain, you could learn to accept it, whatever the consequences. A relationship built on selective truths was little more than a fragile house of cards, vulnerable to the slightest disturbances. Been there, done that. She refused to do it again.

She returned home an hour later to find Victoria on the couch in tears. She took careful steps across the room, slipped by her side, and rested her hand on her shoulder. Victoria turned, embraced Gabrielle in a tight squeeze, and cried. "I'm so sorry about what I did, what I said."

Gabby rubbed Vic's back. "It's okay. Really."

Vic pulled back and eyed her squarely. "It's not okay. I guess the truth is, I miss Reggie, my friend, my marriage, and now I'm too stubborn to admit it. Part of me expected he'd understand what I really needed and just show up for me. I wished he'd find it so impossible to live without me that he'd appear and rescue me from myself. I don't know. The only thing that's clear is that I've taken my frustrations out on you, after you've so graciously allowed me to hide out here. I shouldn't have said anything about Dave. Under normal circumstances, I wouldn't have."

"Whatever your reasoning, I'd rather hear the truth from you now than find out in a text message five minutes before I'm slated to walk down the aisle or before I'm jarred by the sound of tires screeching in the distance."

"You're sweet, but you have every right to be angry with me."

"Oh, don't worry about that. I am," Gabby deadpanned before expelling a little chuckle.

"Did you confront him? Did you ask him why?"

She tightened her lips before replying, "I did."

"And? What'd he say? What reason did he offer?"

Gabby detailed his explanation about the women, about not wanting to be a project. "He didn't want that from me, but he didn't trust me enough to believe I'd give him a chance."

"Hmph. Well, would you?"

She expelled a deep breath and offered silence as her answer; she knew the truth. While she'd fallen in love with the kids at first sight, she may not have fallen for the idea of them over a text. Maybe she would've put up a wall or flat-out rejected him, but she still believed he should've given her a chance to choose.

Vic shrugged. "I dunno, Gabby. I can't imagine what it's like to live with that story. Your wife, the woman you believed to be your soulmate, passes away. And every time you believe you've put the narrative behind you, you have to retell it, over and over again, whenever you meet someone new."

A pit formed in her stomach. That truth was undeniable, but, as is the nature with Garrett women, they hated to be wrong. Exhibit one—Vic.

"I get that. I do. But consider this, just for a moment. He wanted me to know him for who he is, but he's not single with no kids. He's got two brilliant children, Hannah and D.J., and a massive dog. There's an entire life a woman must accept in order to be with him, and if he conceals that life, you don't really know him."

"Call him what you want, but there's one problem you can't ignore. If you don't forgive him, you will miss out on a really good and decent man who wants to love you, and you'll spend your third Christmas in a row alone," she said. "And I'll do you one better than that. If a man had designed a Barbie Dream House for me, they'd have to surgically remove me from him. Surgically."

"A man has done something that sweet for you, a thousand things equally wonderful, if not more so."

Just as Vic opened her mouth to reply, a knock came at the door. Vic started to answer, but Gabby tapped her on the shoulder, signaling her to remain seated. She took slow steps toward the door, part of her hoping that Dave had shown up for her, refusing to let her go. She quickly shrugged off the thought, deciding instead she'd refocus her energy on pursuing her dreams and leave the men alone. She never should've given up in the first place. Still, the butterflies in her stomach took flight as she twisted the knob and opened the door.

Her eyes widened when she saw the man standing before her. He'd arrived with an iPad in his hand and a tepid smile on his face.

"Look what the cat dragged in!" she called out as she sized him up. "Raggedy Reggie."

He appeared as if he'd been wrestling alligators, disheveled and unshaven. He hadn't slept in days from all appearances. She thanked the heavens he didn't smell the way he looked.

"Don't you look like a twenty-pound sack of bad wishes and roadkill. What do you want?" She crossed her arms over her chest and pursed her lips for the sole purpose of giving him the hard time he deserved.

He raised his voice to ensure Vic heard him. "My wife. My beautiful, smart, patient, loving wife. I have something I need her to see."

"You're in a lot of trouble. You'll probably want to run it by me first. What is it?"

"This," he said, handing over his iPad. The calendar showed on the screen.

"What's th— Oh. My. Goodness. You've scheduled her for breakfast, lunch, and dinner…"

"Every day for the rest of my life…well, as long as the calendar would allow."

Yes, a hair on the side of corny, but this was the Reggie she remembered. The one who doted on her sister, the one who treated Vic like a princess. No, a queen, his queen.

"I only want to share my meals, my life, with her. Is she here?"

"I wouldn't cling to the hope of forgiveness, but she's here. You parked next to her Volvo, the one you bought. The question is whether she wants to—"

"Hi." Victoria materialized beside Gabby as if she'd beamed in. "Excuse us for a moment, please, Gabby."

The next thing she heard was Reggie demand, "I want you home, and I'm not leaving here without you."

Gabby reached halfway down the hall before she turned around to snoop. Reggie had crossed the threshold and Vic was wrapped up in his arms.

Gabby smiled.

She loved a happy ending. The hint of sadness still dampening her mood stemmed from Victoria's inevitable departure; she knew she'd be spending Christmas alone.

By the time, she'd changed into a warm pair of pajamas and turned on the TV for a Christmas movie binge, Vic had arrived to break the bad news.

"I won't go home if you don't want me to," she said, her eyes asking Gabby to please want her to leave.

"Go be with your husband. That's as it should be."

"Are you sure you're going to be okay? We'll be back to open gifts first thing in the morning." Gabby could see the hesitation on Vic's face.

"Go! Once I down a couple of mugs of hot cocoa, I'll be out like a light anyway. I'll see you tomorrow."

Victoria walked over and embraced her. "Thank you for everything, Sis. I don't know what I'd do without you.

"And, God willing, you'll never find out," they said in unison.

Gabby choked up a bit when the door shut. She could barely contain her elation at Vic's reunion with Reggie; she hoped he'd learned his lesson. Christmas magic was everywhere.

Too bad it had skipped over her.

On her way to pour her second cup of hot cocoa, Gabby heard a tap at the door...and then another. Someone was standing outside. She peered out of the window and recognized the car in her guest parking space. She flung the door open and propped her hand on her hip.

"Leo?" Her eyebrows scrunched. "What in the...what are you doing here?"

"Wow, you look amazing." He licked his lips and eyed her like a convict preparing to chow down on his first post-prison meal.

"Thank you?" She looked at her Snoopy footed pajamas. He'd been smoking something, or he was blowing hot air. Either way, she opted not to respond to his question, just asked him, "Again, why are you here?"

"I didn't interrupt anything, did I?" he asked, crane his neck to peer inside and see if she had company. "Do you have a minute so we can talk?"

She caught a chill when a stiff winter wind broke across the threshold. "Leo, I'm not angry with you, but you and I have zip, zero, zilch, nada to discuss. Your last text message contained everything you needed to say to me again in this life, and in the next."

"That's what I need to explain. Please, can I come in?"

After a lengthy pause, she stepped aside and allowed him to enter. She found a spot on the chaise lounge, deliberately selecting a one-seater, and cloaked herself beneath a large microfiber throw she stashed for napping and snuggling. He tried to take a seat next to her, but she quickly directed him to the sofa.

"I can't tell you how good it is to see you," he said. She could almost see the word "LIAR" stamped on his forehead.

She refused to feed his ego or his excuses. She pursed her lips with all the attitude she could muster so he'd say whatever he needed to say and scram.

"I've never apologized for the way I ended our marriage."

"Correction, wedding. And no, you haven't."

"In all fairness, you haven't given me a chance, refusing to take my calls and all. But I'd like to tell you how sorry I am for hurting you. You were perfect for me in every way. I screwed it up, not you."

"I appreciate what you're saying, but neither of us was perfect, Leo," she said. "But I can't deny I've always wondered why you couldn't extend me the courtesy of telling me that you didn't want to marry me to my face. I mean, you didn't owe me much. We were adults, and we both signed up for the risks. But you did owe me the common decency and respect of breaking it off to my face."

"To be honest, I was a coward."

Tell me something I didn't know.

"I was afraid marriage meant losing my freedom when the only thing that should've been on my mind is that I'd have you, every day for the rest of my life. I was immature and stupid, then. But I'm a changed man, now. And I suppose it's only fitting that I've realized my mistake and how much you mean to me at *this time* of year."

Gabrielle sat in stunned silence, completely taken aback by his admission. She stood up, and wordlessly paced to the window, looked across the horizon. Her thoughts spun in a million directions all at once.

Well, not a million.

Really, only one.

Gabby realized in that precise moment, when Leo offered an opportunity to resume their journey, the chance to go right back to the way things used to be. She could end her family's questions about her future by replacing Leo…with Leo.

But she was not the same woman and had changed since two years ago; she didn't want the same things.

She turned to him flashing a bright smile. "You're right. It is fitting, but maybe not for the reason you may think. As I stand here right now, I realize that *your swift* exit was the best gift you ever gave to me. You and I were never suited for one another. We differed in every meaningful way, and when you walked, no screeched out of my life with your wheels on fire, you did me the biggest favor ever!"

"What is that?"

"You left a void for the right man to fill. You helped me realize that I can have it all, the renovated Barbie Dream House, the second pancake, the perfect Christmas, just not with you."

"Second pancake? Barbie Dream House? Don't tell me you're seeing someone new?"

"No…no, don't get things twisted, here. I'm not *seeing* someone new. I'm *falling in love* with him…and his two kids…and his big honking dog."

"Two kids? But I thought you didn't want kids."

"That's what I thought. Turns out, I just didn't want to have kids with you. You need to go." She walked to him, grabbed his hand, and dragged him to the door allowing him to stumble along the way. "I've got some preparations to make." She shooed him down the steps without allowing him to get a word in edgewise. "Have a Merry Christmas, a happy New Year, and a nice life!"

She slammed the door and slipped into her shoes. Her new life required the perfect outfit, and the one she needed for this occasion had been collecting dust in the storage room. Time to dig it out.

Chapter 29

Almost Midnight - Christmas Eve

Thirty minutes before midnight and Dave, the kids, and Buddy arrived home from Brian's house just in time to get ready for first gifts. He'd intentionally stayed late to keep them distracted, to avoid confessing the reason for Gabrielle's absence. She'd promised to arrive by midnight so they could enjoy their tradition together, but it was only a matter of time before they figured out that she wouldn't be coming.

They walked in the door, and he darted inside to turn on the tree lights. "All right, monsters. Go brush your teeth and put on your jammies. When you get back, it should be time to open presents."

Buddy disappeared to his bed and returned a minute later with Mr. Squiggles, a rope toy he wouldn't part with if his life depended on it.

The kids stopped in their tracks as they reached the end of the hall and reversed course. Hannah served as the spokesperson. "Where's Gabrielle? We thought she was gonna be here to watch us open first gifts," she whined.

"Yeah! She promised. She wouldn't break a promise. Maybe we should call the cops."

Hannah snapped her fingers. "Or the hospital. When someone's missing, you're always supposed to call the hospital. Where's your phone, Dad? I'll dial."

"Or her mom," D.J. added. "Can we call her mom?"

"We're not calling the hospital or the police. Or her mom. She's not in the hospital nor has she been in an accident."

"You're sure she's not hurt?"

"Well, she's hurt but not the kind that would make her sick. Come sit down with me for a minute. Just a minute or we're going to be late."

They all took a seat on the comfy couch and huddled up next to Dave. Buddy rambled in and sat on Dave's feet.

"What is it, Dad? What's going on?" Hannah asked.

"The thing is...I made a mistake. A big one. What have I told you guys about telling the truth?"

"That you should always tell it, even if you soften the way you tell it. Otherwise, you risk hurting people more by telling a fib."

They nodded in agreement, as if to say *tell us something we don't know*.

"Exactly. The problem is, I didn't take my own advice. I'm not going to tell you every last detail because that's grown-up stuff between Gabrielle and me, but I was dishonest with her about something...something very important, and when she learned the truth, it hurt her."

"Dad!"

"I know. I feel awful about it. I apologized. I pleaded with her to stay, but I'm not certain she can forgive me, not in time to open first presents, anyway."

"Is it too late to ask Santa for help?"

Dave shrugged. "It's never too late to ask Santa for help."

D.J. clenched his eyes shut. Hannah and Dave exchanged glances as they suppressed their grins and shook their heads.

"Mission accomplished. She's coming. I can feel it," D.J. declared. Then he pointed to the clock. "Look at the time! Let's go change into our pajamas. She'll be here any minute."

"D.J." Dave said with exasperation as his footsteps grew faint. A second later his bedroom door slammed.

Hannah pressed Dave's arm. "He's a kid. Let him enjoy his moment. We'll be back in a minute."

Dave watched her scuttle away and listened to her feet patter down the hall. He pulled out his cellphone, scrolled to Gabrielle's number, and stared at it. Then he pushed the phone back into his pocket.

He repeated the same movement five times in a row, desperate to call her, to ask her if she could forgive him. But his gesture required more than a call. It required more than some lame speech. He needed to make a romantic gesture—a big one. He needed to bring her home.

He decided to jump into his car, drive to Capitol Hill, and knock on her door until she talked to him. He ran back to Hannah's room, where both kids were engaged in an unsanctioned pillow fight. He stood there for a moment and waited for them to notice his presence. Finally,

Hannah snatched D.J.'s pillow from his hand and threw both of them on the bed.

"Yes, Dad!"

"Thought you two were getting ready for first gifts?" He shook his head and chuckled. "Put on some clothes."

"Where are we going?"

"To get Gabrielle."

"Yaaaaaay," they cheered jumping up and down.

"Be right back."

He slipped into his shoes, ran to the door to take a quick walk and clear his head; Buddy followed on his heels. "You stay, Buddy. I'll be right back. Sit."

He twisted the doorknob and opened it. His eyes bulged at the Santa standing there with the suit sagging off of them, full beard and all. Santa's fist, which prepared to knock on his door, almost collided with Dave's nose. When he stepped back to duck it, Buddy took off from his hind legs and sailed across the living room; he lifted up his front paws, planted them on Santa's chest, and sent him crashing into the floor. Santa's head banged hard.

A woman's voice, smothered under Buddy's persistent kisses, said, "Hey boy! I missed you, too."

Dave realized at that moment the voice didn't belong to just any woman, it belonged to Gabrielle. She'd come back to him. He fell to his knees beside her, and that's when he saw her eyes, shining, like black diamonds. She was a precious jewel, his jewel.

"Are you okay? Can I get you something? Aspirin? A good attorney?"

She shook her head, perched herself up on her elbows and said, "Actually, I'm looking for an architect. The sweetest, kindest, most considerate architect I've ever known."

"You found him...and I'm the *only one* you've ever known," he said, causing them both to chuckle. "Here, let me help you up." After standing to his feet, he gripped her hands and pulled her up. Thunderous footsteps approached.

"Buddy attacked Santa?" D.J. cried out, almost tearfully.

"It's me," Gabrielle said, pulling the beard from her face. "I promised you I wouldn't miss first presents."

They ran to her and joined together in a group hug before Hannah asked, "But why are you dressed as Santa?"

"It's my dad's. He always used to wear it when he brought gifts to me, so I figured I'd wear it when I bought gifts to you. But the presents are for tomorrow, of course."

They cheered as Hannah tried to peek into the bag and Dave ushered everyone into the house.

"No, no! Not until tomorrow," he said.

Hannah turned to Gabrielle with the brightest smile and shrugged. "I don't need a present. My Christmas wish already came true."

"Awww," Gabrielle said, pressing her hand against her heart. "You two are the best."

"Okay, Munchkins. Can you give us a second?" He glanced down at his watch. "The opening of first gifts will commence in T-minus five minutes."

They cheered and disappeared down the hall, leaving Dave and Gabrielle standing in front of one another, face to face, eye to eye, all defenses down. Nothing except silence between them, a silence Gabrielle quickly filled. "Looked like you were on your way out. I didn't interrupt you, did I?"

He forced a serious expression before responding, "You're right. I was leaving." Then he smiled and said, "I was going to bring you home to me."

"Home?"

"I'm sorry. So sorry. Call it a lapse in judgment. I don't know, but what I can tell you is that is not who I am as a man; that's not what I teach my kids. I tell them the exact opposite, but I need to practice what I preach. I know I hurt you, but you can believe me when I say this—it will never happen again. Ever. I'm going to tell you everything in complete honesty, I promise. When you have morning breath, when your butt looks big in that dress, everything."

She bent over laughing, and the sound sent a nervous jolt through his gut. He was grateful. "Well, you don't have to go that far. I suppose I don't really want the whole truth. Let's restrict your honesty to the things that matter," she said. "Besides, my reaction was bigger than the lie. When I was with Leo, I'd made a laundry list of all the things I didn't want, and I believed myself. But the truth was I didn't want them with him. I'd consented to marry a man with whom I had no real future, no similar interests. He didn't make me laugh. He didn't make me think. He didn't make me pancakes. Frankly, he didn't make me happy. With him, I was no longer single, but I was only content, barely content. That's not the life I wanted to live."

"You deserve more."

"You've given me more. So much more than I could've ever dreamed I wanted, and I believe you when you said you didn't want to be my project. But understand you could never be my project. You're my inspiration, and I'm thankful for every moment we've shared. What we have doesn't come along every day. We owe it to ourselves to give it a try. I want more."

"We'll have more. I'm going to do everything in my power to give you everything you can dream, everything you can imagine."

He looked deeply into her eyes and savored her. His heart hammered against his chest, overflowing with emotion, grateful for the second chance. He locked his arms around her waist and pulled her body until it pressed against his. She reached around his neck and tilted her chin upward, ready to receive him. After teasing her mouth with his, he claimed her lips, surrendering his heart, body, and mind to a passion he never thought he could experience so intensely again. As they began to lose themselves in the frenzy of desire, footsteps trekked up the hall, including the curious sound of heavy paws, bringing their affection to an abrupt halt.

"Dad! It's thirty seconds until Christmas!"

"We made it," Gabrielle said to Dave in a hushed voice.

"Yes, we did," he replied.

Together, they counted down to one and everyone yelled, "Merry Christmas!"

Chapter 30

Christmas Day

One Year Later...

Soft kisses peppered Gabrielle's nose, cheeks, forehead, and finally her lips, drawing her out of her deep slumber. She allowed her eyes to drift open until they greeted the love of her life. He smiled, and his eyes crinkled at the corners. He was beautiful, sweet, her everything.

"Merry Christmas, honey."

"Merry Christmas, sweetheart," she replied, glancing around the room. "Where's the box? I keep finding it in the strangest places."

"Patience. You'll find out what I got you soon enough."

She tried to pull her left hand from beneath the duvet, but as usual, her wedding ring set snagged on the lace. When her hand emerged, she stroked his cheek. "This is our first Christmas together as man and wife. Can you believe it?"

"I know. It's been a whirlwind year. I'm just sorry that I wasn't able to give you the wedding you've always dreamed of."

She turned on her back, looked at the ceiling, and let out a sigh. "It's okay. Really. Like my mom always says, when it all comes out in the wash, the wedding isn't what's most important —the marriage is. Besides, it wasn't your fault. You were game for whatever I wanted. I was the picky one."

"True," he said with a chuckle.

"Dave," she whined as she tagged him on the arm with a playful punch. "I'm sorry. I just didn't want to have some overly expensive, overly formal wedding in some stodgy hotel. I wanted to have a small ceremony in a home, but not Brian's home. Not Vic's home. Our home. Unfortunately, this condo is too small, and we had no luck finding the right house. So, the justice of the peace was just fine. The kids came. Our nearest and dearest showed up. And thanks to Vic calling in a favor with her number one client, they even allowed Buddy in. You and I are together forever. Nothing else matters."

He shrugged and said, "Yeah, I suppose." He tilted his ear to the ceiling as if he were listening for something. "Wow. Do you hear that?"

She craned her neck to hear and that's when she realized he was joking. "Ah, yes, the sweet sound of silence, but I still don't understand why you insisted the kids and Buddy stay at Brian's house last night."

"I insisted because I wanted to give you a special gift."

She turned to her side, patted him on his rear, and wrapped her arm around his waist. "And a special gift you gave me. Twice yesterday evening and once last night. You're just the gift that keeps on giving, aren't you?"

His head fell back as the room filled with their laughter.

"Little do you know...I have something else up my sleeve."

She peeked up the arm of his pajama shirt. "It better be that Sferra duvet I've been begging for. This one keeps snagging my ring. Granted, the Sferra is a little pricey—"

"A million things you could ask for, and you request a duvet," he said shaking his head. "And for the record, it's a lot pricey."

"Yes, but, trust me. It'll last forever." She pinched her lips together. "Judging by the expression on your face, I guess you opted for the foot bath."

"Ye of little faith. Let's get dressed, pick up the kids, and come home and open gifts. How about that?"

She groaned. "Okay, fine. No duvet. At least I've got you. If you're going to disappoint me with the foot bath, the least you could do is make me pancakes."

"Pshhh, of course. What kind of husband would I be if I didn't spend the rest of my life giving you second pancakes?"

She smiled. "Good. That means I get the bathroom first." She rolled her feet over the edge of the bed and checked her phone. Nothing except a text from Vic and Reggie with a Christmas photo of them, the tree, and her ample belly. She was due any day now.

She walked into the bathroom, still a little disappointed by his gift option. It was the last thing she needed to finish up the decor in their bedroom. She wanted everything to be perfect.

"Oh, honey, before you make breakfast, I forgot to ask you how that new job is going. You worked awfully late yesterday."

"I know. The owner is a little bit of a taskmaster. Very demanding and picky about every little detail. But I think we've finally got it nailed down. We can stop and take a look at it on our way to pick up the kids, if you like. You can see some of my work. The owner is presenting it as a gift to his wife later today, but it won't hurt to take a look. Maybe it'll give you a few ideas when we start house hunting next year. Also, I hear they're looking for a decorator."

"Really? Maybe I should take my portfolio, as scant as it is, and throw my hat in the ring."

"I don't know anyone else who'd be more perfect for the job. Sounds like a plan."

House hunting and decorating. She loved the thrill of a hunt and the satisfaction of a finished project, especially as she spent more time helping Vic's clients over the past year. Gabby had even helped stage open houses for other agents. If she could ever start her own company, real estate agents like her sister would bring a significant part of her business.

Dare to dream.

The fact was, they were truly a two-income household, taking care of Hannah and D.J. and the massive ball of fur that was Buddy. Of course, she wouldn't have it any other way, but family life was expensive. Both children seemed to be in the midst of growth spurts and thus inhaling all the food in sight. They'd gone through more pairs of shoes and clothes in one year than she had in five. But nothing could beat the warmth of their hugs, or their unconditional love, or the sounds of Buddy's snores when it stormed outside and the booming thunder scared him. Their ready-made family fit her like her favorite slippers and cotton pajamas on a cold winter's day—almost from day one.

She couldn't wait to see what the rest of their lives had in store. For now, she'd settle for finding out what was in that mystery box.

As they headed up the beltway toward Brian's new home in Silver Spring, Gabrielle couldn't help but be a little nostalgic for last year's weather. The freshly fallen snow blanketed the streets, yards, and rooftops, breathing Christmas into the icy air. This year they weren't so lucky. The overcast skies threatened inclement weather, but the forty-degree temperatures virtually eliminated the hope for the fluffy stuff. Their holiday precipitation would likely consist of a hard, cold rain.

"Dreary day, huh?"

"I think it's beautiful. Perfect. After all, I'm with you," Dave said.

Gabrielle took notice of the highway sign warning that they'd arrive at Brian's exit in one mile. Dave had driven the entire distance in the far-left lane when he should now be in the right.

"Honey. We're almost at Brian's exit. You need to get over."

He ignored her.

"Dave, sweetie, you missed it! Now we're going to have to circle back. Really?"

"What's with you today?" he asked.

"I'm sorry. It's Christmas. I guess I'm just anxious to get the kids back. I can't wait to see their faces when they open their gifts."

"Patience. Patience. Remember, I told you I wanted to show you the project house I've been working on, the reason I arrived home late on Christmas eve."

"Oh, yes. I've started to call this place your work wife. You can't seem to tear yourself away."

He chuckled. "Trust me, you'll see the kids' faces soon enough. And remember they don't go back to school until January seventh. You'll have ample time to get sick of them and wish they'd go back already."

"No! There's never enough time. They grow so fast."

"I'm kidding. Jokes. Simmer down. We're almost there. We'll be in and out in no time."

She lifted her hands to gesture that she'd conceded. "Okay, okay. I'm just gonna sit here and rest my eyes for a minute. It's going to be a long day."

Gabby had almost drifted into a nap when the car stopped, and the engine silenced.

"And we are here!"

She opened her eyes, turned her head, and her jaw hit the floor when she saw the beautiful, brand new mansion in the lot.

It was her Barbie Dream House, standing in front of her tall, majestic, beautiful, perfect, the one Dave had designed a year ago.

She gasped and covered her mouth with both hands and screamed, "Oh my gosh!"

Before she could collect her thoughts and process what she was seeing, Dave had arrived at her car door and opened it. She looked at him and tears immediately flushed down her cheeks. "David Williams. Thank you. Thank you. I can't believe you...I just can't—"

She lost her words inside the moment. She tried to move but couldn't. All she could do was drop her head in her palms and sob. This beautiful, wonderful man had in a single instant erased every bad moment from Christmases past and supplanted them with a blessing and memory that would last her a lifetime.

Dave pulled her hands away from her face and kissed her nose, bringing an immediate smile, and stemming the flow of tears. "Come on, sweetheart. Let's go inside. There's so much for you to see."

She took a quick glance around the quaint, tree-lined neighborhood. "It's so beautiful here. The perfectly manicured lawns. The lush evergreens. And there sure are a lot of cars parked around here. Folks must have a lot of family visiting."

"Something like that."

They walked up the circular driveway which was filled with trucks that looked as if they belonged to the construction crew. But she abandoned that assumption when he opened the door; she couldn't believe her eyes. He'd lined a massive winding double staircase with red roses, poinsettias, and white Christmas lights. An "Our Wedding Day" banner had been hung across the top rail. At eye level stood hers and Dave's nearest and dearest. The kids, siblings, parents, their closes friends, all dressed for a special occasion.

It can't be, she thought. "What is this?"

Everyone yelled, "Surprise!"

"It's your Christmas wedding. Your dress is waiting in our master bedroom suite. The dining room is set up for our wedding, and the reception is in the basement. All we need is you."

She questioned why he spoke those words; they only served to send the tears streaming down her face again. She fell into his arms, sobbing again before Vic collected her and escorted her upstairs.

"How did you guys do this?" she asked, her voice still trembling.

"Dave kept you focused on the empty box, while he planned and arranged everything. He loves you, you know?"

She pushed open the double bedroom doors to see the California king bed covered with the Sferra duvet she'd requested. More tears. She couldn't stop them. He'd given her everything she wanted and so much more.

"I can't believe with everything he's done, he remembered the duvet."

"Come on, sis. Let's get you dressed."

She opened up the walk-in closet slash dressing room to see it hanging there, the Vera Wang she'd always wanted but she'd foregone because Leo had wanted her to wear his mother's gown. "It's breathtaking," she said. "I'm ready."

The ceremony room made Gabrielle dizzy with the excitement. A tulle canopy had been draped from the ceiling, strung along with the paper snowflakes the kids told her they needed for a holiday cabaret. As it turned out she'd made decorations for a wedding she had no clue was about to happen.

White linen-covered chairs topped with red bows were separated by an aisle runner and helped frame the room, setting the bride's guests apart from the groom's. An arch of white lights served as the altar. There Pastor Brooks and Dave stood, waiting for her.

Gabrielle glided to the melody of "Canon in D" as she took careful steps. At the end of the short aisle, her James Bond-attired groom awaited. The officiant was the son of the Reverend who'd married her parents. Vic, her matron of honor, stood there with her paunch belly, the direct result of her rejuvenated marriage. Gabby had received the greatest gift, the family she never knew she'd been waiting for her entire life.

After they exchanged vows and affirmed their "I dos," their guests proceeded to the basement to indulge in hors d'oeuvres before the reception commenced, while Dave pulled Gabby by both hands. "Come with me. I want you to see something."

Dave guided Gabrielle through a mini-tour of the first floor, an expansive and bright space with a contemporary design and floor-to-ceiling windows that allowed light to flood every room. He led her to a door and guided her through a short hall and then a second door which was closed.

"Open it," he said.

She twisted the knob, pushed it open, and covered her mouth with both hands. "What is this? A she-shed? For me?" Seconds later she realized he'd posted a sign and what it read. "Gabrielle's Designs? I don't understand."

"It's your office, design studio."

"You mean?"

"Quit the job you hate. Start your own company."

"But what about—"

"Don't worry about the money. I've got plenty saved, and I've made some pretty good investments. One of my best friends was a Wall Street broker, remember? We're going to be fine. Nothing matters to me if you aren't blissfully happy."

She couldn't contain her jubilance. "How can I ever give you even a fraction of what you've given me?"

"There is no you anymore. And there is no me. There's only us. I can't calculate the value of the gift of love, understanding, and gladness you've brought to the lives of the kids and me. We're happy when you're happy. And, quite frankly, I couldn't watch you trudge off to that government job another day. You always look as if the Grinch stole your soul."

She chuckled. "You are a miracle. In a single day, you've made a lifetime of wishes come true in every way."

"That reminds me. Now, there's just one more surprise. A very small one."

"What is it?"

He reached into his pocket and pulled out a sprig and held it over her head.

"Mistletoe?"

"Remember you said if all of your wishes came true in a day, you'd eat it."

She laughed. "You really think I'm gonna eat that? Dream on. But, hold it over my head; I most certainly will take a kiss."

"Is this how you pictured us? Is this what you imagined?"

"No, not even close," she said. "We're more, so much more, than I ever could've dreamed."

He chuckled and stroked his finger along the curve of her cheek. "Merry Christmas, my beautiful Gabby."

She lifted her lips toward his and whispered, "Merry Christmas, my dear, sweet, wonderful Dave."

The End

If you enjoyed this novel, please stop by and leave a review at your favorite site—and thank you so much for reading!

About the Author

K. L. Brady, a D.C. native, started her writing career in the pages of diaries when she was seven or eight years old. But it wasn't until her fortieth birthday and an Oprah "Live Your Best Life" moment that she finally answered her calling and wrote her first novel–The Bum Magnet. The originally self-published novel was picked up by Simon & Schuster in a two-book deal and K.L. hasn't looked back since, penning the follow-up, Got a Right to Be Wrong and self-publishing the first books in two young adult series and a spy thriller series based on her twenty-year career in the U.S. Intelligence Community.

A certified nerd girl with a love of all things Star Wars, Big Bang Theory and Star Trek, she has a B.A. in Economics and an MBA. She also holds memberships in the Maryland Writer's Association, Romance Writers of America, Sisters In Crime, and International Thriller Writers. She's addicted to writing and chocolate—not necessarily in that order—and currently lives in the Washington D.C., area with her son.

Website link: http://www.klbradyauthor.com
Facebook link: https://www.facebook.com/KLBRADY/
Pinterest: https://www.pinterest.com/authorklbrady/
Twitter: https://twitter.com/KARLAB27

Join my newsletter for news on the latest releases, chances to get free books and early review copies, and special contests for newsletter readers only! (Note: We never spam; newsletter issued once every 3 months.)
http://tinyurl.com/klbradynews

OTHER BOOKS BY K.L. BRADY
Women's Fiction – Chick Lit
Free ebook - Acquired (A Billionaire Brother Romance) – Only at www.klbradyauthor.com
Fate brings Nicki and Devin together during an unexpected trip to the Caribbean, sparks fly in their May-December romance, and they fall hard and fast. But the highly-coveted piece of property, one they both need to further their goals, stands between them and happiness (43,000 Words).

The Bum Magnet
After a lifetime of bad relationships, a woman decides to go on an introspective journey to find out why she attracts to the wrong men—a journey hilariously complicated by a new love interest.

Got a Right to Be Wrong
One week before her wedding day, a woman with a lifelong struggle with trust issues finds out a life-altering secret about her fiancée and questions their future.

12 Honeymoons (Clean)
After a nasty break-up that lands her court, a D.C. socialite, struggling to find her purpose and love, gets arrested (again) and is forced to perform community service.

The Playmaker Series – Sweet romance
Her Perfect Catch (Clean)

A struggling sports writer finds the story of her lifetime, and love soon follows, during a trip to the Super Bowl.

The Player's Option (Clean)
When sports agent Ty Baker and C.J. meet at a pro-football conference, sparks fly, and they can both see love in the end zone...until disaster strikes. Each learns the other is trying to steal their biggest client and cut-throat competition threatens to tear them apart.

The Eligible Receiver (Clean)
Jet Jamison is hot, successful, wealthy, and can have any woman he wants, the one he truly needs still eludes him, that is, until Veda enters his life. A chance meeting with Jet begins with a sparring match and ends with love at second sight. But she's got a secret that threatens to tear them apart.

The Playmakers – 3-Book Box Set (Clean)
Her Perfect Catch, The Player's Option & The Eligible Receiver
Are you ready for some love and football? This funny and sweet box set contains heartwarming romances featuring sexy professional football stars who deliver hot, flirty days and cozy nights.

Five Golden Rings - A Christmas Novella (Clean)
A.J. and Kristie serendipitously "fall" for one another at the National Tree Lighting in Washington D.C. As fast as destiny brings them together, Murphy's Law pulls them apart.

Love's in the Cards – A Novel (Clean)
In this second-chance romance, a greeting card company owner's life is sent into a tailspin when her business is

acquired by the ex-boyfriend who dumped her. (Coming October 2020)

Seven Minutes of Christmas Magic (Clean)
Sparks fly when greeting card company Vice President, Mia, ruthlessly steals Nixon's parking space before a Christmas party—and then steals his heart. Too bad he's been tapped to destroy her career. (Coming November 2020)

Young Adult - Romance
Worst Impressions (Clean)
In this modern retelling of Pride and Prejudice, shy, basketball loving, tomboy Liz Bennett meets star high school quarterback Darcelle Williams and sparks fly—and she'd like to set him on fire.

Soul of the Band (Clean)
A bullied, inner city teen gets a chance to start a new life when, after her mother's mental breakdown, she is forced to move to a small town in Ohio and joins the high school band.

Spy Thrillers – The J.J. McCall Series (S.D. Skye)
The Bigot List (A J.J. McCall Novel #1)
An FBI Special Agent and her partner are drawn into an unsanctioned hunt for an intelligence community spy when Bureau sources are killed, and an internal investigation threatens to land them atop the suspect list.

Situation Critical (A J.J. McCall Novel #2)
An FBI Special Agent and her partner lead an intelligence community task force ordered to find moles throughout the intelligence community, and its first case targets the White House.

The Shadow Syndicate (A J.J. McCall Novel #3)

The FBI task force heads to New York to shut down a sleeper spy funding network, landing them in the middle of a burgeoning war between a Russian organized crime organization with links to diplomatic spies and the Italian mafia.

SpyCatcher — 3-Book Box Set
The Bigot List, Situation Critical & The Shadow Syndicate
Read the first three J.J. McCall Novels in one great set!